* * *

With a confident smile, "Melissa" hit the phone's send button.

"This is Ray Ortega. What's up?"

"Ray, it's me. I've got the disk. Call Jane and tell her to extract me right away."

"Goddammit, Kristie! You're just supposed to be planning a backup strategy. What the hell's going on?"

"I'm perfectly safe. Salinger is my prisoner, bound and completely unconscious."

"Kristie, where are the bodyguards?" Ray's voice had grown steady and commanding.

"Outside the door. Salinger gave them instructions not to disturb us. But eventually, they'll probably check. That's why I've got the gun on him. If they come in, I'll threaten to shoot their boss. The plan is flawless, but I'm a little anxious to get it over with. So please call Jane."

"How many guards?"

"Two."

"Okay. Go to the door. Poke your head outside and give them your biggest, sexiest Melissa Daniels smile. Then shoot them—once each—in the head."

"What?"

Dear Reader,

We invite you to sit back and enjoy the ride as you experience the powerful suspense, intense action and tingling emotion in Silhouette Bombshell's November lineup. Strong, sexy, savvy heroines have never been so popular, and we're putting the best right into your hands. Get ready to meet four extraordinary women who will speak to the Bombshell in you!

Maggie Sanger will need quick wit and fast moves to get out of Egypt alive when her pursuit of a legendary grail puts her on a collision course with a secret society, hostages and her furious ex! Get into *Her Kind of Trouble,* the latest in author Evelyn Vaughn's captivating GRAIL KEEPERS miniseries.

Sabotage, scandal and one sexy inspector breathe down the neck of a determined air force captain as she strives to right an old wrong in the latest adventure in the innovative twelve-book ATHENA FORCE continuity series, *Pursued* by Catherine Mann.

Enter the outrageous underworld of Las Vegas prizefighting as a female boxing trainer goes up against the mob to save her father, her reputation and a child witness in Erica Orloff's pull-no-punches novel, *Knockout.*

And though creating identities for undercover agents is her specialty, Kristie Hennessy finds out that work can be deadly when you've got everyone fooled and no one to trust but a man you know only by his intriguing voice.... Don't miss Kate Donovan's *Identity Crisis.*

It's a month of no-holds-barred excitement! Please send your comments to me, c/o Silhouette Books, 233 Broadway Ste. 1001, New York, NY 10279.

Best wishes,

Natashya Wilson
Associate Senior Editor, Silhouette Bombshell

Please address questions and book requests to:
Silhouette Reader Service
U.S.: 3010 Walden Ave., P.O. Box 1325, Buffalo, NY 14269
Canadian: P.O. Box 609, Fort Erie, Ont. L2A 5X3

KATE DONOVAN

IDENTITY CRISIS

Published by Silhouette Books

America's Publisher of Contemporary Romance

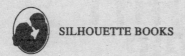 SILHOUETTE BOOKS

ISBN 0-373-51334-8

IDENTITY CRISIS

KATE DONOVAN

is the author of more than a dozen novels and novellas, ranging from time travel and paranormal to historical romance, suspense and romantic comedy. An attorney, she draws on her criminal law background to create challenges worthy of her heroines, who crack safes, battle wizards and always get their man. As for Kate, she *definitely* got her man and is living happily ever after with him and their two children in Elk Grove, California. You can e-mail Kate at kate@katedonovan.com.

To my husband, Paul,
for bringing out the Bombshell in me.

Prologue

"Well, Ms. Daniels, that about wraps it up for now." Ray Ortega, director of the Strategic Profiling and Identification Network, leveled his stare directly into a pair of sparkling green eyes. "You've probably figured out from our questions that a position here at SPIN involves more than traditional profiling. We also design false identities for undercover operatives. Do you think you'd enjoy that sort of thing? Creating a three-dimensional person with a history, identification and personality, then inserting that person into an existing community without detection?"

"Actually, sir, I think that's the part of the job I'd *really* excel at."

"I like your confidence," Ray assured her. "And your credentials are impressive. But—" he began gathering up the papers in front of him "—we have several other applicants, so I'm afraid we won't be able to give you our decision until early next week."

"Wait!" Colonel Ulysses S. Payton, a heretofore-silent member of the interview team, motioned for Ray to stay seated at their elongated table across from the interviewee. "*I* have a question for Miss Daniels."

The young woman smiled. "Yes, Colonel?"

"You're not only pretty and well educated, you're an Olympic-grade athlete! Why *this* job? What's the point of earning a black belt in karate, or becoming a sharpshooter, if you're hiding away all day working at a computer?"

The candidate gave a slight nod, as though acknowledging the aptness of the question. Then she explained, "I'll be using my skills as a resource, so that I can create believable identities and workable strategics for government agents. My imagination is my universe, Colonel. It's all I need. And there's no place on earth I'd rather be than at SPIN headquarters, assisting agents in the field."

"It's a danged waste if you ask me," the soldier muttered.

"With all due respect, sir, you're focusing on the wrong part of my résumé." The emerald eyes shone with pride. "I graduated summa cum laude from Yale with a double major in psychology and criminology, then went on to get my Ph.D. from Stanford. Professor James Clark, one of the world's most highly respected profilers, has dubbed me his most gifted student. I'm published in the field, most recently with an upcoming article for the *New England Journal of Psychology.*" She turned her attention toward Ray. "Did you have a chance to look at the article I sent you?"

He nodded, remembering the insightful, well-written work. "It was excellent. And as I said, your qualifications are impressive."

"Everything about her is impressive," insisted Colonel Payton.

"Looks like we're all in agreement." Ray was on his feet before anyone could protest. "Ms. Daniels, it's been a pleasure. Here's my card. If you think of anything else, don't hesitate to call."

"I look forward to hearing from you." She stood and shook the hand of each interviewer in turn, then headed for the door and disappeared without a backward glance.

"Amazing girl," Payton observed. "Built, too. Is there really any doubt in your mind, Ortega? Where are you gonna find someone better? A leggy redhead with a brain and a black belt—if I were twenty years younger, I'd hire her myself!"

Despite his annoyance at the remark, Ray knew better than to object. After all, Colonel Payton was the president's best friend and adviser. Wasn't that how the guy had gotten himself on the SPIN interview panel in the first place? It was all politics. But the choice of a new "spinner" was ultimately Ray's alone, so why sweat it?

He even sent a perfunctory smile in the colonel's direction. "I agree, sir, she's an impressive prospect. But something about her bothers me. I just can't put my finger on it."

"Let me guess," interrupted the third interviewer, Ray's fellow profiler, David Wong. "She's too sexy? Too smart? Speaks too many languages?"

"Okay, okay." Ray was laughing in spite of himself. "I'll admit, she's perfect. *Too* perfect. That's what bothers me. If I had set out to design the ideal candidate for this job—"

A dull but insistent warning bell sounded in his brain, and he pulled out his cell phone, then punched in his secretary's number. "Beth? Did the original transcripts for Melissa Daniels ever arrive from Yale?"

"We got them a few minutes ago, boss. Want me to bring them over?"

Confused, Ray murmured, "No. Thanks anyway," and ended the call.

"What is it, Ray?" Wong demanded. "Didn't she check out? I followed up on her references myself, and every-one—including the dean—sang her praises."

Ray stopped him with a wave of his hand. "Don't worry, she's legit."

He was about to go further, to admit that they were right, and Daniels was the hands-down best candidate, when a buzz from his cell phone preempted his attention.

Murmuring "Give me a second, will you?" he flipped open the phone and gave his habitual salutation. "This is Ortega. What's up?"

"Hi, Mr. Ortega. You said to call if I thought of any-thing else."

"Ms. Daniels?" Ray arched an eyebrow in the direction of Wong and the colonel. "Sure, go ahead. The others are still here."

"Good, because there's one tiny matter I'd really like to bring to your attention."

"There's *more?*" He had to laugh, wondering what fur-ther credentials she could possibly have. "Shoot."

"Well, sir…" The candidate gulped audibly. "Every-thing on my résumé is a fabrication."

"Huh?"

"I made it all up. Every bit of it."

Stunned, Ray tried to think of something to say, finally settling for, "Where are you, Ms. Daniels?"

"Right outside the door. But my name isn't Daniels. It's Hennessy. Kristie Hennessy."

"Hennessy?"

"And I should probably warn you, I'm going to look very different the next time you see me."

He shook his head, not trusting himself to respond to that.

"Shall I come back in, sir?"

"Yes. Absolutely," he assured her, turning his full attention to the doorway.

"So? What's going on?" Wong demanded. "What new information did she give you?"

"Huh?" Ray had almost forgotten his colleagues were in the room, so intent was his focus on Daniels—or rather Hennessy—and the door that would readmit her.

But facts were facts, and the other interviewers had a right to know, so without taking his gaze off the doorway, he announced with a self-mocking smile, "Congratulations, gentlemen. It appears we've got ourselves a new spinner."

Chapter 1

"Say your prayers, blondie, because tonight, I'm gonna flatten you!" Kristie Hennessy aimed a high-flying kick straight at her target's smiling face and shouted, "Take that!"

The five-foot-high bop bag careened backward, dipping nearly to the floor, then bounced back up, still grinning.

"Curse you, Betty Bop!" Kristie's fists began to pummel the bag with feigned ferocity, interspersed with high kicks. "Take that! And that!"

Her aim was getting better, and she congratulated herself as she danced around the toy, attacking it from every direction. This was so much more fun than hitting and kicking the twin-bed mattress that was still propped against the wall of her spare bedroom, having served as her target for weeks while she worked through the introductory lessons of a kickboxing videotape.

"No more faceless enemy," she crowed. "Just two blondes kicking each other senseless. There's a dumb-blonde joke in there somewhere, Betty, but I can't think of a good punch line."

Landing a final kick, she stood back and bowed to her synthetic opponent, which had been painted to resemble a popular computer-game heroine sporting yellow hair, ample—albeit two-dimensional—breasts and a gold leotard.

Turning to catch a glimpse of her own ensemble—cut-off jeans and a gray halter top soaked with sweat—Kristie grimaced. Not exactly a superheroine, but that was okay with her. After all, she didn't plan on ever putting these skills to use. She just liked understanding what her operatives went through so that she could design more effective cover stories for them.

Because you're Super-Spinner, she reminded herself playfully, acknowledging that she was indeed living a kind of fantasy, thanks to having been lucky enough to land a job in Washington, D.C., with the Strategic Profiling and Identification Network, otherwise known as SPIN. Where else could she hope to spend hours every day brainstorming by phone with agents from the FBI, DEA and ATF, as well as detectives from sophisticated metropolitan police departments like the NYPD and LAPD?

Although closely associated with the FBI, SPIN had been designed and established as a separate federal entity working on a contract basis with various law-enforcement agencies. Sometimes the task was straightforward, such as profiling a suspect or confirming a profile that had already been developed. Other times, a spinner became immersed in a particular case by designing an undercover identity for an agent and then providing phone support for the duration of the operation. The contracting agency decided the level of support needed, and budgeted the project accordingly. SPIN's own internal budget was small, focusing on high-tech equipment and a core staff of profilers and strategists.

In her six months with the agency, Kristie had demonstrated an aptitude and commitment that had earned her the respect of her team, the confidence of director Ray Ortega and a portfolio of complex and highly sensitive cases that absorbed her every waking thought.

And at the moment, the most absorbing of those assignments was the assistance she was providing to Special Agent Justin Russo of the FBI, who in turn was assisting police in locating a kidnapped child.

"Justin, why don't you call?" she entreated her favorite operative aloud as she stripped off her drenched clothes and headed for the shower, taking the cordless phone with her into the bathroom, just in case. "It's almost nine o'clock. You always call by eight, so what gives?"

Turning up the spray of hot water until it was at full force, she stepped into the shower and allowed her muscles to relax.

He'll call. He always does. He's not like McGregor, thank heavens. The world could be coming to an end and he wouldn't think to pick up the phone.

McGregor, McGregor, McGregor...

Of all the agents she had worked with thus far at SPIN, Will McGregor was the most confounding to Kristie. No matter how many times she came through for him—designing identities, profiling informants, strategizing her heart out—he had never once contacted her for follow-up. And certainly never to say thank-you. The FBI agent was darned independent, and while she knew from his psych evaluation that it was simply his nature, she still resented it.

All the other operatives phoned her routinely during active cases. And her favorite—the intrepid Justin Russo—spoiled her rotten, calling each and every night to report, amuse and flirt. He had even named her "Essie," insisting that her official contact name, S-3, was too impersonal for such a beautiful and talented girl.

Beautiful and talented…

She sighed as she turned off the water and began to dry herself. In actuality, Justin had no idea what she looked like. None of the operatives did. That was part of Ray Ortega's system—complete anonymity for the spinners.

In contrast, she knew *everything* about her operatives—or, at least, everything their files could tell her, plus whatever she could manage to glean over the phone. Which made the phone-free situation with Agent Will McGregor all the more frustrating.

Forget about him, she advised herself. *McGregor's a loner. Always has been, always will be. Just be glad Justin and the others are more sociable.*

As if on cue, the phone began to ring, and she dashed for her desk so that her home copy of the kidnapping file would be close at hand. Then she took a deep breath and answered with a crisp, professional, "This is S-3. Please identify yourself."

"Hey, Essie."

"Justin! Thank heavens. Is everything okay?"

"Yeah. We wrapped this one up tonight. I can only talk for a minute, but I knew you'd want to know."

"Wrapped it up?" Kristie sank into a chair, completely unnerved. "What does that mean? Did you find Lizzie? Was she…?"

"We didn't find the body yet," he murmured. "The local authorities are gonna take it from here. We made the arrest. Got the confession. The rest is just…well, they can handle it from here."

The body.

Those two words told her all she needed to know.

"At least she didn't suffer much," Justin was insisting. "Apparently, she fell and hit her head. Never regained consciousness. And there was no sexual assault. That's a blessing, right? I'm not saying death is preferable to that, or vice versa, but——"

"Don't worry, Justin. This is no time for political correctness. If the choice is between death and molestation, there's no choice at all."

"Right."

His mournful tone reminded her that he must have gone through hell the last few hours, so she forced herself to find the bright side for both their sakes. "It really is a relief that she didn't suffer. We can be grateful for that."

"Yeah. Real grateful."

"Try not to think about it anymore tonight. Just be proud that you brought that bastard to justice before he could hurt anyone else." A million questions invaded the spinner's brain. "What finally made Horton confess? Did a new witness step forward? And why didn't he tell you where he hid the—the body? That doesn't make much sense."

"Horton?" Justin sounded as confused as Kristie. "You thought it was *him?* Why?"

Kristie winced. "You're saying it wasn't? Sheesh, I was so sure. Who was it then?"

There was a long silence. Then Justin murmured, "I didn't see anything in the file to indicate he was your top suspect. I mean, he was on your list, but so were seven other people."

"What difference does it make?" she demanded. "Tell me who did it."

"Tell me why you thought it was Coach Horton," he countered.

"I don't know. Instinct, I guess. But I didn't have any facts to back it up, which is why I didn't highlight him in the file. You know Ray's rule—we can follow any hunch we want in-house, but if there's nothing in the file to support it, we have to be objective in the analysis we send to the field. And now I see why," she admitted, half to herself.

She had been so sure Horton was the kidnapper. Had felt it in her bones, so much so that she had spent two long hours in Ray Ortega's office, trying to force the facts into the traditional abductor profile. All because her gut told her she was right, and until now, her gut had never betrayed her.

But Ray didn't believe in gut instinct, or hunches, or female intuition. And apparently, in this case at least, he had been right.

So?" She returned to her no-nonsense approach. "Who killed poor Lizzie? The neighbor with the motorcycle?" When the agent didn't answer right away, she felt a twinge of foreboding. "Justin? Who was it?"

"The kid."

"Pardon?" It didn't make any sense for a moment, then she realized he was referring to the victim's fourteen-year-old brother, Randy, and she gasped the boy's name in disbelief.

"Yeah. It's been rough all around," the operative confirmed. "As if that family didn't already have enough grief."

Kristie was shaking her head, still stunned. "When you say he confessed, what exactly do you mean?"

"I mean he did it. He *told* us he did it. He's racked with guilt, Essie. They had to sedate him, and even then, he was a mess. It was one of the most painful things I've ever had to witness."

"Oh, Justin. How horrible."

"It was an accident. The kids had an argument, then Randy pushed her, and she hit her head. When he realized she wasn't breathing, he panicked and threw her in the river. They're dragging it again as we speak, so it's only a matter of time."

Kristie struggled not to picture how Lizzie Rodriguez's little body would look after six days in icy water. The poor, sweet angel...

"This is so awful, Justin. Do you know what made Randy decide to confess? It's been almost a week. Why today?"

"I asked him that. And he said..." The agent's voice trailed into silence.

"Justin? What's wrong?"

"Tell me why Coach Horton was your top suspect."

"Pardon?"

He exhaled audibly. "I spent the whole day at the school, conducting another round of useless interviews. Just when I was leaving, Randy approached me and said he wanted to turn himself in. I was surprised, because I had been watching him in the cafeteria during lunch. He was talking to his friends, and it was the first time I'd seen him look halfway relaxed since—well, since I got here. I remember thinking to myself, the days are probably getting a little easier, but I bet the nights are still a bitch. Missing his baby sister. Hearing his mom cry."

"Go on."

"I even mentioned it to the vice principal—that the kid's mood seemed to be improving. And she said the staff were all trying to be sensitive and supportive. To be aware but not crowd him. Then she said she saw Horton take him aside after lunch—probably to do that very thing. You know, give him moral support. Horton's a part-time guidance counselor as well as the track coach, you know, so it made sense."

"Randy talked to the coach this afternoon? And then out of the blue...?" Kristie stopped herself from finishing the sentence, prompting the agent instead. "So? What did he say when you asked him 'Why today?'"

"He said Coach Horton reminded him that he was just a kid. That he shouldn't carry his grief inside. That no matter what he said or did, his teachers and parents and community cared and would support him. It made sense, Essie."

"It still does," she assured the agent. "That's just the kind of thing a really good guidance counselor would say. I just didn't think..."

"You didn't think Horton was a 'really good' one? Why not?"

She took a deep breath, then admitted, "Instinct, pure and simple. I'll admit he didn't fit the profile in several key respects. At least, no more than any of the other men the cops questioned. But there were those two years of his life, in his late twenties, when he suddenly didn't have a real job. I just kept coming back to that."

"His mother was dying. Emphysema, right? She needed him to come home. And she had enough retirement money so he could afford to help her full-time. That's what the file said. His relatives and neighbors made it sound like he was a frigging saint," Justin added, his tone slightly frantic. "But you don't think so? Is that it? You think... what?"

"I guess I don't think anyone's a saint," Kristie admitted. "And I don't think twenty-eight-year-old men who've been holding themselves out as Mr. Macho for years suddenly quit their jobs and break their engagement to their high-school sweetheart and move home to play nursemaid for two whole years—no matter *how* sick their mom is— unless there's something else going on."

"Geez, Essie, don't say that." Justin heaved an exaggerated sigh, then muttered, "Okay, say it. Your gut instinct has been flawless in every case we've worked together. Almost eerie. So...?"

Her heart was pounding again. "Either I'm right or I'm wrong. Obviously. But if I'm right—"

"If you're right, Lizzie might still be alive? *That's* what you're thinking? Based on what?"

"Horton wants the search directed elsewhere. Away from him. Buying himself more time—more time to spend with Lizzie. He doesn't really think he's going to get away with it, but he wants it to last as long as possible. It's right there in his file, Justin. I see it, even though I can't explain it." Kristie's voice almost cracked with desperation. "He's not finished yet, Justin. We still have time."

"Damn, Essie, I want that to be true."

"I know you do. Her big brother does, too. So—" She took a deep breath, then exhaled and instructed him briskly, "Just do exactly what I say."

Kristie had promised Justin Russo she'd wait a full half hour before putting their plan into action, allowing plenty of time for him to smuggle a phone into Randy's room at the juvenile detention center. The agent was risking his case by putting her in touch with a detainee without alerting defense counsel, and was probably risking his career as well, all because of his faith in a woman he had never met.

Now it was up to Kristie. Or rather, up to Melissa Daniels. Because Kristie Hennessy definitely intended to delegate this particular assignment to her red-haired counterpart. Melissa had gotten her this great job, and had been a virtual operative for several of her most challenging assignments. Now she was going to crack this kidnapping case.

The spinner propped three pictures on a shelf in front of the phone for inspiration. The first was a photo of fourteen-year-old Randy Rodriguez, a typical boy with bravado to spare, yet gentleness behind his soft brown eyes. According to all reports, Randy had played hero in his five-year-old sister's life since the very day she'd been born.

Little Lizzie Rodriguez. She had the same brown eyes and dark hair as her brother and was just as adorable. Staring back at Kristie from the second photo, her eyes danced as playfully as the teddy-bear emblem on her pink polo shirt.

Each of those photos was an inspiration, but given the chutzpah needed for this endeavor, Kristie focused on the third picture—a computer-generated image of Melissa Daniels. Long legs and a perfect body, cut-and-pasted from the Internet and clad in black leather. Luxurious red curls framing a face that was based on Kristie's, but with shamrock-green eyes, sharper cheekbones and a sinfully generous mouth, all accentuated by sultry makeup and a saucy smile.

When she was just about as psyched up as she could hope to be, Kristie glanced at her watch, confirmed that it was time, then took a deep breath and reached for the no-frills cell phone she kept in the top drawer of her dresser.

She didn't dare use her home phone to make this call, knowing that SPIN monitored and taped it. Her cell, on the other hand, wasn't registered, since she had purchased it solely for the purpose of making private calls. Not that she generally made any such calls, but she had always hoped her love life might one day reactivate itself, and when it did, she didn't want anyone, much less Ray Ortega, listening in.

Meanwhile, this phone's day—or rather, its night—had apparently arrived.

Bracing herself, Kristie entered the phone number, then began to count the rings. One, two, three—

"H-hello?"

The plaintive voice brought a lump to the spinner's throat, but she banished it and spoke confidently into the phone. "Hi, Randy. My name is Melissa Daniels, and it's my job to help little girls in trouble. I'm six feet tall with flaming-red hair and a black belt in karate. And I'm not afraid of a damned thing in the whole damned world. How does that sound to you?"

Dead silence greeted the announcement.

"Randy? Are you still there?"

"I already told the police—"

"I know what you told them. I also know *why* you told them that. I'm very proud of you, Randy, but you and I both know there's more to be done, don't we? And we have to act fast. Right?"

"I don't know."

"That's because you've never done this before. But I've

saved *hundreds* of children, so I know exactly what to do. Just stay on the phone with me, and keep listening to my voice, and everything will be fine. Okay?"

He didn't reply, but the sound of rapid breathing told her he was beginning to panic.

"Take a deep breath, sugar. I'm going to ask you a question, and you're going to answer it yes or no. And after that, we're going to go find Lizzie and bring her home. Okay?"

A small sob that sounded suspiciously like his sister's name was his only response.

"Are you ready for the question, Randy?"

"Y-yes."

"Okay. When Coach Horton talked to you today—"

"I can't talk about him! Please don't make me! If I do—"

"If you do, he'll hurt Lizzie? That's all I needed to know." Kristie's pulse began to race. "Horton told you she's alive, right? That's why you confessed—to keep her alive. You did the right thing. The smart thing. The only thing. And now with your help, I'm going to make sure he never has a chance to hurt her again."

"You don't understand! He doesn't *have* to do anything to her. He already did it."

"Did what?"

"He buried her in the dirt, in the middle of the woods, and he's the only one who knows where she is. If he gets arrested, we'll never find her and she'll run out of air. Oh God, now what? I *promised* him—"

"Randy! Listen to me. Take a deep breath." She waited a moment, then demanded, "What color hair do I have?"

"R-red."

"And what am I afraid of?"

"Nothing," he whispered.

"And how many little girls have I saved?"

The boy was silent for a few seconds, then answered in a voice rich with innocent hope. "Hundreds?"

"You bet your ass, sugar. So, what do you say we make it hundreds plus one?"

Chapter 2

The next morning, SPIN headquarters was buzzing with news of Kristie's successful—albeit unconventional—foray into fieldwork. Never in the three-year history of the elite service had a spinner directly contacted a suspect or witness, much less interrogated one.

"We should have known you'd be trouble after the way you made monkeys of us at the interview," David Wong told her as they sat drinking coffee in one of the spacious cubicles that housed the tools of the spinning trade—reference books, faxes and phones, along with the most sophisticated computers, software and peripherals available anywhere.

Kristie laughed with delight. "Don't look at *me*. Melissa deserves all the blame for that interview. And she deserves some credit for last night, too. But really, it was Justin Russo's willingness to bend a few rules that saved Lizzie's life. I hope he's getting some strokes, too."

"Any update on the little girl's condition?"

"She's doing okay, all things considered. Thank heavens that creep didn't really bury her." Kristie shuddered, remembering the first tense minutes after Justin had arrested Horton. The coach had refused to talk without a lawyer, and the cops had been frantic, not knowing where to start digging. Meanwhile, a small team had torn Horton's house and vehicles apart, and once again, resourceful Justin Russo had come through, spying an almost imperceptible variation in the striped wallpaper that decorated Horton's bedroom. Seconds later, Justin had pried open a flat-paneled closet door and had pulled little Lizzie Rodriguez into his arms.

Patting Kristie's hand, David told her, "Why don't you ask Ray for the rest of the day off? You must be beat."

"I'm fine."

"Kristie!" Ray's secretary called out from across the expanse that separated the spinners from their boss's office. "Ray wants to see you," Beth added.

"I'll be right there," Kristie called back, pleased that she was finally going to hear her supervisor's reaction to the prior evening's adventure. Ray had taken a big chance hiring her, given her lack of on-the-job experience, and in her first six months at SPIN, he had become both mentor and friend, praising her talent and giving her some of the best cases. Now his faith in her had been justified. She could only imagine how proud he was.

"You might want to tilt his office blinds closed, just in case this turns out to be the big day," David suggested slyly.

"Pardon?"

Her friend grinned. "People have been hugging you all day. I figure when Ray takes his turn, you guys might not be able to stop. And frankly, it's about time."

"Me and Ray?" Kristie glared. "Are you nuts?"

"No, just perceptive," he said, chuckling. Then he seemed to realize he was the only one laughing, and cleared his throat. "Sorry. Taboo subject."

"It's not taboo. It's not a subject at all. Ray and I are just friends."

"Right."

"David! I'm serious. There's nothing going on."

"I know that. You're both too disciplined to have an affair on the job. I just thought—" He shook his head. "Are you saying you don't have the hots for him? Not even a little?"

"Of course not." She glanced toward Ray's office to confirm he wasn't watching, then insisted, "Ray and I are two peas in a pod. We like the same music, the same books, the same movies. We've got the same skills, tastes and political views. We're the proverbial twins separated at birth."

"Yeah? Well, do the guy a favor," David suggested dryly. "When he finally cracks and pours his heart out to you, *don't* tell him you love him like a brother."

Kristie groaned in frustration. "You've seen us together, attacking the crossword puzzle and laughing on break, and you think it's romantic. But it's not. We're just kindred spirits. There's no chemistry. No longing glances or any of that."

She sighed as she added, "Don't get me wrong. The guy's gorgeous. I'd have to be dead not to notice that. But there's no spark. Nothing. *Nada.*"

"Fine. My mistake. Forget I said anything."

She studied him warily. "You're his best friend. Has he said something to you?"

"Nope."

"But you really think…?"

David shrugged his shoulders. "Obviously I was wrong."

She smiled, relieved. "Thanks for scaring me to death."

"Whatever."

He was too quick to look down at his shirtfront, picking at some microscopic piece of lint, and she realized he wasn't yet convinced. And considering how well he knew Ray, that was beginning to worry her.

"I'm not his type, David. You of all people should know that."

"I should?"

"You've met his ex-wife, right? I found out all about her when I was doing research for my job interview. Red hair, green eyes, svelte. There was another girl, too, one he was engaged to when he was in the army. Angela something. Same type as the wife. And that senator from Ohio that he had a fling with. The one with the gorgeous auburn curls. That's how I got the idea for Melissa Daniels. Red wig, green contacts, flashy makeup and a push-up bra. The works." With a wicked smile, she admitted, "It was dirty pool, but I wanted to throw him off guard so he wouldn't notice any little imperfections in my cover story. I did my best to impersonate his favorite female fantasy."

David arched an eyebrow. "You intentionally made Ray fall for you?"

"Not for *me*. For Melissa." Kristie gave her fellow spinner a halfhearted glare. "This is nuts. If it's true—if he really does have a harmless little crush on me—it's a simple case of transference."

Yeah. Tell him that," David drawled. "It'll make him feel so much better."

"Hey, you two." Beth bustled over to the spinners and

scolded them playfully. "For some reason, Ray thinks he's in charge. And since he can see the two of you sitting here gabbing, I can't exactly cover for you."

Kristie shot a quick look toward the office, and was again relieved to see that Ray wasn't watching them. Not that there was anything to watch. And not that Ray shouldn't look at her whenever he wanted—

"Thanks a lot, David," she muttered. "You've completely freaked me out."

"Sorry. Just remember not to use the b-word when tou talk to him."

"B-word?"

"Brother."

Grimacing, she nodded, then hurried to her boss's glass-walled office.

"Ray? Beth said you wanted to see me."

Without looking up, he told her, "Close the door and take a seat, Kristie. I'll be with you in a minute."

She was relieved to note that the blinds were wide open. And he wanted her to sit on the other side of the desk from him. Business as usual. No sexual tension. He barely seemed to know she was there.

Slipping into a chair, she took a moment to study him. He was a truly handsome man with a ramrod build, raven-black hair and an endearingly boring habit of wearing a white shirt and conservative tie every single day.

Would she have been attracted to him had they met under other circumstances? Probably not. She was a firm believer in chemistry, and there simply wasn't any between them, at least, not on her part.

Realizing that a full minute had passed in silence, she murmured, "If this is a bad time, I can come back."

"I'll be with you as soon as I finish this list."

"Sounds mysterious. What kind of list?"

He raised his gaze to hers, stunning her with the cold gleam in his usually sweet eyes. "I thought it would be easier if we went infraction by infraction."

"Oh." She coughed to clear the surprise from her throat. "I get it."

"You 'get' it? That's all you have to say for yourself?" Exploding out of his chair, he began gesturing wildly. "What the hell were you thinking?"

"Ray—"

"Don't 'Ray' me!" He took a deep breath, visibly getting his temper under control, then sat back down and began tapping the items on his list. "You used an *un*registered, *un*monitored cell phone for SPIN business. That alone is a basis for dismissal, and it's the least of your offenses."

She squirmed, then offered lamely, "I was afraid if a monitor heard what we were up to, they wouldn't understand. And there wasn't time—"

"Five minutes! That's all it would have taken to call me and clear your plan—"

"And you would have said no!"

"You bet your unregistered cell phone I would have said no. And I would have been right." He raked his fingers through his thick black hair. "It worked out great. I'm as happy as anyone that the Rodriguez girl is safe. But there were other ways to accomplish it. Ways that didn't jeopardize Russo's career, not to mention mine."

She mentally cringed, but didn't dare interrupt.

"Do you understand what a disaster it would have been if you'd been wrong? You would have single-handedly destroyed our relationship with the local cops—guys who were busting their asses to find that kid. They didn't deserve to be made fools of. Plus, you would have ruined the prosecutor's case and probably gotten us sued for violating the brother's civil rights."

"I knew Randy wasn't guilty, Ray. So I knew none of that would happen."

"You're a frickin' genius," he agreed dryly.

"I didn't say that. But it went well—"

"Did it? Since there's no tape of the call, I'll never know exactly what you said to that kid. But the unofficial story is you promised him his sister was still alive and you were going to find her. What if Horton had already killed her? Dammit, Kris, what were you thinking?"

"I had a feeling—"

"Screw feelings and hunches and all that crap," he advised angrily. "I don't believe in that baloney, and neither should you. You're good—*great*—because you make inferences other people miss. You connect the dots in a coroner's report or a psych test or an interrogation transcript. That's the second most important part of your job, and you're terrific at it."

"And the first most important part of my job is being able to articulate my theory to the field agents based on facts." She gave a heartfelt sigh. "I've heard you say that a million times. And guess what. I tried, but I couldn't. I *knew* it was Horton, but I couldn't put my finger on why." Completely deflated, she slumped in her chair and admitted, "I screwed up."

Ray snorted. "Is this where I'm supposed to tell you it's okay because it all turned out for the best?"

"No. Not at all." She studied her hands for a second, then summoned the nerve to ask, "Am I fired?"

"Yeah, right. I'm gonna fire you the same day I'm ordered to give you a commendation."

"Ordered?" Her gut twisted into a knot. "By whom?"

"Your secret admirer. Ulysses S. Payton."

Kristie groaned, knowing how much Ray resented the colonel's license to meddle in his project. "I don't want a commendation from *him*."

"You don't have a choice. It's already part of your record, just like the telegram from the kids' parents, praising you—or rather, Melissa—for saving both their children. Congratulations," he added bitterly.

"I'm sorry, Ray."

"Just tell me it's never going to happen again."

"It won't. I promise. It was a unique, once-in-a-lifetime screwup. I take full responsibility, and I give you my word it will never, ever happen again."

"There's enough blame to go around," he murmured. "I should have seen this coming with you. You're too involved with your cases. And way too chatty with your operatives. I've given you latitude because you're—well, because you're you. That ends today."

"I'm not me anymore?" she quipped, but when his eyes flashed, she told him quickly, "I'm just joking because I feel so guilty about letting you down. And just for the record, it wasn't your fault. You made the rules very clear to me. I knew I was breaking them."

"With Russo's help. That stupid screwup."

"Don't blame Justin."

Ray snorted again. "If anything, I blame him the most. He's an experienced agent. He should've known better than to let you call the shots."

"He was desperate. After six days of frantically searching for that sweet little girl, he believed he had failed. The poor guy felt like crap when he called me. Then I promised him we could find her if he did exactly what I said.

That's the only reason he smuggled a phone into Randy's cell. So don't judge him, please?"

Her boss eyed her intently. "New rules, starting today. Is that understood?"

"New ones? Wouldn't it be enough if I just started obeying the old ones?"

"You'd think so, wouldn't you?" Ray agreed. "But no. You apparently need some extra ones. So here goes. I want you to register any and all personal telephone lines and cell phones with us from now on. We'll randomly monitor them just like we do everything else."

"Fine with me. What else?"

"Start using your backups. That's what they're there for."

Kristie grimaced. The thought of slaving over a scenario and getting it perfect, only to abandon it for twelve full hours every night was unbearable. She had faith in her fellow spinners, but knew in her gut no one could run her cases as well as she could.

Ray leaned back in his chair and rubbed his eyes, clearly frustrated again. "You can't live this job twenty-four hours a day, Kris. It affects your objectivity."

"And objectivity is the key to good spinning? I believe that as much as you do. But the field agents never call at night unless it's an emergency, and in emergencies, it's especially vital for the original spinner to take the call."

"This isn't a negotiation." He exhaled sharply. "Do you understand that you've got to get a life? Make friends. Go to parties. Go on dates! It'll make you sharper. More valuable to everyone, especially the field agents."

"I *have* a life. I don't just sit by the phone and wait for operatives to call at night, you know."

When he arched a disbelieving eyebrow, she explained, "I exercise. And study. I actually have a lot on my plate."

"You *study?*" He chuckled. "What's left for you to learn? I thought you knew it all."

"If you must know, I'm teaching myself Italian. And a little Greek. And kickboxing, too. All the things I lied about in my interview that impressed you so much."

"You're teaching yourself kickboxing?"

"I have a great video."

His tone was gently mocking. "You can't learn self-defense that way, Kristie. Let me set up some lessons for you. Or I can teach you myself. I have a black belt in karate—"

"And I have a pink belt in pacifism," she retorted. "I don't need self-defense training. I just want to understand what my operatives go through. It's a Zen thing—mental, not physical."

"Zen kickboxing?" Ray chuckled again, then shook his head as though to clear away the congenial moment. "Starting today, you're using your backup."

"But—"

"If something happens that your backup can't handle, he or she will contact you, even if it's three o'clock in the morning. You've got to trust them to do their jobs half as well as you do yours."

"Like I said, the operatives don't call in the middle of the night unless it's an emergency. Which means the backup is going to have to refer the call to me anyway. It just seems like a waste of time."

"Emergencies?" Ray reached for a pile of folders and flipped open the top one. "According to this file, you specifically told Will McGregor that he should contact you—day or night—with any question or concern, however small." Raising his gaze, he repeated in disgust, "However small?"

"Okay. I went a little overboard. And for the record, it didn't have any effect. McGregor has never once contacted me. Not at night, not during the day. Not for anything, big or small."

Ray surprised her by grinning at that. "Drives you nuts, doesn't it?"

"No."

"Sure it does. It bugs you that he won't let you play virtual field operative. He does his job his way, not yours. That's why I've been assigning so many of his cases to you. So you'd learn the division of labor around this place." His voice softened. "Just for the record, McGregor never contacts any spinner once the case is under way. Not even me. So don't take it personally. But do try to learn a lesson from it."

Leaning forward, he explained, "You and McGregor are a great team. Every assignment you've had with him has been an unqualified success. Why? Because you prepare a flawless background report and identity for him, and he takes it from there. End of story."

"He really doesn't call you either?"

Ray confirmed with a nod. "I used to handle all his cases personally because they're invariably hot potatoes. But I've never once spoken to the guy in my capacity as a spinner. And only rarely as the director of SPIN. To him, we're just an anonymous resource. Because he's a true professional."

"I'm sold," she assured her boss. "From now on, I'm putting a new note in my file. Something like, 'If you have a nonemergency question between the hours of midnight and 6:00 a.m., please contact my backup.' How's that?"

"Six hours off? No way." Ray leaned forward. "Seven p.m. to 7:00 a.m.—and all day Saturday and Sunday."

"I'm okay with seven to seven on work nights, as long as the operative is in the same time zone as us. Otherwise, I'll have to adjust it. And weekends are tricky—"

"Did I mention this isn't a negotiation?" he asked, clearly struggling not to smile. "But it's a step in the right direction, so I'll take it for now."

"And?"

The smile became a full-fledged laugh. "Yeah, you're back in my will."

Kristie sighed in relief. "I really am sorry, Ray."

"Stop apologizing. You're a pain in the ass, but you also saved that kid—both kids, actually—so you're getting another chance. Don't blow it. And Kris?"

"Yes?"

He walked around to her side of the desk and grasped her chin in his hand, then looked deep into her eyes and murmured, "Nice job."

She bit her lip, unsure of how to respond, especially in light of David's remarks.

Then Ray made the decision for her, stepping back and reminding her gruffly, "I've got tons of cleanup to do today, thanks to your little prank. And you've got a new red folder waiting for you on your desk, so get cracking. Your moment of glory is officially over."

It was a relief to head back to her SPIN cubicle, tucked in a corner with a view of treetops and clouds. She knew that some people would balk at the industrial furniture and artificial lighting, but to Kristie, this high-tech workspace was heaven.

She checked her messages—three new ones in the last half hour, all complimenting her on the Rodriguez case. Then she reached for the new assignment Ray had left on her credenza, but a ring from her priority line, which was reserved for operative assistance, stopped her.

As always when an operative made contact, her pulse quickened, preparing her for a new challenge. But her voice remained calm, professional and reassuring. "This is S-3. Please identify yourself."

"This is Special Agent Justin Russo. I've got a grateful fourteen-year-old here who wants to talk to Melissa Daniels. Any chance of that?"

"Absolutely. Put him on."

Randy's voice was filled with awe. "Hi, Miss Daniels."

"Hey, sugar. How's life?"

"Better. Because of you."

Choking back an un-Melissa-like gulp, Kristie reminded him, "The way I hear it, Lizzie's big brother was the one who really came through for her. So, fill me in. Have they let you visit her yet?"

"Yeah, we've been coloring together all morning. The shrinks want her to draw pictures. To see how messed up she is, I guess. And so far, she hasn't drawn any monsters or anything. Just our house. And our dog. And us."

"Those were the images that made her strong during those terrible days. In her heart, she knew you'd find her, some way, somehow."

"It was you," the boy insisted. "My mom wants you to come to dinner so we can thank you in person."

"Tell her I'd love to, but it's against the rules."

"Yeah. That's what Agent Russo said. But I was thinking…"

"Yes?"

"I'll graduate in four years. Then I've gotta go to college. But after that, I want to help you rescue children. I'll even do it for free, and get another job on the side or something."

Touched, Kristie murmured, "You've got what it takes, Randy. That's for sure. And you've got years to decide the best way to help. Look how many people played a part in saving Lizzie. The cops, the FBI, the witnesses, me, you— and now the psychologists, who are *still* saving her."

"Yeah, but I want to do what you do."

"Sugar, you'd have to get some major surgery before you could do *that*."

She could hear him blushing through the phone, and congratulated herself impishly for the Melissaesque quip. "Give Lizzie a hug for me, sugar. And put Agent Russo on again."

"Okay. Bye, Miss Daniels."

"Bye, handsome."

Justin was laughing when he got back on the line. "What did you say to the poor kid?"

"Hmm?"

"Never mind. We've got important business to discuss."

"Oh?"

"Yeah. I'm taking the next two weeks off."

"You deserve it."

"Right. This case has been a killer. So I'm headed for Tahiti, and I want you to come along."

Kristie sighed. "Take a real girl, Justin. You don't know anything about me. I could be old enough to be your grandma. Or married. I could even be a guy."

"I'll take my chances," he retorted, then his tone softened. "It doesn't have to be romantic, Essie. We're friends, right? I just want to get to know you. To thank you for what you did. Plus, you need a break, too. I'm sure Ortega'll give you time off after what you did last night."

"After what I did last night, he gave me a lecture, all about the rules of spinning. I broke most of them, you know. But even I respect the one about socializing with operatives."

"I socialize with other agents all the time, and that doesn't keep me from being objective when it counts," Justin muttered. "It's a bullshit rule, Essie. Ask Ortega to make an exception, or I might just have to take matters into my own hands."

"What does that mean?"

"It means I know where SPIN headquarters is located, more or less. Maybe I'll spend my vacation on a stakeout instead of an island. That's what I do for a living, remember? And I'm pretty good at it. If I want to meet you, I can and will."

"Okay, that's enough," she scolded him. "I know you're kidding, but the monitors might think you're serious and get us both in trouble. So just be a good little agent and tell me you're going to Tahiti."

Justin growled. "I forgot about that monitor bullshit. Yeah, yeah, I'm kidding."

"And?" she prompted him.

"And I'm going to Tahiti for mindless sex with beach bunnies."

"That's better."

"You oughta take a break, too. And if any monitors are listening," the agent raised his voice and warned, "get your own lives and stop listening to ours!"

Kristie laughed fondly. "Have fun in Tahiti, Justin. Drink something frosty and tropical for me."

"Will do. And I'll call as soon as I get back."

"Assuming we have an active assignment together," she reminded him, still wary of the monitors.

"Stupid bullshit rules," he repeated in clear disgust. "Take care, beautiful."

"Bye, Justin."

As she hung up the phone, she remembered what the agent had said. They were friends. Nothing romantic about it. Just like Kristie and Ray.

Glancing toward her boss's office, she saw him standing there, watching her through the glass wall, his hands on his hips. Without hesitation, she smiled and waved, and to her delight, he smiled and waved back—his old self again.

So much for David's lame-brain theory, she told herself happily, then she opened the new folder—red, which meant it was politically sensitive and on a fast track—and settled down to spin.

Chapter 3

The street was semideserted on her walk home from work, which suited Kristie just fine. It would give her a chance to mull over the details of her new case, so that she could design just the right cover story for the young female agent who would be infiltrating a posh sorority on an Ivy League campus.

Of course, it would have helped to know the agent's mission, but as with most red folders, this one came with strings attached. Nowhere in the file did it reveal the nature of the wrong that would be righted, which told the spinner it was either so highly classified, it couldn't be shared with someone at her level of clearance, or it was some sort of quasi-political vendetta. Perhaps the precious daughter of some high-ranking U.S. government official had become involved in some grade-tampering scandal with her sorority sisters, and SPIN had been enlisted for damage control for fear the episode would reflect on the official's agency or party.

It annoyed Kristie to think she could waste hours of precious spinning on such an undeserving case. Then she reminded herself that it was part of the job. These assignments, however distasteful, helped keep SPIN well financed, even in hard times. And as bad as it was occasionally for the spinners, Ray had it worse. As the director, he was constantly forced to do political favors, most recently and repugnantly, for the president's adviser Colonel Ulysses S. Payton. Kristie remembered the chauvinistic jerk from her interview, and knew that his meddling in SPIN affairs had grown along with his power within the administration in general. The thought that her first commendation had come from so ignominious a source made her want to kick a bop bag.

If Ray can put up with Payton, you can be a sport about this sorority caper, she told herself briskly. *It might even be fun. Just give your imagination free rein on this one.*

But something else had captured her imagination—the sensation that someone was following her. Surprisingly, the idea didn't frighten her. After all, she was just three blocks from home on a well-lit, well-traveled street. It was simply intriguing, especially when she reminded herself of what Ray had said—that there was no such thing as instinct or intuition. Forcing herself to pay closer attention, she realized she could actually hear a second pair of footsteps. And unlike the sounds from the soft-soled shoes she had changed into just before heading out of the office, these were the dull *clop-clop-clop* of men's dress shoes.

Not instinct. Just observation and deduction.

And it definitely didn't require instinct for her to guess the identity of her stalker.

You just had to prove your point, didn't you, Justin? she grumbled silently, remembering the agent's threat to arrange a face-to-face meeting.

Several other SPIN employees lived in her neighborhood, and the last thing she needed was to be seen socializing with a field agent, so she ducked down an alley, then turned and planted her hands on her hips, ready to give the agent a piece of her mind. But it wasn't clean-cut Justin Russo who strode right up to her. It was someone much scarier.

"Ray!"

His golden-brown eyes were wide, his voice strained. "What are you doing in an alley? Are you insane? What if I'd been a mugger?"

"Then I would have kicked your ass," she quipped.

"What?"

Kristie winced. "I'm kidding, Ray. I knew you weren't a mugger. From your shoes."

"Pardon?"

"Men's dress shoes. Not exactly designed for a quick getaway." She tapped her temple with her index finger. "Analysis. Not instinct."

"You were willing to bet your life on the fact that muggers never wear dress shoes?" His scowl deepened. "I still don't get why you went down the alley. You didn't know it was me."

"The truth?" She squirmed but admitted, "I thought it might be Justin."

"Russo?"

"Get a grip. I was wrong. It's just…" She tried to smile, failed, and grimaced instead. "He joked about it today on the phone. About meeting me. I heard the footsteps of a well-dressed, athletic, clearly good-looking guy, and jumped to conclusions."

"Athletic and good-looking?" Ray chuckled. "Nice save. Come on. I'll walk you home."

"Not so fast, Ortega."

"Huh?"

She eyed him sternly. "You interrogated me. Now it's my turn. Why were *you* following *me?*"

"I wasn't." He cleared his throat. "Not really. I was just trying to catch up to you."

"Oh?"

"Yeah. I wanted to talk to you before you left, but I got a call. Then you took off. So I followed. I would've called out your name, but I didn't want to startle you."

She stepped closer, intrigued by the fact that he seemed uncomfortable. "Talk to me about what?"

He flushed. "I was a little rough on you this morning."

"And so?" She flashed a playful smile. "You wanted to apologize? But instead you scared me half to death?"

"You didn't look scared."

"And you don't sound apologetic."

"Touché." Ray inclined his head toward the brightly lit street. "Walk with me."

When he cupped her elbow with his hand and steered her toward home, she reminded herself that it meant nothing. She wouldn't even have noticed the intimate gesture if not for the Curse of David Wong.

You're a dead man for psyching me out like this, she told the absent spinner. Aloud, she prompted Ray, "You said something about an apology?"

"And now I'm saying something about self-defense lessons."

"Pardon?"

He shrugged his shoulders. "If you're going to take chances like the one you just took, you need to get some sensible shoes—not just tennies—and you need some in-struction. Like I said, I can give you some pointers. Or you could take a real class—"

"I took a self-defense class in college. Eye-gouging, nut-kicking, thumb-bending—all sorts of violence." She flashed a teasing smile. "I'm a lover not a fighter."

"Yeah, well, you might not like the kind of lovemak-ing a mugger has in mind."

"How many times do I have to tell you, I *knew* it wasn't a mugger. Sheesh, if this is your idea of an apology, I don't think I want one."

They had reached the vestibule of her apartment build-ing, and she glared playfully as she inserted her key in the lock. "If I invite you up, do you promise not to nag me?"

Ray laughed. "I promise."

He took her arm again as they climbed the two flights of stairs leading to her unit. "I haven't been here since you moved in."

"I only found it because of you. And it's been such a great place. Big and quiet. Just what I needed."

She stole a sideways glance, knowing that their em-ployer-employee relationship made outside socializing awkward for such a rule-oriented guy. He could be bud-dies with David, a married male, but an unmarried female subordinate was a different story.

So why was tonight different? Was this part of the apol-ogy? Or was David right, and Ray was going to make some sort of move on her?

In any case, she was determined to be a good hostess, so she quickly unlocked the door, pushed it open and mo-tioned for him to enter. "Ta da."

He walked past her, then whistled appreciatively as he surveyed walls lined from floor to ceiling with bookshelves. "It looks completely different. Nice, but different. I see now where your paycheck goes."

"Books make expensive wallpaper, as my uncle says. But it never goes out of style."

She bustled past him, depositing her keys and belongings on the coffee table and turning on lights. "I have a bottle of champagne in the fridge. Want some?"

"Champagne?" His brown eyes warmed. "What's the occasion?"

She flushed, hoping he hadn't mistaken her careless hospitality for a romantic overture. "No occasion. I just don't have company very often."

He seemed about to respond—most likely to remind her of his advice to get a life—then he just shrugged instead and wandered over to the doorway of the spare bedroom, where he promptly began to laugh. "What's this?"

"If you're referring to my sparring partner, she has a name. Betty Bop."

"Unbelievable. Let's hope you get attacked by a micromugger."

"She's short but wily." Kristie joined him, smiling toward the five-foot-high toy. "I figure if I can kick *her* in the head, I can easily reach most guys' groins. That's the target of choice, right?"

"Right. Unless they have a gun."

She nodded. "That's the one thing Betty can't do for me."

"The *one* thing?"

Kristie eyed him sternly. "Since you're here, maybe I'll put you to work. Come on." She dragged him by the arm back into the living room, then picked up a wooden ruler from her desk. "Hold this like a knife. Let's see if I can kick it out of your hand."

Ray groaned. "I was kidding. If you ever get mugged by a guy with a knife, submit. They taught you that in self-defense, didn't they?"

"Submit? Not bloody likely," she told him in her best Cockney accent. Then she instructed, "Come at me like you're going to attack me. But don't worry, I'll aim for the ruler not your hand, so you won't get hurt. I just want to see if I can disarm you."

"Take my word for it. You can't."

Kristie glared. "It's not like I'm completely untrained. My grandparents forced me to take aikido for two years in high school, and I still have most of the movements down. Plus, I'm almost finished with the video kickboxing class. So bring it on, Ortega. Unless you're afraid."

"Fine," Ray grumbled. "Let's get this farce over with." Then he gripped the ruler in his right palm and moved toward Kristie.

She took careful aim and kicked, but in the split second it took for her to move, Ray had expertly shifted the "weapon" to his left hand, freeing up the right to grab her by the ankle the moment her foot reached its aborted target. Then he flipped her to the floor.

The impact knocked Kristie's breath from her chest, and before she could even hope to react, Ray was on her, pinning her securely while pressing the blunt edge of the ruler to her throat.

And for a split second, she was terrified—not by the fall, or even by the weapon, but by Ray's cold, vacant eyes. It was almost as if he were in a trance.

Then her fear was replaced by a heady rush of admiration and she murmured, "Can you teach me to do that?"

Ray seemed startled by her voice, and quickly shrugged to his feet. Then he laid the weapon carefully on the desk.

"The lesson is over. And I'll take a rain check on that champagne. I've got a lot of work to do tonight."

"Wait!" Kristie scrambled to join him, ignoring a twinge of pain in her shoulders and spine. "You have to eat dinner, don't you? We could get a pizza."

"Some other time."

She didn't want to let him leave. Not this way. So she demanded lightly, "What about my apology?"

"That's over, too." He hesitated, then touched her cheek. "Did I hurt you, Kris?"

"Of course not. I told you, I took aikido. If nothing else, I know how to fall."

"See you in the morning then?"

She nodded, watching in confusion as he let himself out of the apartment.

The episode had reminded her that she didn't actually know much about Ray Ortega despite their close office relationship over the past six months. Picking up the ruler, she turned it over and over in her hand, remembering the answer he'd given her the one and only time she had tried to quiz him about his past.

Four years in college; four in the military; four years I don't talk about—not ever. And now SPIN. That's all you need to know about me.

And Ray being Ray, "not ever" had meant just that. They had never discussed it again. Still, Kristie had speculated about those four years, imagining covert operations so highly classified, Ray still wasn't allowed to discuss them. She had assumed he masterminded those ops, but this impromptu demonstration with the ruler suggested he might have done more than just plot strategies—he was perfectly capable of executing them, too.

She was sure she had just caught a flashback to Ray's

past life and the thought fascinated her. She also realized he hadn't made a romantic move on her despite having her flat on her back. So much for David's theory.

Her SPIN line rang at that moment, and she assumed it was her boss, calling from his cell to put a cap on the evening's adventure. Still, she answered with her SPIN-approved salutation. "This is S-3. Please identify yourself."

"This is Will McGregor," a deep, gravelly voice informed her. "I know it's late, so if this is a bad time—"

"It's fine," she interrupted him, her imagination shifting instantly to her favorite file photo of the thirty-two-year-old FBI agent. It was a black-and-white shot, but his eyes, which she knew were blue, still managed to have an effect on her every time she happened upon the picture in his folder.

Coughing to dispel any breathlessness from her tone, she asked briskly, "What can I do for you, Agent McGregor?"

"There's a problem with the setup on the Mannington case. We may have to scrap it. I thought I'd give you a heads-up so you can start doing whatever it is you do to come up with something else."

Her heart sank. "What kind of problem? It seemed so perfect."

"Yeah, I thought so, too," he admitted. "Your usual brilliance. But Manny isn't following *his* usual pattern, so I haven't had much of a chance to establish a rapport with him."

Kristie frowned. "You mean he's not coming to the bar? Or he won't talk to you while he's there?"

"He's been a no-show for four nights straight. I'm willing to be patient, but at some point, it makes more sense to retool, right?"

"Four nights?" She shook her head, remembering the details of "Manny" Mannington's file. For more than ten years, the barfly had chosen one particular bar, Rafferty's, to frequent at least five nights a week. According to reliable sources, one could usually set one's watch by Manny's comings and goings, especially on Wednesday nights, otherwise known as All-You-Can-Eat Hot-Dog Night.

What on earth was going on?

"Are you sure he's in town?"

"Yeah, just staying home."

"Impossible."

"I read the file, too," McGregor assured her. "But facts are facts. He isn't coming to the bar."

"You said he's been a no-show for four nights straight. But you've been there for over two weeks. That means there was contact at the beginning?"

"Yeah, it went like clockwork." McGregor chuckled. "That toy-salesman cover you designed for me seemed stupid, but you were dead-on right. It provided endless topics for casual conversation with the guys. Manny in particular has fond memories of Christmases past, and luckily, I remembered enough from my nerdy grade-school days to be able to sound professional."

"I'll bet Manny played with G.I. Joe, right?"

"Yeah. How'd you know?" He paused. "You're something else, S-3."

With the cordless handset pressed firmly to her ear, Kristie moved to her computer. "You're sure he's at his house? Let's see if he's online."

"You can do that?"

"I did it a couple of times last month, when I was working up his informant profile. You can learn a lot about a person by watching them surf. Hold on, I'm just about—

there!" She studied the screen. "He's very active. Looking for something. Shopping, or rather, scavenging. Mostly the auction sites. Hold on."

"What's he shopping for?"

"A blue 1969 Mustang convertible in near-mint condition." Kristie bit her lip. "There's nothing in his background to indicate he's a car buff. This doesn't make sense, unless…" She scrutinized one of Mannington's online offers closely. "He doesn't just want low miles and great condition. He wants this baby right away. What would make a bagman so desperate to acquire a particular car?"

Wracking her brain, she arrived at only two possible conclusions. Either this was a favor for "the Boss," or it was a gift for Manny's debutante wife. Those were the only two people in the world that could keep the loquacious socializer out of Rafferty's on Hot-Dog Night.

"It's got to be the wife," she murmured, grabbing the duplicate file from her desk and scanning it anxiously. "Maybe her birthday's coming up."

Locating the relevant information, she grinned. "Or worse. Her birthday was four days ago. And I'll bet poor Manny missed it. And now he's in the doghouse and out of the bed."

McGregor whistled softly. "That's gotta be it. The man's insane for that woman, and it's not hard to figure out why. Five foot ten with state-of-the-art implants. And if half of what he says is true…well, never mind."

Kristie laughed. "We'll get those lovebirds back together in no time. The Bureau gave SPIN a big budget for this case, so acquiring the Mustang quickly shouldn't be a problem, even if we have to do a little restoration. As soon as we hang up, I'll respond to Manny's inquiry using one of our auction pseudonyms."

"Like I said, you're something else. Thanks for the help. Give me a call if you need anything on my end."

"Wait! We're not done."

"We're not?"

"Uh-uh. We've been given an amazing opportunity here, McGregor," she insisted. "Manny's vulnerable. We need to find a way to take advantage of that."

"Just get the car. I'll take care of the rest."

Kristie smiled at his take-charge, impatient tone. A loner, just like everyone said. But it was time to teach him the usefulness of partnering with a spinner.

"Won't you please hear me out?" she asked, and when he grumbled something that sounded vaguely like permission, she forged ahead. "Manny won't be back to Rafferty's for a day or two. But you should go there later tonight. And instead of being your usual charming self, you'll drink too much and mope at the end of the bar. When the bartender asks what's wrong, you'll resist talking about it at first, then you'll end up pouring your heart out to him."

Pleased that McGregor hadn't yet interrupted her, she continued. "You'll tell him all about Melissa Daniels, the girl you've been seeing. She's beautiful, wild, sexy, temperamental—and unbelievably jealous. She saw you having an innocent drink with your secretary and dumped you on the spot."

A warm chuckle came over the phone line. "What're you doing to me, S-3? I've got a reputation to protect with these guys."

Kristie laughed, too. "You don't really care what the rest of them think, right? You just want to be friends with Manny."

"You figure when he gets back, he'll hear about my broken heart and think we're…what? Kindred spirits?"

"Right. He'll probably start coming to the bar as soon as he knows the car is on its way. But until it's actually delivered, he'll still be in the doghouse in his wife's eyes. You'll have a few days to cry in your beers together."

"It's not a bad idea," McGregor murmured.

"And as far as your reputation is concerned, all you need to do is tell the guys about some of your sex-capades with Melissa, and they'll see you as a stud not a wimp."

The agent was laughing again. "Sex-capades?"

"Right. You can draw on your own experience, or if you'd like, I could come up with some for you. Either way, lay it on thick. Like the story of the first time you met her. At a toy convention in Vegas. How the two of you had so much chemistry, you couldn't wait to get upstairs to your hotel room, and ended up tearing each other's clothes off in the elevator. Likewise with the first dinner date—you picked her up in a limo but never made it to the restaurant. Just drove around all night making wild, passionate love. And don't even get me started about the first airplane trip you took together!"

"Those are the same sorts of stories Manny tells about his wife."

"Right. He knows all about stormy relationships. The kind that can consume a person if they're not careful. Jealousy, breakups, gut-wrenching arguments, exquisite make-up sex—the most obsessive, destructive, exhilarating addiction possible. Show him you and Melissa have— or rather, had—that sort of thing, and he'll be putty in your hands."

McGregor was silent for a moment, then proclaimed, "It's effing brilliant."

Kristie exhaled in relief. "I'll have a courier bring you a snapshot of her tomorrow for your wallet. Something sexy but classy. We'll rough it up so it looks like you've been carrying it around for a while."

"You have a picture of this Melissa?"

"Computer generated. I use her a lot. She's sort of a virtual operative. She usually has red hair and green eyes, but if you'd prefer something else, name it."

He was silent for a moment, then said simply, "You decide."

"Okay, red it is. Do you need anything else from me?"

When he was silent, she asked warily, "McGregor? Is something wrong?"

"I can't keep calling you S-3. What's your real name?"

Startled, she gave a nervous laugh. "You know I can't tell you that."

"I'm gonna call you Goldie then."

"Pardon?"

"Because you spin lies into gold."

She smiled with delight. "That's sweet. And so much nicer than calling me Rumpelstiltskin."

"Huh?"

"From the fairy tale."

"Right. Rumpelstiltskin from the fairy tale. Is there anything you don't know?"

"Minutia is my life," she assured him. Then she added fondly, "Knock 'em dead at the bar tonight. I'll arrange the sale of the car right away. With any luck, Manny'll be back in Rafferty's tomorrow."

"It's not exactly a life-or-death situation," he reminded her. "Find the car tomorrow. I'll call in the afternoon for the update."

She wanted to protest, but knew it might scare him back into loner mode. So she contented herself with saying, "Good night, Agent McGregor. And good luck." Then she hung up the phone and turned her attention to composing an offer irresistible enough to lure Manny Mannington into their trap.

And if she succeeded and decided to call McGregor back after all—just to give him a thoroughly professional and unemotional update—what monitor could possibly object to *that?*

Chapter 4

It took Kristie six hours to locate a car for Manny Mannington, and while the mileage was higher than he had specified, she knew a SPIN crew could roll back the odometer and spruce up the details enough to fool the bagman and his bride. Predictably, Manny was eager to consummate the transaction as soon as Kristie made e-mail contact with him, and by 2:00 a.m., West Coast time, they had a deal.

Elated, she tried to reach McGregor in his San Diego hotel room but was only able to leave him a message. It was tempting to suggest he call her back regardless of the hour, but again she wanted to respect the loner in him, so she provided highlights of her coup in the message itself. Tomorrow would be soon enough to share the rest of the details. And she had to admit, her neck and shoulders were bothering her, courtesy of Ray's knifing lesson, so she forced herself to be sensible and crawled into bed.

Coups aside, she was still achy and groggy the next morning. So she dressed in jeans and a black knit pullover instead of her usual bargain-basement suit before heading to SPIN headquarters, where Ray Ortega was waiting in the reception area.

"My office. Now," he instructed her.

She followed him into the room and closed the door. "Am I in trouble again?"

"There's a basic self-defense course starting the first of next month at my health club. I want you to enroll."

"I told you, I already took a course. Plus, I have Betty Bop as my personal trainer. I'm ready for the big leagues." She smiled. "But if your offer to teach me personally is still open, that's a different story."

"Last night reminded me why I can't do that," he told her, adding gently, "How's your back?"

"I'll live." She gave him a hopeful smile. "If you hadn't pulled that little switcheroo, I still think I could have kicked the ruler out of your hand."

He chuckled. "Yeah, actually, it was a good kick. Just save it for the bop bag from now on." Clearing his throat, he added gruffly, "Let's get down to business."

He handed her two sheets of paper, then motioned for her to sit down, while he moved to his seat behind the desk. "Sign on the dotted line. Unless you want to consult a lawyer first."

She scanned the first page, which was a consent form allowing SPIN to monitor her cell phone. "No problem. Can I borrow a pen?"

Ray handed her one. "It doesn't explicitly exempt conversations with your aunt and uncle, but you have my word that we'll respect your privacy on those calls."

Kristie gave him a grateful nod. "We rarely call each

other these days, since they're always traveling, and the time zones don't match up."

"That must be rough."

"On me? Hardly. I mean, they raised me and I love them to death, but after I left for college, the relationship went back to how it was when my parents were alive. Loving but distant." She winced, knowing that the words didn't do justice to the huge sacrifice her childless aunt and uncle had made for her. "They're always there for me, and vice versa. But they have to travel so much, we use e-mail to keep in touch."

"That's covered on page two."

Grimacing, she turned her attention to the second sheet of paper. "My personal e-mail accounts? Are you going to bug my apartment, too?"

"Do we need to?"

She shrugged as she signed. "What a week."

"I know. But you saved a little girl's life. That counts for a lot."

"Not only that—" she began, anxious to tell him about McGregor's call, but his secretary interrupted, buzzing him loudly on the intercom.

"What is it, Beth?"

"Someone named Jane Smith is on her way up. She claims she's an old friend."

"Shit." Ray inclined his head toward the door. "Excuse me, okay? We'll pick this up again later."

"Who's Jane Smith?"

When his only answer was to arch an eyebrow in mock reprimand, she jumped up and saluted just as playfully. "I'll be at my desk if you need someone to yell at later, sir."

"Get going, smart-ass."

His tone was light, but Kristie wasn't fooled. He didn't want her to be around when the mysterious Jane Smith arrived.

Intrigued, she stopped at David Wong's cubicle on her way to her own. "Hey."

"Hi." He leaned back in his chair and studied her casual outfit, then arched an eyebrow. "Late night?"

She nodded.

"Hot date?"

"Knife fight." She plopped herself into his extra chair. "What do you know about a woman named Jane Smith?"

"Why do you ask?"

"Because she's on her way up. And Ray won't tell me who she is."

David glanced toward the glass-walled office. "It's need-to-know information. And *you* need to butt out."

"Lovely." She rolled her eyes. "I'm not leaving until you sing like a canary. Starting with the name. It sounds fake."

He shrugged. "I never met her. She worked with Ray a long time ago. That's all I know. Honest."

"There she is." Kristie watched intently as a tall woman with shortly cropped brown hair emerged from the elevator and strode toward Ray's office. The visitor's navy blue pantsuit was smartly cut, and she appeared to be in her midthirties. Not particularly pretty, but so confident she immediately owned the place. "Good grief, David. I never met a real dominatrix before."

"Shush."

"Tell me about her. Please?"

"I don't know anything," he insisted. "And even if I did, I've got work to do. And that ringing in your ears is your operative line, if that matters to you."

She jumped up. "McGregor! I've got to get that." Sprinting for her cubicle, she managed to grab the receiver one instant before the call rolled over to voice mail. "McGregor?"

"Goldie? Great. I was about to leave a message on your voice mail, but wasn't sure whether to address it to you or Melissa."

She sank into her chair, delighted to hear his sexy voice, but also a bit sheepish over answering her SPIN line as informally as she'd done. "Did it go well last night?"

"Better than well. Manny was so relieved about the car, he showed up at the bar just as it was closing."

"And? Did you commiserate together?"

"I didn't want to overplay it, so I just slipped out of the place without even talking to him. But the bartender got an earful from me before that. If we're real lucky, he filled Manny in. If not, I'll do it tonight."

"Perfect." She moistened her lips. "The car will be ready today, but I'll delay delivery until Friday. That should give you plenty of time to bond."

"Yeah. I think this will work."

A shiver of pride coursed through her. "Call me tonight, okay? I won't be able to sleep until I hear how it went."

"It could be three in the morning your time," McGregor protested. "You'd better learn to pace yourself, S-3. This could go on for weeks, you know."

"Kristie!" It was Beth, calling to her from across the room, then motioning toward the closed door to Ray's office. "He wants to see you right away."

Kristie could see through the half-opened blinds that Jane Smith was still in Ray's office. Conflicted, she murmured, "McGregor? I have to go. But I'll call you back—"

"Not necessary. I just wanted to say thanks. Take it easy, Goldie."

She winced as a click echoed through the phone wire. He had sounded so final.

And after all we've meant to each other, she reprimanded him, only half joking. But as frustrated as she was over the FBI agent's attitude, she had to admit that the prospect of meeting Ray's mysterious visitor was a great consolation prize.

She only wished she hadn't dressed so casually today of all days. But there wasn't time to change into the spare suit she kept hanging in her cubicle, so she settled for smoothing a few loose hairs back into her French braid, then hurried to Ray's office.

"Come on in, Kristie." He motioned for her to take a seat at the round conference table in the far corner of his office, where his visitor was already sitting. "This is Jane Smith. She runs a counterintelligence unit for the CIA."

CIA. Kristie tingled as she joined them at the table, but quickly reminded herself that six short months ago, the initials F-B-I had impressed her, too, and now it was just another acronym.

"Nice to meet you," she told Jane Smith.

She could see now that the woman was older than she'd appeared from afar, perhaps in her midforties. Fine lines surrounded her pale blue eyes, and a few gray hairs were sprinkled among the chestnut ones.

But it was the agent's attitude that really made an impression on the spinner. Take-charge, despite the fact that this was someone else's turf.

"May I call you Kristie?" the woman began.

"Yes." She was tempted to ask if she could call the

agent Jane—assuming that was her real name, which seemed doubtful.

The visitor arched an eyebrow. "You're getting quite a reputation. Did you know that?"

"A reputation?"

Smith nodded. "Your skill as a profiler makes sense, since you concentrated your studies on abnormal psychology. But your talent for strategizing. Improvising. Creating opportunities out of thin air. That's impressive. To what do you attribute it?"

"Curiosity maybe?" Kristie shrugged. "I'm pretty eclectic in my interests, and I like figuring out how and why things work. Or don't work. Especially the way seemingly innocuous variations can affect a result. In other words," she added cheerfully, "I'm a nerd."

The agent nodded in apparent agreement. "The tiniest detail can spell the difference between success and failure. And in my line of work, the difference between life and death. I suppose that's the same for your so-called spinning, although on a less dramatic scale."

"It's dramatic enough for us," Ray retorted.

Smith gave him an amused look. "You haven't changed. Still competitive as hell." Turning her attention back to Kristie, she said, "I've asked Ray to loan you to me for a couple of days. He's going to say yes because the president wants him to say yes. Isn't that right, Ray?"

"Loan me to you?" Kristie's pulse quickened. "To design a strategy for one of your operations?"

"A backup strategy. My best people have already come up with the primary plan, and it's as close to foolproof as possible, given the multitude of 'variations' as you call them. But this job is important—as important as anything I've ever done, and definitely more important than anything *you'll* ever handle. So—" she smiled grimly "—I decided to get an outside opinion."

Kristie's ego bristled, and she expected Ray to defend the importance of work done at SPIN, but he simply said, "We're willing to help within certain parameters."

"Which are?"

"You'll brief us. *Both* of us. Then you'll go away. Kristie will design the scenario under my supervision, and when she's done, we'll send it over. If you have questions, the three of us will meet."

"You're afraid I'll try to steal her away from you?" Smith rolled her pale blue eyes. "Believe me, that's not on the agenda. What I like most about this girl is that she's a civilian. Trained by you—the best profiler in the business, and a pretty good strategist in your own right."

When Ray ignored the compliment, the agent shrugged her shoulders. "Kristie can bring a fresh perspective to this. That's all I need. So your rules are fine with me. In fact, I wouldn't have it any other way."

Barely able to contain her excitement despite the tension between Ray and the agent, Kristie demanded, "What's the assignment?"

"You'll find what you need in here." Smith pulled a folder from her briefcase. "It's fairly straightforward. Your security clearance is something of a joke, so the details are sketchy. But that shouldn't matter. All we're asking you to do is plan a good old-fashioned heist."

"Pardon?"

"I *thought* that would intrigue you." The agent's eyes twinkled. "Our target is a wall safe, hidden in an inner room in a mansion in Palm Springs, California. We have reliable intel on the layout and the security. But we'll only get one shot, so we want to get it right."

"What's in the safe?"

"A disk, maybe two, containing the names and positions of half a dozen moles in sensitive positions in federal government. We've known for some time that the owner of the mansion, a shipping magnate named Kenneth Salinger, was working for the other side. We've been watching him, and were about to move in when we heard about the disk. We want it."

"I don't mean to sound naive, but if you know exactly where it is, and you have grounds to arrest Salinger, why not just—"

"Get a warrant?" Jane Smith burst into laughter. "Why didn't *I* think of that! My God, Ray, she's priceless."

Ray shot her a silencing glare. "It's a reasonable suggestion. I suppose you're saying Salinger has some sort of contingency in place?"

"He and his people are armed with remote devices," Jane confirmed. "They'd blow that safe in an instant if they thought we were on to him, much less arresting him." To Kristie she added, "If we showed up out of nowhere at his front door, the disk would be destroyed before our people could start down the hall. Our best chance is to sneak in and get it, then arrest him." She stood up and secured the latches on her briefcase. "We originally planned on going in this weekend. Salinger's hosting a cactus show on the premises and we could easily put someone there undercover. But instead we're going to use it as an opportunity to gather additional information, so we may have more for you in a couple of days.

"Meanwhile, just look over the file. Start getting a feel for it. Do whatever it is you do to research the alarm systems, et cetera. And get to know Salinger—he's a real piece of work." Smith's tone softened. "You'll undoubtedly have questions. That's fine. I'll come back on Friday to answer them. And if you want my team to gather particular intel during the cactus show, just make a wish list, and they'll see what they can do. Is that clear?"

"How soon will you need the final product?" Ray asked.

"There's another big event at Salinger's house in three weeks. Some sort of art auction. We'd rather not wait that long, but access is such a bitch in this situation, we don't seem to have a choice. Unless of course your spinner comes up with something we missed."

Kristie raised a finger to interrupt them. "I have a question."

"Another one?" Jane Smith's reaction was almost a sneer. "I hope it's better than the warrant brainstorm."

The spinner silently counted to ten, then leveled a no-nonsense stare directly into the agent's eyes. "You're CIA. This is a domestic operation. Is jurisdiction a factor here?"

"Homeland Security is coordinating this. And my team is detached to the FBI as consultants. But believe me, we're running the show. Do you have a problem with that?"

"Me?" Kristie shrugged. "I just don't want to break any laws."

"Since when? You talked to that juvenile detainee without his parents or attorney present," Jane Smith reminded her coolly. "If it hadn't been for that little stunt, I wouldn't be here even if you were the best strategist on the planet. So save the holier-than-thou attitude for the folks back on the farm."

"That's enough," Ray warned.

The CIA operative laughed. "I agree. Kristie? Study the files. See what you can come up with. We're particularly interested in the best routes for entry and for escape."

"Although technically, once you get in and acquire the disk, you don't really need to get out. Just execute the arrest warrant, assuming you really have one," Kristie suggested.

When Jane Smith winced, Ray chuckled with pride. "Sounds like Kristie has all the information—about your mission *and* you—she needs. See you Friday."

"I can hardly wait." The agent gave them a haughty glare, then swung her briefcase off the table and strode out of the office.

"Wow, I hope she's not someone you care about, Ray, because—" Kristie paused for emphasis, then insisted "—what a bitch."

"That's the general consensus." He patted Kristie's hand. "Be careful, okay? Help them out, but run everything by me first. She's a dangerous woman. Good at her job, but ruthless and ambitious."

"You guys have a past?"

"We worked together for a couple of years. Not a time I'm particularly fond of. But it taught me a lot. Now I'm teaching you. Don't trust her."

Kristie cocked her head to the side. "For example…?"

"For example, I wouldn't be surprised to learn she's not after a list of moles at all."

"Wow. What do you think she wants from that safe?"

"Who knows? It probably is a disk of some sort—she'd want to be accurate about that detail so that your plan takes size, weight, et cetera, into account. But the contents of the disk are anyone's guess. All we know for sure is, this op will further her career. And if we're not careful, it'll do so at our expense."

"That's pretty cynical."

"But accurate. She's always been that way. But now that

she's getting a little older—a little slower—I'm guessing she's even more desperate. Ergo, more dangerous."

The spinner sighed. "Okay, I'll be careful."

"Good. But have fun with this, too." He touched her hand again. "It's a helluva compliment. And she was right about one thing—you're something special. Thanks for making SPIN look good."

Kristie felt her cheeks redden. "Like she said, I was trained by the best. So…" She gathered up the Salinger file. "I guess I'd better get started."

"Yeah. I'll transfer all your active assignments to David for the next few days."

"Ooh, that reminds me. Guess who called last night. Will McGregor."

Ray seemed genuinely surprised. "Why?"

"That toy-salesman cover wasn't working because the target was busy trying to get out of the doghouse with his ingenue wife. Forgot her birthday."

"Sounds like the Bureau needs to send someone else in. With a different cover. David can take that on."

"McGregor and I worked it out. Came up with the perfect birthday present, *et voilà!* The assignment's back on track, and McGregor and Manny have something to bond over."

Ray arched an eyebrow. "What time last night did McGregor call you?"

"This all happened before I had a chance to announce the new rules. The new *old* rules, I mean."

Ray laughed. "I'm not worried. It's McGregor, after all. He's not going to make a habit of it, so no harm done."

"Right."

She bit her lip and Ray seemed to notice right away, demanding, "What now?"

Kristie flashed what she hoped was an innocent smile. "When you tell the operator to direct my calls to David, make sure that doesn't include Justin Russo. Okay?"

"Russo?" Ray practically spat the name. "I thought he was in Tahiti."

"He is. But he'll be checking on Lizzie Rodriguez's condition. If he calls me with an update, I want to hear it."

Ray's scowl disappeared. "Yeah, okay. Calls from Russo will go directly to you. And when you hear about the kid's condition, let me know right away, too."

"You're such a softy," Kristie told him, adding nonchalantly, "And calls from Agent McGregor should come directly to me, too, okay?"

The scowl returned. "Didn't I just say David will take over your assignments?"

"You also said McGregor won't make a habit of it. Which means if he calls, it'll be important. And it'll be about Melissa. David can't possibly deal with that."

"You dragged Melissa into another case?" Ray's frown returned. "Someday you and I are gonna have a long talk about you and your alter ego."

"And meanwhile?"

"Sure, McGregor's calls can go to you. But don't hold your breath. Like I told you yesterday, he's a professional."

Kristie suspected Ray was right. McGregor wouldn't contact her again—or at least, not without a little encouragement. So she called him that evening just to touch base. "Did the photo of Melissa arrive?"

"Yeah. She's pretty hot," he said teasingly. "The guys at the bar are gonna love her."

Kristie's cheeks warmed. "I promised to concoct a few stories for you about her. Such as, you met her at a doll show. She was wearing a ruffled sundress and a wide-brimmed straw hat. Very sexy. Very Southern plantation."

McGregor's deep laugh rumbled over the monitored line. "Southern plantation, huh? No wonder I went nuts."

"You never stood a chance."

"Yeah, I'll bet." He cleared his throat. "Is the photo based on you?"

"It's computer generated," she insisted. "If there's nothing else, Agent McGregor, I'd better get back to my new assignment. Feel free to call if you need me. Or if you just want to brainstorm a little. We're a team now, you know."

"Yeah, I'm starting to get that," he admitted. "I'll check in tonight. Take it easy until then."

And right on schedule, he began calling her in the middle of the night as soon as he'd left the bar, updating her on his heart-to-heart talks with Manny, who had almost instantly proclaimed McGregor to be the brother he had always wanted. And while the lovesick thug still didn't discuss "business" with his new friend, he did begin telling other secrets, and McGregor was pleased with the progress.

Kristie, on the other hand, craved victory not progress. "I keep trying to think of some way to catapult this to the next level," she told the agent in frustration. "Something you can say to him to make him trust you so completely, he can't resist sharing details about the syndicate."

"Patience, Goldie," McGregor advised her. "Some things are worth waiting for. I promise."

Did he mean it to sound so seductive? she wondered. So prophetic?

Some things are worth waiting for...

"Okay," she told him, struggling to keep her tone cool. "We'll be patient."

"Right. Manny's like a fish. We've got him hooked. Now we've just gotta reel him in."

So much for seduction, she told herself with a wry laugh, but aloud she insisted, "I'm all ears, McGregor. Educate me."

To her surprise, he proceeded to do just that, giving her a string of examples from his own early undercover experiences. And while the nominal reason was to teach her the value of patience, she was sure he was also trying to strengthen their newfound connection. The stories were work related, but also profoundly personal, providing glimpses into his life that she hadn't dared dream she'd ever get.

She needed those moments, not just for the visceral thrill and occasional romantic vibe, but also to keep her from becoming obsessed with the Salinger file, which was easily the most challenging case she had ever faced.

And even if it wasn't, she was determined to design a scenario that truly knocked the socks off a certain bitchy CIA agent.

As for Salinger himself, Kristie was learning he was one scary guy. No criminal record, but the CIA file identified him as the mastermind behind several "accidents" that were undoubtedly assassinations. He had made a fortune in shipping, which provided both the financial means and the network for his anti-USA activities, while also allowing him to be perceived by the community as a respectable businessman. He left most of his dirty work to a certain bodyguard known as the Axe—a psychopath devoted to serving his boss's interests.

Salinger's defining characteristic was his thirst for revenge, which translated into a profound hatred for his native country. It drove his every waking thought, fueled by his certainty that his younger brother's death in the Gulf War had been orchestrated by high-level U.S. officials to prevent a lucrative contract for one of the president's campaign contributors. According to the CIA's file, there was no truth to Salinger's suspicions about his brother's death. But given Ray's cynical assessment of Jane Smith, Kristie reserved judgment on whether the file was accurate on that issue.

Meanwhile, she focused her attention on the target: Salinger's Palm Springs estate. It was an oasis, carved from the desert, irrigated by the snowcaps of the nearby mountain ranges and resplendent with every luxury known to man, including a private golf course.

The triple-crowning glories of the place were Salinger's world-renowned cactus garden, his collection of priceless paintings, housed in a rotunda-style gallery in the center of his home, and the art gallery's domed skylight, fashioned from delicate Italian glass that had been tinted blue and white to resemble a sky filled with clouds.

If Jane Smith's intel was correct, the safe containing the disk was hidden behind one of the paintings in the glass-roofed gallery. And the more Kristie studied the situation, the more convinced she became that she had to see that gallery in person. Providing the reconnaissance team with a wish list seemed inefficient, when she could go on the scouting trip herself. And since the venue would be a harmless garden party, there was no danger at all, either to the mission or to Kristie personally. The actual operation would still be weeks away and by then, she would be safely back to the East Coast.

She wondered if Jane Smith would see the wisdom in allowing Kristie to attend. Or would the agent just use the

suggestion as an opportunity to ridicule SPIN—and Kristie in particular? And even if the agent could be convinced,
Kristie knew Ray Ortega would never allow her to actively
participate in an operation, however harmless.

But he might just agree to send Melissa Daniels.

Chapter 5

"No. Absolutely not."

"Ray—"

"It's out of the question. You don't have the necessary training. You could blow their entire operation."

"Training? For a flower show?" Kristie rolled her eyes. "I'd just be observing, sketching and making notes. Piece of cake. I've already started designing Melissa's cover identity." To Jane Smith she explained, "Melissa Daniels is a virtual operative I use sometimes. She can be adapted to fit almost any situation."

The CIA agent arched an eyebrow at Ray. "Since when do you send your spinners into the field?"

"Since never. And I'm not going to start now."

"It isn't fieldwork, it's research," Kristie protested. "At a public event with a bunch of cactus lovers. What could possibly go wrong?"

"We all read Salinger's file," Ray reminded her. "The guy's a pervert. He's got a closet as big as my office filled with sex toys! I don't want you anywhere near him."

"What file did *you* read?" Kristie demanded playfully. "They aren't sex toys. Just costumes."

"Just costumes? That's supposed to make me feel better?"

She laughed. "So he makes his girlfriends dress up for him. I'll bet rich guys do that all the time. Poor guys, too, for that matter. It's not perverse. Just healthy fantasizing."

Ray's eyes narrowed, and she knew he was picturing the contents of the closet as described in the CIA's file: harem-girl outfits, mermaid fins, angel wings. And of course, the staples, from leather and metal to silk and satin.

"Salinger's not going to try anything kinky at a public event," Jane murmured. "And Kristie's right about one thing. She'd notice things my operatives might miss. We need to be dead on with this one, Ray. The security of the whole intelligence community depends on it. If she's willing—"

"I am. It sounds safer than the Laundromat, which is where I usually spend Saturday afternoons." Kristie flashed a confident smile. "I give you my solemn word I won't do anything to jeopardize the operation."

"It's settled then. Get us your cover story by tomorrow morning and we'll arrange for this Melissa to be admitted. What's your preference? Press pass? Fellow cactus lover?"

"Press pass. We'll say she's a reporter from Sacramento, flying down to cover the event."

"Good. You'll need to use a different last name for her, since you've apparently used Daniels before. You can fly out with us Saturday morning. After the show, we'll debrief you and then send you back, safe and sound."

"Make arrangements for two," Ray advised. "I'm going with her."

"That's not necessary," Kristie began, but Jane interrupted them both with a cheerful, "Don't worry—we don't let civilians walk around unescorted. She'll have at least one baby-sitter. Maybe two. I want them to be *my* people though. It's been six years since you did any fieldwork, Ray. Let us handle it. I promise we'll take good care of your girl."

Kristie grimaced but didn't say a word until Jane had left the office. Then she turned to Ray and smiled in sincere apology. "Don't be upset. I'll be careful. I promise."

"As Kristie, you're careful. But as Melissa—" He gave a weary chuckle. "Can you picture her at a garden party? She's too flamboyant. The whole idea is to blend in."

"I'm going to put her hair up. And tone down her makeup. She'll do great. I promise."

He hesitated, then exhaled in apparent surrender. "Just try not to get yourself killed, okay? I've got plans for you."

"What kind of plans?"

"For one thing—" his demeanor grew tentative "—I'm going to stop taking my problems out on you."

"Pardon?"

"This is the long-awaited apology, so sit back and enjoy it."

"Oh." Kristie gave him a sympathetic smile. "It's not necessary, Ray."

"Sure it is." He hunched toward her, his expression sincere. "The other morning—when I lost my temper with you after you had just saved Lizzie Rodriguez's life—it wasn't you I was really mad at."

"It was Colonel Payton, right?" she guessed. "Because he ordered you to give me a commendation? I'm still mortified about that."

"You deserved the recognition. But yeah, it was tough to take, coming from him."

Kristie nodded. "Everyone knows SPIN is your creation. It's unfair that the president lets that—well, that Neanderthal—interfere with your judgment."

"The president's a strange guy," Ray said, rubbing his eyes. "If it weren't for him, there wouldn't be a SPIN at all. He's the one who listened to my idea, supported it, got me funding in a tough budget year."

"Because he recognized its potential. And yours."

"And I'm grateful," Ray insisted. "But he's got a blind spot when it comes to that jackass Payton. They were best friends in grade school, did you know that?"

Kristie nodded again. "President Standish has the proverbial weight of the world on his shoulders. Obviously. So it kinda makes sense that he'd enjoy returning to simpler times by associating with his childhood friend."

"Exactly. He sees the mischievous boy, not the reprehensible man. Unfortunately, it's getting worse. The rest of us—the Cabinet members, me, the first lady—used to have tremendous influence. Influence we earned through years of loyal support and counseling. I see that lessening every day."

"Standish still relies on you a lot, though. Right? It seems like at least once a week you have to drop everything and take a call from him, or even go to the Oval Office."

Ray seemed about to contradict her, then jumped to his feet instead. "This was supposed to be an apology, not a therapy session. I was pissed at Payton and took it out on you. I'm sorry. End of story."

She arched a disapproving eyebrow. "FYI, that temper still needs a little work."

Ray chuckled. "Go plan a cover for Melissa that won't attract too much attention. And Kris? Take this seriously, okay?"

"It's a *garden* show."

"It's Jane Smith. You would have been safer with a mugger in that alley, believe me."

After a brief practice round with Betty Bop that evening, Kristie showered, then slipped into bed with a stack of files. She needed to review the final details of her undercover identity, and to study up a little more on cacti, but was distracted by a photo of Will McGregor that had slipped out of the Mannington folder on her nightstand.

There he was, rugged yet disarming, with his square jaw, wavy black hair and steady blue gaze. She could almost hear his voice teasing her, and felt a familiar shiver. Then as though in answer to her thoughts, the phone rang.

Taking a deep breath to steady herself, she answered with a brisk, "This is S-3. Please identify yourself."

"Essie?"

"Justin!" Delighted, she pretended to scold the errant agent. "You've been neglecting me. I was sure you'd call sooner than this. How's Tahiti? Any word on Lizzie?"

"She went home today."

"Oh, Justin. How wonderful."

"Yeah. Her mom says she had some friends over to play and it went pretty well. Plus, she has a clean bill of health—physically, I mean. No permanent damage. No infections. That sort of thing."

"They must be so relieved. Can you imagine?"

"Nope. Life here is pretty shallow. Just sex, tequila, sun and surf. It's an empty existence."

Kristie laughed lightly. "In other words, you're in heaven?"

"Only one thing's missing, so hop on a plane, will ya?"

"I'm actually going to do that tomorrow, but I'm going to—well, somewhere else. If you need to call me—"

"I won't. It's just good to hear you're getting away from that monitor-infested workplace for a while. Are you visiting friends? Family? Some lucky stud?"

"It's SPIN business, so I can't give details. But I'm so glad you called."

"I'll be back in a week, and I'll call you then, even if I don't have business to discuss. Hear that, monitors? Screw you one and all."

Kristie laughed. "Bye, Justin. Thanks for the Lizzie update. Have fun."

"Yeah. Take care, beautiful."

She bit her lip as she hung up the phone. Agent Justin Russo—a man every bit as good-looking and talented as Will McGregor—had become a true friend. Just like Ray.

McGregor himself, on the other hand, had become—well, the closest thing to a date she'd had since she started spinning.

On impulse, she grabbed the phone and dialed McGregor's cell-phone number. He answered on the second ring, his voice deep and rumbly. "This is McGregor."

"Hello, Agent McGregor, this is S-3."

"Goldie? Excellent timing. I was just about to call you."

"With an update on the Mannington case?"

"What else?"

The electricity in his tone intrigued her. Either he was pumped at the sound of her voice, or something great had happened on the case. She wasn't sure which she hoped it was, but opted for, "Did you make progress with Manny tonight?"

"He spilled his guts *way* ahead of schedule."

"That's great!"

"Whatever they're paying you, it isn't enough. You're a genius."

Her cheeks warmed. "What happens now?"

"I already turned the information over to the U.S. Attorney, who practically wet himself with excitement. They think they can break the whole drug ring now, thanks to you."

"And to you. You must have been pretty convincing."

"Yeah, I went on and on about my wild ride with Melissa. And Manny just ate it up." The agent's voice rang with enthusiasm. "I thought I'd be stuck on this gig forever, and here it is, all wrapped up in a couple of weeks. Must be a record. I'm giving you full credit in my report. You and Melissa, that is."

She snuggled happily under the covers. "Do you have a pen handy? I want to give you my personal cell-phone number. I'm going out of town for a couple of days, but you can always reach me this way."

"An unmonitored line?" He chuckled. "Sounds too good to be true."

"Actually, it's monitored."

"You're kidding. Don't you spinners have any rights?"

"It's sort of a probationary thing," she admitted with a sigh. "I used my personal line for SPIN business recently, which is a clear violation of protocol. To make matters worse, the person I called was a suspect. In other words, I'm lucky they didn't fire me."

McGregor whistled softly. "That was you? I should've

guessed. We heard a rumor about a profiler who saved a kid." His voice grew strident. "They should be giving you a medal, not punishing you."

"It was unprofessional on my part. One miscalculation and that child would've been dead."

"True. But your instincts were sound. And anyway—" his tone softened "—it's tough to be professional when kids are involved. I know that from experience."

Kristie flipped his file back open and located a picture of twenty-four-year-old Ellie McGregor. "Your sister went through something similar, right?"

He was silent for a moment. Then he muttered, "You know about Ellie?"

"It's my job to know things. I can't design identities for you—for any of my operatives—without knowing a lot about them."

"So you have access to all our secrets, but we can't find out Jack Shit about you? How's that fair?" he demanded. Then his voice grew wistful. "What does my file say about Ellie?"

Kristie measured her words carefully. "Not a lot. Just that she was part of a children's-theater company when she was fourteen. Two other girls made accusations against the director for improper behavior. He was tried and convicted. Ellie was a star witness. For the *defense*."

"She still claims the guy didn't lay a hand on her," McGregor murmured. "She says the other girls just made up the story out of spite. Because they couldn't get good parts in the plays. Ellie, on the other hand, got great roles. The question is, why?"

Kristie could hear confusion and bitterness in his voice. Not to mention helplessness. "Maybe she got those parts because of talent. The file says she still does some acting."

"Yeah, when she's not doing drugs or staying out all night with—" He broke off, then insisted, "I don't want to talk about it."

"Okay."

"I'll never know whether she was abused by the director or not," he said with uncharacteristic vehemence. "What I do know is she's been abusing her*self* ever since. Because of the publicity, I think. It was eight long months of constant media scrutiny. Our friends. Family. Boys at school. *Everyone* treated her like she'd been molested. It took on a life of its own."

"Poor Ellie."

"Yeah." He exhaled loudly. "Can we talk about something else?"

"Of course."

"What's Melissa wearing tonight?"

She laughed. "You're going to get me into trouble with the monitors, Agent McGregor. Do you want my cell number or not?"

"Let's have it."

She recited the number, then wished him, "Good night, McGregor. Sweet dreams."

"Can I ask you one more thing?"

"I guess so."

"I know you used a picture of yourself to create Melissa. I'm guessing it's pretty close, except maybe for the eye color and hair color. So, what are you? My money's on blond—"

"Good night, Agent McGregor." She slapped the receiver back into its cradle, but not before she heard a laugh come rumbling over the line.

What are you doing? she asked herself in disgust. *Jane Smith's car will be here at 6:00 a.m. to take you to the air-*

*port. You need to be sharp. Rested. Ready to run with the
big boys. So stop playing phone-footsie with a guy you've
never met, and get some sleep!*

From the moment she hefted her travel bag into the
back of Jane Smith's SUV at six o'clock the next morning, Kristie's senses went into overdrive. The idea that she
was actually going to visit the location of one of her operations, after six months of working through files and
computer simulations, made her head spin. And for a
bonus, it was the CIA!

Per Smith's instructions, the spinner had dressed for
comfort in jeans and a gray hooded sweatshirt, with her
hair freshly washed and pulled back in a ponytail, her face
scrubbed and free of makeup. The plan was to transform
her into "Melissa O'Hara" during the private jet flight to
Sacramento. Thereafter, she would catch a commercial
flight to Palm Springs, check into her hotel and proceed
to Salinger's desert estate.

Still, she wished now that she had dressed either professionally or stylishly. She felt like a kid next to the CIA
agent, who was wearing a smartly tailored black suit, and
who barely acknowledged Kristie's presence in the back
seat. Instead, Smith spent most of the ride barking orders
into her cell phone. The only other occupant of the vehicle was the driver, who kept his eyes straight ahead and
never uttered a word.

Once aboard the jet, the focus of attention quickly
shifted, and Kristie was pelted with information from both
Smith and a man named Pritchert, who dryly referred to
himself as the spinner's "baby-sitter."

"Just don't talk to anyone. And don't touch anything,"
he advised her. "Use the rest room at your hotel before you

leave for the show, 'cause I've got orders not to let you out of my sight for more than sixty seconds at a time. I don't want to piss off the garden-club biddies by following you into the ladies' room."

It was clear to Kristie that Pritchert found the assignment beneath him, and she could imagine why. He looked more like an assassin than a bodyguard—lifeless eyes, sunken cheeks, thin lips frozen in a perpetually sarcastic smile. She suspected he had been handsome once, and he clearly still saw himself that way.

Maybe the jaded routine works for some girls, Kristie told herself. It *definitely* didn't work for her, but to be fair, Pritchert didn't seem to find Kristie attractive either. She was clearly just a nuisance in his eyes.

"Pritch will arrive separately about ten minutes ahead of you," Jane Smith was explaining. "He'll be hanging around the metal detectors when your cab pulls up. Once you make it through, he'll latch on to you. The story is that your paths have crossed before, which makes sense, since he's posing as a photographer from the San Francisco area."

Kristie pursed her lips. "Metal detectors at a cactus show? I know why Salinger wants that, given his sidelines. But I'm surprised the garden world is willing to put up with it."

"Believe me, they've been dying to get a glimpse of his cactus collection. They'll put up with anything," Smith told her. "Just make sure Pritch checks the contents of your handbag before we land."

"Yeah, if you've got any gadgets with you, leave 'em behind."

"Gadgets?" Kristie rolled her eyes. "I'm armed with a pencil and notebook. Period. But I'm guessing you're going to feel a little naked without your gun?"

He reached into his duffel bag and pulled out a small pistol made of white plastic. "Don't worry, baby. Daddy's gonna take good care of you."

Kristie ignored the obnoxious remark, focusing on the weapon instead. "It doesn't have any metal parts?"

Pritchert pulled it apart, revealing three small steel components, which he quickly removed from the plastic casing. Then he took a fountain pen out of his jacket and demonstrated how the metal pieces fit perfectly inside the writing implement. "I'll pass the pen through with my keys and change."

"It's amazing," Kristie admitted.

"Show her your new lipstick, Janie," Pritchert said to Smith.

His boss scowled for a moment, then reached for her purse and located a shiny tube, which she handed to Kristie.

"This is a gun?"

Pritchert chuckled. "Not quite. But it's definitely a weapon. Clockwise from that position, it's lipstick. Counterclockwise, it sprays a neurotoxin from a tube in the bottom that can paralyze a three-hundred-pound man instantly. So don't screw around with it."

"Wow." Kristie examined it carefully. "How long do the effects last?"

"Five or six minutes," Jane told her. "You can keep it as a souvenir if you want. Our way of thanking you for the assistance."

"Who knows? It might come in handy if the Axe takes a shine to you this afternoon," Pritchert interjected, his tone once again disrespectful.

"From what I've seen in his file, he's just as likely to take a shine to *you*," Kristie retorted, refusing to acknowledge that indeed her one trepidation about this reconnaissance assignment was the thought she might run into Salinger's sociopathic bodyguard, Axel Holt.

"That's enough bickering," Smith warned them, then she spoke directly to Kristie. "I don't remember seeing anything like that in the Axe's file."

"You mean, that he likes guys?" The spinner shrugged. "I didn't mean that. Just that he probably gets off on causing pain, not traditional sex. So either a man or a woman would do."

"I see now where their little agency got its name," Pritchert muttered. "She can put any spin she wants on the intel, and we're supposed to be impressed."

Jane silenced him with a glare. "We land in three hours, children. So let's get down to business, shall we?" Striding to the back of the cabin, she unzipped a hanging garment bag. "Here's your outfit, Kristie. What do you think?"

The spinner joined her quickly, admiring the classy yet sexy lines of the two piece linen dress. The ivory-toned top was sleeveless with a collared neckline that formed a deep V. The emerald skirt was short—but not too short—and pleated. "It's just perfect."

"You said you wanted to supply your own undergarments and shoes, correct?"

"Right. They're in my bag."

"Let's have a look." Pritchert hefted Kristie's suitcase onto an empty seat, and before she could protest, he was rummaging freely. Pulling out a pink lace garter belt, he grinned. "This assignment is looking up."

Jane turned to Kristie. "It's going to be awfully warm in Palm Springs. You might just want to skip the stockings."

"Stockings are part of Melissa's routine," the spinner explained, ignoring Pritchert's sarcastic chuckle. "I'll be fine. After the winter we just had, warm sounds wonderful."

Jane hung the dress back on its hook and went over to the suitcase, and while she didn't paw through the clothes the way the male agent had done, Kristie still felt uncomfortable enough to offer further explanation. "Since I'm spending the night in the hotel, I brought enough Melissa-style clothes to wear to the restaurant, gift shop, whatever. I'll wear the wig then, too, obviously. But when I'm in my room, I'd rather wear my own things. That's why I brought the warm-ups. And the robe."

"Interesting," Jane murmured. Then she cleared her throat and added more briskly, "It's too early to change. Or to put the wig on. But we can start with your makeup if you'd like, while Pritch runs some slides for you. We have a couple of good shots of the service area behind Salinger's house."

Kristie nodded, appreciating the opportunity to close her suitcase, and to refocus on the upcoming challenge. True, it was just a garden party, but she was still entering the world of a cold-blooded killer guarded by a clinically insane henchman. Melissa or no Melissa, she needed to start taking that seriously.

But you've got your toxic lipstick. And a CIA assassin who's sworn to protect you, she reminded herself philosophically. *What can possibly go wrong?*

Chapter 6

"Name and organization?"

"My name's Melissa O'Hara. What's yours, sweetie?"

The uniformed guard looked up from his clipboard for the first time, then flushed, clearly disarmed by Melissa's smile. Or maybe it was the generous glimpse of her breasts afforded by the linen outfit that pleased him. "I'm Ed. Nice to meet you, Miss O'Hara. They'll give you your name tag once you've gone through the detector. Do you have anything on you that might set off the alarm?"

"It's all me under these clothes," she assured him breezily.

"Well then…" He cleared his throat. "We're confiscating cell phones. You'll get it back when you leave."

Once she had handed him the phone, he added, "I'll take your handbag, too, if you don't mind. Just for a second."

"That's fine, handsome. I feel safer knowing you're checking everyone so closely today."

He beamed as he set the purse on a conveyor belt while motioning for Kristie to pass through the metal detector. With a playful smile, she sauntered to the other side, collected her handbag and name tag and headed for a nearby refreshment table, where Pritchert, in a white polo shirt, khakis and aviator-style sunglasses, was waiting per their plan.

He handed her a glass of champagne. "I didn't know Melissa was such a hot babe."

"You saw her on the jet."

"No, I saw Kristie Hennessy in a garter belt and red wig." He ogled her without apology. "Melissa's a whole other story."

"She's out of your league, sweetie. Just try to concentrate on the mission, okay?"

"Mission?" asked a soft voice from behind them, and Kristie turned to stare, flustered, into the suspicious eyes of their host, the notorious Kenneth Salinger.

Fortunately, Pritchert fielded the situation. "Mr. Salinger, right? Thanks for having us, sir. I'm Jason Safire from Bay Area Travel Treasures. This ravishing beauty is Melissa O'Hara. *Her* mission is to look great. Mine is to try not to get fired. Which is what will happen if I blow another assignment. Luckily, it looks like this story's gonna write itself. I don't think I've ever seen such an impressive show."

"Thank you." Salinger turned his full attention to Kristie. "I'm tempted to call you Scarlett, Ms. O'Hara."

"And shall I call you Rhett?" she answered, trying to echo his mood.

In an instant, she knew she had miscalculated the remark, as the flicker of interest in his eyes disappeared. He apparently hadn't been flirting at all. But he *had* been intrigued—willing to chat—and in one word, she had blown the opportunity.

This time, when he bowed, it was stiff and formal. "Enjoy yourselves."

"Smooth," Pritchert said, when their host was out of earshot. "Good thing you weren't supposed to seduce him."

"I can't believe I said such a stupid thing."

"If it's any consolation, that would've worked on me. In fact, it did."

She grimaced. "Thanks, I think."

Pritchert laughed. "Stay put for a minute, will you? I want to find a rest room and assemble the g-u-n. Shouldn't take more than forty-five seconds or so. Just sip your champagne, keep your head down and don't talk to strangers."

"I'll be in the cactus garden—"

"What did I say? Stay *put*. Enjoy the bubbly. Like you keep saying, this is just a garden party, not an actual op."

"I notice you're not drinking."

"I'm a martini kind of guy. If one of those sexy maids brought me a nice dry one, believe me, I'd drink it."

Kristie shook her head in mock disapproval. "They're waitresses, not maids. Although you wouldn't know it from those silly uniforms," she added, wondering how the bevy of servants could possibly carry their huge silver trays and negotiate these crowds, given the fact that their uniforms consisted of tight black microskirts, black bustiers with white lace sleeves, and stiletto heels.

"Those dresses aren't silly. Just sexy. Like those French maids in porno movies."

"Don't you have something to build?" she drawled in disgust.

He nodded and strode away toward Salinger's elegant white stucco mansion.

Moving to a bench, Kristie pretended to sip her drink while she studied her surroundings. She also took the opportunity to scold herself for overplaying Melissa. Hadn't Ray anticipated just that, saying she was too flamboyant for a garden party?

Pritchert had made a good point, too, reminding her she wasn't supposed to seduce Salinger. In fact, repulsing their host would work in her favor, allowing her to wander and sketch without fear of attracting attention.

Just keep a lid on the outrageous remarks, she cautioned herself. *A little more "Kristie Hennessy in a red wig," a little less "man-eating nympho."*

Pritchert returned, bringing with him two plates piled with appetizers, including bits of batter-fried cactus, miniature tamales and green chilies stuffed with cheese and fried to a golden brown. "Miss me?"

She rolled her eyes. "Let's get to work."

The spinner quickly discovered that the photographs and other intelligence provided in the Salinger file had been extremely accurate. Yet none of it had done justice to this magnificent estate. One had to see the graceful lines of the house in context, with the lush green golf course in one direction, the Santa Rosa Mountains rising out of the desert in the other.

Kristie and her companion wandered through the crowd, causally studying the house and grounds. Although Pritchert had a digital camera, the spinner took the time to make sketches, knowing that it forced her to observe every last detail.

When they were deep enough into the desert landscape to be certain they could not be overheard or monitored, they were able to relax and talk more freely, always with one eye on the guests and their hosts.

"You'd better draw a couple cactuses," Pritchert suggested. "All you've done so far is the house." He took her hand and led her to a towering saguaro. "This one's the best. Straight out of the Wild, Wild West."

Kristie nodded. "It must be at least twenty-five feet tall. How did they manage to move it here from Arizona without killing it? Not that it matters. It can't survive here for long." She felt a surge of anger. "He calls himself a cactus lover then does something like this?"

"Lighten up," Pritchert advised. "Here. Take my picture next to it." He stood beside the giant cactus, holding his arms out and up in imitation of the saguaro's spine-covered appendages.

Kristie set her drink and hors d'oeuvres down on a bench, then used the agent's camera to capture the shot. "Now move over there. To those pretty prickly pear. I read about them last night. They really are native to this region, so they'll thrive here."

Pritchert laughed. "They're ugly. You've got crummy taste."

"Really? You've been eating prickly pear yourself all afternoon. Those little fried *nopalitos*. According to my books, they have tons of vitamins. So eat up. And have some respect."

"You know, it's just a cover. You aren't really supposed to like cactuses."

"Cacti, not cactuses." She lowered her voice. "It's just so frustrating not to be able to get into the private areas of the house." She gave him a hopeful smile. "Can't we invent some excuse? Pretend I'm sick or something? I want to see the hallway leading to the gallery, and if possible, the gallery doors themselves."

"Can't be done. They've got it roped off, and Salinger's men are everywhere. Guests are confined to the dining room, the entry hall and two guest powder rooms. One move beyond those parameters and you'll be a dead spinster."

"Very funny."

His tone softened. "Do you want to run your ideas by me? This is a little out of your league. Maybe I can help."

She hesitated, but had to admit it could be useful, so she sat on the bench, then patted the seat for him to join her. "There are two challenges I can't really solve yet."

"Only two?" He held up his hand and began to count on his fingers. "We have to get on the grounds and up to the house without being spotted. Then past the alarm on the house itself. Then the alarm on the gallery doors. And assuming we can do all that, we've got to crack the safe without setting off the explosives. That's four challenges at the very least."

"We've got the make and model of the house alarm," she countered. "I've got the gallery-door system narrowed down to two models—either one being easy to disarm. Cracking the safe is a piece of cake—"

"Huh?"

She smiled. "He's got it rigged with plastic explosives, right? I've studied four jobs he financed, and each time, the device was the same. You'll be able to neutralize it in seconds, then use some of the C-4 to blow the lock. Or bring a device of your own if you're not confident about that. Either way, piece of cake."

Pritchert gave her an approving whistle. "Not bad for someone from a boutique agency."

"A what?" She glared. "Boutique? That's what you think of us?"

"No offense," the agent insisted. "So? What are the two challenges you can't overcome?"

"Like you said, getting onto the grounds without detection. I just don't see how it can be done. I think Jane's right—you'll have to wait for three more weeks for that auction. The operative who attends will have to hide on the premises until the other guests have gone, then sneak into the gallery."

"Check. So? What's the second unsolvable obstacle?"

"Guessing which painting the safe is behind," Kristie told him. "There should be about twenty, but we only have definite intel on six, and none of those seems to be the likely ones, based on Salinger's profile."

"We'll just check behind all twenty, right? That's doable, even with a short timeline."

"Unless some of them are booby-trapped. That's what I'd do if I were him."

"Yeah, that makes sense." The agent patted her knee. "Doesn't sound like there's much point in staying around. Everything you need is in the gallery, and there's no way we can get in there today. Stay here while I take the g-u-n apart, then we'll go for one last sweep of the place."

"Okay." She bit back her disappointment, admitting that he was correct. One last look at the driveway and golf course would be a good use of their last hour. After that, she might even break down and really have a glass of champagne, rather than just pretending to sip one.

It hasn't been a complete waste of time, she consoled herself. *You confirmed that your scenario is fairly solid, at least as far as it goes. And it's only a backup plan anyway. Jane Smith probably won't even use it. Meanwhile, you got to see this gorgeous place. Maybe someday you'll win the lottery, and you'll know just what kind of home you'd like to build.*

If the house was impressive, the grounds were even better. She adored the way Salinger—or more likely, his landscaper—had paired the living cacti with some equally beautiful man-made works of art, including religious statuary and intricate stone structures inspired by the grand pyramids of Central America.

But as wonderful as these sights were, her attention was always drawn back to the two-story white brick edifice itself. She had already sketched what she needed of it, but was so charmed by the way it blended into the desert that she turned to a fresh page and began to draw again.

Then without warning, the sketchbook was snatched from her hands and she turned, stunned at first by the action, then by the all-too-familiar accusatory gleam in Kenneth Salinger's hazel eyes.

"This is a cactus show, Miss O'Hara. I can't help but wonder why you're so interested in my home."

She gulped as she realized he was even more suspicious than last time—enough so that he had brought along a bodyguard.

At least it isn't the infamous Axe, she consoled herself nervously. *Just try to act natural. This is a party and you're his guest.*

Salinger was paging through her notebook in disgust. "Two drawings of plant life. The rest are my house and grounds. Explain that."

Melissa had failed the spinner once tonight, but Kristie Hennessy wasn't going to get herself out of this one, so she took a chance and allowed her alter ego to field the question. "The explanation is simple. I'm a fraud."

"What?"

She gave her shoulders a little shrug. "I like flowers as much as the next girl, preferably in a long white box with a nice little love note. But my passion is art. And architecture. In particular, the blending of nature and man-made works of brilliance. I came here to write a piece on cacti, because that's the only freelance assignment I could get. But this place—your house, your statuary—I'm intoxicated by it. And in my defense," she added with a wry smile, "I took good notes. And those two specimens I drew—they're the most impressive ones, don't you agree?"

Salinger opened his mouth as if to answer, then shook his head instead, and turned his attention back to her sketchbook, examining it page by page. Finally he murmured, "You have exquisite taste, Ms. O'Hara."

"Scarlett," she reminded him.

He looked up in time to catch her playful smile, and burst into laughter. "You should show this side of yourself more often. Charming, but not so obvious."

"In my defense, most guys like the other me," she said with a wry grin. "Subtlety is wasted on them."

"It's their loss," Salinger assured her. "Tell me more about this passion for blending nature with art."

Kristie's pulse quickened. "Me? Tell you? It's your specialty, isn't it? I mean, look what you've done out here. I can only imagine what the inside of the house looks like. Plants everywhere, right? Lots of natural light. Grass cloth on the walls?"

"And a vibrant blue sky overhead."

She cocked her head to the side. "You painted the ceiling to look like the sky?"

"Better," he murmured. Then he offered her his elbow. "Come with me. There's something I'd like to show you."

* * *

Although she could barely breathe, Kristie somehow managed to chat with Salinger as they walked to the house while the burly bodyguard followed at a respectful distance. She couldn't help but wonder what Pritchert would do if he saw where she was going, and with whom. The CIA agent had come to respect her, hadn't he? At least a little. Would he trust her instincts? Or would he pull out his plastic gun and try to save her?

Salinger's staff of gray-suited henchmen were everywhere as the couple made their way down a wide hall leading to the gallery. Kristie knew she was taking a risk of exposure, but only a slight one. And the payoff? She was going to see the inside of the gallery. It was the only way Salinger could show her the blue-and-white skylight. And once inside, even for just a minute or two, she could catalog the paintings in her memory, so that she and Ray could figure out which one a man like Salinger would use to hide his safe.

If she could accomplish this one task, she could validate SPIN's participation. Even if Jane Smith didn't choose Kristie's scenario for the actual operation, the CIA team would benefit from this piece of vital information.

A stocky guard—presumably armed—was standing in front of the double doors leading to the gallery. Salinger instructed the fellow in an authoritative voice. "Miss O'Hara and I would like some privacy. Turn off the room alarm and the closed-circuit system, but stay here. If we need you, we'll let you know."

"Yes, sir," the guard assured his boss. Then he used a key card to open a hidden panel in the molding. Flipping a switch, he then swung the gallery doors open and stepped aside to allow Kristie to enter. At the same time, the body-guard who had accompanied them from outside moved a short distance away and growled instructions into a walkie-talkie, ensuring that the gallery cameras were being turned off.

Heady with anticipation, Kristie gave her host an encouraging smile, then stepped over the threshold and into the pitch-black rotunda. Meanwhile, Salinger pressed a light switch on the wall, and the motorized cover that shielded both the skylight and the artwork from the elements began to slide open, allowing the rays of the hot desert sun to illuminate the room.

And for just a moment, the spinner forgot why she was there. She could only drink in the beauty of the gallery's graceful lines, the rich mahogany paneling, luxurious Oriental carpets, and last but not at all least, the paintings, ranging from landscapes to portraits.

The space was almost devoid of furniture, save for an iron table that held a graceful brass urn, and an oversize, circular upholstered piece that seemed to be half bed, half ottoman. Covered with forest-green velvet, the bed was centered directly under the skylight.

Kristie wondered how many females had been seduced on that monstrosity while staring up at the dazzling artificial sky. Or perhaps it was Salinger who did the looking up while the women did all the work!

Don't think about stuff like that, she ordered herself. *You'll freak yourself out.*

She hadn't yet looked up at the skylight, despite the fact that it beckoned to her. As silly as it seemed, she instinctively knew that once she saw it, it would distract her from her mission again, and that was something she couldn't afford. She had to concentrate on committing a list of the paintings to memory, so that she and Ray could plan the rest of the heist to their mutual satisfaction.

"Look up," Salinger whispered in Kristie's ear.

She hesitated, gazing into his eyes instead, and was charmed by the depth of his pride and anticipation. Then with theatrical precision worthy of Melissa Daniels herself, she walked over to the ottoman and sat on the edge, took a breath, leaned back onto it until she was fully reclined, and gazed at the ceiling for the first time.

"Oh my gosh." Her hand flew to her mouth in complete, unadulterated delight. The blue of the glass was so deep, so luminescent, it truly disappeared, leaving only the sensation of sky. And the huge expanses of white seemed to actually billow in the wind, moving before Kristie's eyes in some bizarre and beautiful optical illusion.

No description in a file could ever do this justice, she raved to herself, and the thought jarred her, reminding her why she was there. Sitting upright, she gave Salinger an apologetic smile. "I almost got lost in it."

"That happens all the time."

She stood and crossed the room to him. "You've created something amazing here. I hope the paintings are half as wonderful."

"See for yourself."

Finally! The invitation she had needed. All she had to do now was walk quickly around the perimeter, memorizing. Then she'd make an excuse, return to the party and let her baby-sitter usher her back through the metal detector and out to the safety of an awaiting taxi.

She was no longer worried about Salinger's intentions toward her. He would be a gentleman. Disappointed, perhaps, if she left so abruptly. After all, she wasn't naive enough to think he'd brought her here just to admire his artwork. But he also wasn't going to force himself on her. She was practically certain of that.

The reconnaissance operation was more or less over, except for the memorizing, so she hurried over to the first painting, a sweeping landscape. "Lovely," she murmured. Then she took a few steps sideways, allowing herself to view the second piece of art, a portrait.

"Take your time," Salinger said, gently chastising her. "You needn't leave when the others do. In fact, I'm hoping you'll agree to dine with me."

She was glad he couldn't see her wince, and she summoned her best Melissa attitude before responding with, "After all those hors d'oeuvres, I'm not sure I could eat another thing."

He stepped closer, murmuring in her ear, "I'm sure I could find something with which to tantalize you."

She winced again, remembering that despite his polished demeanor, he was a killer. Ruthless and vengeful. And on a more mundane note, he had a closetful of outfits for fantasy role-playing with his girlfriends. Was he expecting *her* to play dress-up after dinner?

As quickly as it had come, the sense of beauty and class that had reassured her now vanished, and she knew she had to take a quick scan of the remaining paintings and then feign a convincing stomachache, complete with vomit if necessary.

"I'd particularly like to hear your reaction to this piece," he told her, steering her toward a dark, brooding work depicting a woman lying on a bed, her arm outstretched, her eyes closed.

Kristie noted that there was nothing erotic about the painting despite the boudoir setting. Instead, the effect was melancholy bordering on distress. And touching, in an amateur sort of way.

"Who is she?" the spinner asked, her voice hushed.

"Someone important to the artist, right? But not a lover or anything like that."

"She's his mother."

"Oh, I see." Kristie bit her lip. "Is she...? Well, is she dying?"

"Very perceptive. In fact, the work is entitled *Forever after Death.* So you may assume she has just expired."

"Wow." Kristie was honestly intrigued. "It has a haunting quality. Really remarkable, actually."

"But odd, don't you think?"

She turned to him, surprised. "Odd?"

"Look at it again. Something's not quite right. Tell me what it is."

He was challenging Kristie. Or maybe he was challenging Melissa. Either way, she couldn't resist, so she turned back to the painting and studied it carefully. "It seems pretty realistic to me. But maybe..."

"Tell me."

"This huge fern is a little out of place. I mean..." She bit her lip, not wanting to offend his taste in art. But facts were facts, and this painting simply wasn't very good. And even for a lousy painting, the placement of a big plant in the foreground was amateurish. "Lots of people have ferns in their bedrooms, but in this case, by placing it in the forefront, the artist blocked our view of the mother a little. Why would he do that?"

"Look here." Salinger pulled a magnifying glass from his jacket pocket and held it in front of the dying woman's outstretched hand. "What do you see?"

When Kristie squinted she could barely make out traces of green on the mother's otherwise pale hand. "I don't get it. She had paint on her hand when she died?"

"What kind of paint?"

"What kind? Well, it's shiny. And—Oh!" Kristie's gaze moved rapidly from the green stains on the mother's tiny hand to the giant fern. And to her shock, she could see it! A full-size handprint among the fronds. Fingers outstretched...

Without thinking, she reached for the painting, instinctively wanting to place her own hand over the imprint of the mother's, but Salinger grabbed her wrist, instructing sharply, "Don't!"

"Oh, I'm sorry!" She backed away, truly distraught. "My God, it's so bizarre. Almost like a magnet. The artist's mother put her hand there, in the wet paint. Actually touched the painting, right? Maybe just moments before she died! It's amazing."

She realized Salinger was staring at her, so she apologized again. "I know better than to touch an oil painting. I'm really sorry."

"But it was like a magnet? Isn't that what you said?" Salinger's eyes glistened. "You're so like her."

"Her?" Kristie's stomach knotted, and she had to force herself not to back farther away. Not just from the painting this time, but apparently from the artist himself.

"Don't be frightened," Salinger murmured. "Here." He stepped up to the wall and pressed his fingers against a panel, which sprung open to reveal a control station. Then he leaned forward, allowing his retina to be scanned by a thin, blue beam.

Turning to Kristie, he announced, "You can touch it now. I *want* you to touch it."

The haze of morbid fascination cleared from her brain, and she was a spinner again, thinking more rapidly than ever. Planning. Imagining. Knowing.

This was the painting that hid the safe. It had to be. She could walk out now, knowing she had the information Jane Smith needed for a successful operation.

Except there was still the problem of getting the team into the gallery in the first place. And a million other tiny things that could go wrong if they waited.

But if she did it now, with the painting identified, the guards banished, the alarm turned off...

Not daring to look directly at Salinger, she moved past him, up to the painting, and placed her hand over the image in the fern, her fingers spread open to exactly match the imprint. Then she touched it, first lightly, then with an intensity she knew he wanted her to demonstrate.

"Tell me," he whispered.

"I feel her spirit." Kristie didn't have to fake the lump in her throat. She was scared to death at what she was thinking, yet also energized beyond belief. All she had to do was reach into her purse—

Patience, Goldie. Some things are worth waiting for.

Taking a deep breath, she turned away from the painting, pushed past Salinger and flung herself onto the ottoman, wailing softly. Then she opened her purse and fumbled inside, pulling out a tissue and dabbing her eyes. When Salinger took a step toward her, she held up her hand, pleading with him to wait.

"I need a minute. And..." She smiled tearfully. "I must look awful."

"You look beautiful."

"Still..." She pulled a compact out, and flipped it open, taking the time to study her reflection critically.

Patiently.

Only then did she dare to bring into view the shiny silver tube of lethal lipstick Jane Smith had given her.

As a souvenir...

Chapter 7

Exhaling sharply, the spinner sprang from the ottoman with the base of the lipstick tube directed straight into Salinger's disbelieving face. Then she twisted the mechanism counterclockwise, allowing the spray to hit him full force. In less than an instant, he slumped to the floor.

Silently cheering Melissa for the performance of a lifetime—and thanking Will McGregor for the undercover tip—Kristie Hennessy took over. After all, this was *her* forte.

Tying her host's hands behind his back with his necktie, she then bound his feet with his belt. It was tempting to stuff his handkerchief into his mouth for good measure, but his breathing was already weak, thanks to the toxin, and she didn't want to take the risk of asphyxiating him. And she had five whole minutes left before he started coming around, didn't she?

It now seemed to be a fairly straightforward game plan as she confidently swung the frame of the painting away from the wall on a hidden hinge, exposing a sleek safe.

So far so good, she told herself, remembering how she had instructed Pritchert to first disarm the explosive device that protected the lock. Then she could use a small portion of the plastic compound to blow the safe open.

Sliding her finger warily along the edges of the safe, she surprised herself by accidentally revealing a second hidden compartment in the wall panel. As with the first one, it contained a retinal scanner.

"Good news, bad news," she told herself. There was apparently no need to worry about disarming the explosives. She could open the safe legitimately, but there was a catch. She had to get Salinger's eye into place!

At times like this, you need a guy like Pritchert, she had to admit, sure that Jane Smith's agent would simply cut the eyeball right out of the bad guy's head. Settling for a less violent, more labor-intensive approach, she returned to Salinger's limp body, dragged him over to the painting, and hoisted him against the wall, then inched him up toward the scanner.

Ray's going to be so proud of you, she told herself. Then she pictured her supervisor's face, contorted with disbelief, and decided to focus on McGregor's rugged visage instead. But even McGregor might think this a bit foolhardy. And Jane Smith? Kristie didn't know her well enough to predict.

But the bottom line was, it was working. Flawlessly! They had to give her credit for that at least, didn't they? The plan was so perfect—so foolproof—she wasn't the least bit frightened. She might as well have been in her cubicle at SPIN, plotting away. It was all so ordinary and efficient.

By the time she had Salinger's dead-weight body close to full height she was panting, but still managed to steady his head, then edged it over until the eye was right in front of the scanner. She held his eyelid open, and with inspiring precision, the light beam moved across his retina. Then with a gentle click, the latch on the safe was released.

Perfect!

She allowed the body to slide to the floor, then pulled open the door to reveal stacks of bills of every denomination, along with rich velvet bags she suspected held fabulous jewels.

Those could have been yours, Melissa O'Hara! After all, you reminded him of his dead mother.

Giddy, the spinner pawed through the loot until she found what she was seeking—a small cache of computer disks. Three yellow, one black. There was no way of knowing which one contained the names so she took all four.

Stuffing them inside the waistband of her skirt for the moment, she dropped to her knees beside Salinger's still, silent form. Patting him down, she carefully removed any item that could possibly house the remote detonator, including his watch, a fancy ballpoint pen and his wallet. The alarm on the safe could be on a timer and might reactivate at any moment, she knew. The last thing she needed was to trigger an explosion at this point in her perfect plan.

Then she turned her attention to the final two items needed for complete success—Salinger's gun and his cell phone. Rocking back on her heels, she double-checked the pistol to confirm it was fully loaded. Then she entered Ray's private number on the phone's keypad, but before pushing the Send button, she took a moment to further steady herself, breathing in and out slowly and deliberately, sending her body a signal that the danger was over.

And it was true. Thanks to the pistol that could be aimed at Salinger's temple at a moment's notice, she could effectively control any guard who decided to enter the room. No one would dare endanger Kenneth Salinger, and so they would stay back, or better yet, run away, rather than force Kristie to blow the boss's brains out.

And chances were, the guards wouldn't even dare step foot in the gallery in violation of Salinger's order in the first place. At least, not before Jane Smith and company arrived and took over.

With a confident smile, she hit the phone's Send button, and to her delight, Ray answered on the first ring.

"This is Ortega. What's up?"

"Ray? It's me."

"Hey, I've been worried sick! Does this mean you got out of there without getting stuck on a cactus?"

She laughed. "Even better. I've got the disks. Can you call Jane and tell her to extract me right away? I'm in the gallery, and—"

"*What?* Goddammit, Kristie! What the hell's going on?"

She held the phone a distance from her ear, amused by his roar. Then she explained, "I'm perfectly safe. Salinger is my prisoner, aka my insurance policy. Just have Jane send her team in—"

"Your prisoner?"

"Bound and gaggable, and completely unconscious. With his own pistol aimed straight at his head." Her voice rang with pride. "You should have been here, Ray. It was a heist, just like Jane said."

"Kristie, pay attention now." Ray's voice had grown steady and commanding. "Where are the bodyguards?"

"Outside the door. Salinger gave them instructions not

to disturb us. But eventually, they'll probably check. That's why I've got the gun on him. If they come in, I'll threaten to shoot their boss, and they'll back off. I'm perfectly safe, and the plan is flawless, but I'm a little anxious to get it over with. So *please* call Jane."

"How many guards?"

"Two. The others are policing the rest of the house."

"Where's Jane's operative?"

"My baby-sitter?" she drawled. "I have no idea. But—"

"*Listen* to me. Are you sure the gun's loaded?"

"Good grief, Ray, you sound like Pritchert. I know what I'm doing."

"How many rounds?"

"Ten."

"Check the safety."

"It's a Glock," she informed him. "No external safeties."

"Okay, fine. You're still wearing the wig, right?"

"Yes, but—"

"Have you seen the Axe?"

"He's been completely absent. Salinger probably gave him the day off. Psychos and garden parties aren't exactly a good match."

"Okay then. Go to the door. Poke your head outside and give them your biggest, sexiest Melissa Daniels smile. Then shoot them—once each—in the head."

"What?"

"Do it!" he commanded. "Then come back to Salinger's body and shoot *him* in the head. Then get the hell out of there. Mingle with the crowd. Ditch the wig if you can, in case someone saw you going in the house with Salinger."

"I'm not shooting anyone," Kristie told him firmly. "I don't need to, Ray. Salinger will be my protection. They wouldn't dare endanger their boss's life. That's the beauty of my plan."

"Except Salinger isn't the boss."

Kristie froze. "What?"

"It's the Axe, Kris. He's the boss."

Her mind began to swim. "The Axe?"

"Listen to me." Ray's voice was clearer—more inspiring—than she'd ever heard it. "You trust me, don't you?"

"Yes."

"Then just do what I say. Go to the door. One shot to the head for each guard. You have to do it now, before the Axe gets involved. He'd shoot Salinger himself to keep you from getting those disks."

She shook her head in stubborn denial. "The file doesn't say anything about the Axe being in charge."

"You didn't have clearance. This is top-secret info, Kris. And you were just supposed to be going there for recon."

Her stomach churned. "Oh no."

"Suck it up, Kristie. Go to the door. Shoot the guards. Then come back and shoot Salinger. Got it?"

Panic was spreading fast through her nervous system. "I don't think I can, Ray. Shoot three men? And one of them is unconscious!"

"Three quick shots—boom, boom, boom. Nothing to it. Then I can call Jane to rescue you. Just don't let any blood splatter on your clothes."

"Oh, God…" She jumped to her feet and started to pace. "There has to be another way!"

"Dammit, Kristie! Just do it."

"Wait!" She forced herself to review the various scenarios they had designed and discarded over the last few days. Only two ways into the gallery—the double doors and the skylight.

Which meant there were two ways out.

"Maybe I can shoot my way out after all," she murmured, half to herself.

"Good girl. Go to the door, count to three—"

"I've got an idea, Ray. It's complicated, but I think it'll work. Just hang up and call Jane. Tell her I'm hiding the disks in a big brass urn in the gallery so I won't be caught with them on me. If something goes wrong—if I get killed, or if somehow the explosives get triggered—the disks should be protected there."

"Kristie—"

"Just *do* it," she insisted, echoing the confident tone he had been using on her just moments before. Then she turned the phone off and placed it back in Salinger's pocket.

He was beginning to stir, and she considered giving him another spray of neurotoxin, but decided she might need that for one of the guards. Instead, she dragged her host into a sitting position and brought the butt of the pistol down so hard on the back of his skull, she was sure she had cracked it.

"Sorry," she murmured as he slumped into a heap. Then she sprinted across the room to the brass urn and pried open the lid.

She hadn't expected it to be filled with anything, let alone ashes, and realized with a shiver that these were probably the remains of Salinger's mother.

Well, at least no one will be opening it unexpectedly, she decided as she buried the four disks, resealed the jar and moved it off the iron table and onto the ground, lay-

ing it carefully on its side. The CIA would be able to re-
trieve the disks later. Then she carried the table itself over
to the double doors. After confirming that the dead bolt
was in the locked position, she wedged the table against
the handles, further deterring any entry into the room.

Her next step was to make it appear as though the safe
had been frantically rifled, so she scattered the bills, jewels and other contents on the ground.

Then she kicked off her shoes and took off her stockings, one by one. The first she looped around Salinger's
torso, tying the ends firmly, but leaving just enough room
for her to wriggle inside with him later. Then she used her
second stocking to make a loop around her wrist, leaving
room again, this time so that she could slip her other hand
through when needed.

Her plan was simple. She would convince the guards
that someone else had robbed the gallery, assaulting both
Salinger and Kristie, and tying them up with Kristie's—
or rather, Melissa's—stockings. She'd pretend to be terrified, which would be easy, since a part of her actually was.
She'd plead to be allowed to use a rest room, which would
offer her a safe hiding place until Jane arrived to rescue
her.

Peeling off the top of her outfit, she draped it on the ottoman, making it seem as though she had been undress-
ing for Salinger.

"That's it," she told herself, adding wryly, "Maybe it
would have been easier to just shoot the three guys and be
done with it."

Retrieving the pistol from beside Salinger's body, she
went to the ottoman and lay on her back, staring up at the
skylight.

"Okay, Melissa. You're back on deck," she told her alter

ego grimly. Then she took a deep breath, aimed carefully, and fired shot after shot after shot.

Cracks formed instantly before her mesmerized eyes, then the delicate glass shattered into thousands of sparkling blue and white shards that rained down onto her. She shielded her eyes, but otherwise allowed herself to be covered with bits of glass in every shape and size.

In an instant, men were shouting Salinger's name and pounding frantically on the door, and Kristie allowed herself to be scared to death, knowing it would show in her face when the guards finally gained entry. The dead bolt and table wouldn't delay them for long, so she quickly executed the last four steps of her plan, sliding the pistol under the ottoman and out of sight, gagging herself with Salinger's handkerchief, sprinting over to his body and squirming inside the stocking loop so that she appeared to have been tied inside with him, then, finally, forcing her hand through the loop on her wrist so that she was effectively bound.

A series of shots sounded from the far side of the door, and she knew the guards were blasting the dead-bolt lock. They would be inside the gallery within seconds now, and she began wriggling so that the stockings would abrade her arms, midriff and wrists. Then she tried to scream through the gag in her mouth again and again, hoping that her voice would sound strained and hoarse by the time the guards untied her.

"You must be insane!" she shouted to herself at the top of her lungs, although the only sounds she actually made were muffled squeals. "Ray's going to kill you! Why didn't you just shoot them like he told you to?"

Her throat burned from the effort—and her arms and wrists were nearly raw from all her squirming—when a sharp, cracking sound announced the final breaking of the doors, and three guards stormed into the gallery, guns drawn.

"Boss!" The man who had accompanied them from the garden to the house was the first to reach Salinger and Kristie. Dropping to his knees, he tugged at the stocking that bound them together. Then with a roar of frustration, he pulled out a switchblade and cut them free.

Kristie screamed at him through her gag, begging him to help her, but it was a second man who grabbed her, dragging her to her feet and yanking the handkerchief downward, freeing her mouth.

She wailed in protest. "Ow! Be careful!"

"Shut up," he warned, his lip curled in a menacing snarl. Then he turned to his companions. "Frank, secure the house and grounds. No one leaves. *No* one!"

"Okay, Axe." The man who had been guarding the gallery doors sprinted out of sight, barking into a walkie-talkie as he went.

The sound of that name—Axe—curdled Kristie's blood, but she forced herself to draw closer to him rather than away. Using a voice that was half-grateful, half-accusatory, she insisted, "What about *me?*"

"Shut up," he repeated. "Mike, how's Salinger?"

"Alive, but out cold."

Axe grabbed a walkie-talkie from the guard's hand and shouted into it. "Listen up! Find a doctor. There's gotta be one in that crowd. Salinger's hurt."

"I'm hurt, too!" Kristie turned to the guard named Mike and said pleadingly, "They almost killed me."

Mike gave her a sympathetic shrug, his gaze momentarily focused on her chest, where her breasts were show-cased by the Melissa-style push-up bra. Taking off her top had apparently been a very, *very* good idea, despite the humiliation factor.

Axe spun her back around so that his penetrating gaze was locked with hers. "What the hell happened in here?"

"I don't know," she insisted, allowing her panic to bubble into her voice. "One minute we were kissing. Over there." She used her bound hands to gesture toward the ottoman. "Then the glass broke, and guns started blasting, and men came down on ropes."

"Ropes?"

"Wires, maybe. I don't know. It happened so fast."

"How many men?"

"Three. One of them pinned me down—and he was a real creep about it! The other two hurt Mr. Salinger. They pushed his face against that wall, and opened the safe, and then they hit him on the head with a gun. Then the creepy guy pulled off my stockings and used them to tie us up. See?" She waved her wrists in his face. "Can't you undo this? It's digging into my skin."

Axe glared. "Stop whining. What else happened?"

"That's it. They left as quickly as they came. It all happened *so* fast. I thought they were going to murder us." She threw herself against the sociopath, burying her face in his shirtfront. "Thank you for saving me!"

"Stupid bitch," he muttered, pushing her toward Mike. "Here, take her."

The guard steadied her, then used his knife to free her hands. She immediately laced her arms around his waist, hugging him with all her might. Then she stepped back and smiled tearfully.

Three other armed men had arrived in the meantime, and Axe growled orders at them to seal the exits, secure the perimeter and keep the crowd quiet. When they'd left, he knelt next to Salinger and began to shake him roughly. "Salinger? Can you hear me?"

"He's out," Mike told him.

"Where the hell's that doctor?" Axe's gaze traveled around the room, taking in the shattered remnants of the skylight and the strewn contents of the safe before settling on Kristie.

His eyes narrowed. "Three men on cables?"

"I think there were three. It all happened so quickly."

"You and Salinger were screwing around when it happened?"

"No! Just kissing." She folded her arms over her half-naked chest. "He was being a perfect gentleman. We were having s-s-such a g-good time—"

"Don't cry," he warned between gritted teeth. "Or I'll kill you myself."

"Look at my bra! It's filled with pointy pieces of glass. So is my hair. I need something to wear. I need to use a rest room." She put her hands on her hips. "You can't just bully me, you know. Mr. Salinger won't like that."

"Shut up, bitch." Axe strode to the ottoman and picked up her jacket, which was covered with iridescent splinters and plainly unwearable.

"I've got a polo shirt in the trunk of my car, Axe," Mike offered, his voice tentative. "She can wear that if she wants."

Kristie turned to him and beamed. "You're so sweet."

"Yeah, you're a frigging Lancelot," Axe confirmed with a sneer. "All right, take her upstairs to Salinger's room. Let her find something in that freak-show closet of his. But don't let her out of your sight. And no screwing around. Be back in five minutes."

Kristie bit her lip to keep from smiling in relief, then

began to gather up her purse and its contents, knowing that the lipstick might just be her ticket to freedom.

"Leave that stuff."

"I need my makeup at least—"

"Salinger's got everything you need in his room." Axe grabbed the purse and eyed the contents with suspicion.

"Come on," Mike suggested, draping his jacket around Kristie's shoulders, then ushering her toward the door.

"Five minutes," Axe repeated. "Don't let her out of your sight. And *don't* let her use the phone."

"Okay, Axe." Mike grabbed Kristie's hand and tugged her into the hall, warning under his breath, "Stop arguing with him. Do you want to get yourself killed?"

"N-no." She grasped his hand tightly. "Thanks for helping me."

"My pleasure." He slipped his arm around her waist and guided her up the grand staircase that led to the second-floor sleeping quarters.

A few steps from the top, they encountered two armed guards who reported that every room had been checked. There was no sign of the intruders.

Mike advised them to join the Axe in the gallery for further instructions, then propelled Kristie down a hallway to Salinger's quarters. Once inside, he gestured toward a walk-in closet. "Wait'll you see this."

"I'll be out in a second," she began to promise, but the guard entered the closet with her, reminding her he wasn't allowed to let her out of his sight.

"That's fine with me. I never want to be alone again after what I've been through today," she assured him, taking off his jacket and handing it to him, then turning her attention to her new surroundings.

One glance confirmed the outlandish rumors about Salinger's fantasy life. Not only did the closet contain all the classics—belly dancer, parochial schoolgirl, cheerleader and the ubiquitous French-maid uniform—but all possible accessories as well, including a variety of wigs, assorted bondage implements and some intriguing occult paraphernalia.

"Wow."

The guard grinned. "Yeah. Salinger knows how to have a good time. I'd tell you to pick out something racy, but the Axe'd probably have a fit."

Kristie flashed a coquettish smile. "I'd love to wear something special for you. You practically saved my life." Stepping closer to the guard, she murmured, "I know he said we couldn't screw around, but is it okay if I kiss you? Just to say thanks?"

The guard nodded, clearing his throat.

Think about McGregor, she advised herself as she slid her arms around Mike's neck and moistened her lips, but the ploy didn't work. She was still repulsed.

Fortunately, the guard did the rest of the work for her, grabbing her by the waist and pulling her hard against himself, crushing his mouth eagerly to hers. Shocked but also fascinated, she allowed it to happen without actually kissing him back. And to her disgusted amusement, Mike didn't even seem to notice her lack of participation.

Predictably, his hand began to paw the contents of her bra, giving her an excuse to yelp and jump free of him. "The glass is cutting me," she told him with a pout.

"Take it off."

She giggled, then turned to survey the contents of the closet. "What should I wear? How about this?" She held up a black leather bustier and microskirt in one hand, and a matching pair of knee-high boots in the other.

"Yeah." His voice was thick with arousal. "Hurry up."

Kristie's smile was now genuine, and she kept her gaze locked with his as she donned the boots, glad to know her toes would have some protection from the kickfest to come.

Then she straightened up and moved her fingers to the front clasp of her bra. The guard's jaw actually fell open, and she almost felt guilty, knowing he was about to see stars rather than the nipples he was salivating over.

Flashing one last, sexy smile, she propelled her booted foot into his engorged crotch with all her might. He howled, and as he fell to his knees, she grabbed a heavy crystal gazing ball from a silver stand on a nearby shelf and slammed it into his jaw, knocking him sideways to the ground.

From his pitiful groans, she could tell he was barely conscious and completely disoriented, so she flipped him onto his stomach, then slapped handcuffs on his wrists. After securing his feet with a second set of cuffs, she gagged him with a silk scarf, then patted him down as she'd done with Salinger.

"Déjà vu," she announced, liberating his Glock from his shoulder holster and his cell phone from his belt. After cracking him on the back of the head with the firearm, she keyed Ray's number into the phone.

"Don't talk," she instructed as soon as he answered. "I'm fine. Is Jane on the way?"

"She'll be there in four minutes. Where the hell are you?"

"Tell her I'll be dressed as a waitress. There are dozens of them, so I shouldn't have a problem disappearing into the crowd. Tell her I'll have black hair, not red."

"Kristie—"

"Gotta go. Just get me out of here, okay?"

Snapping the phone shut, she jumped to her feet and stripped off the boots, followed by her bra and skirt. Then she wriggled into a French-maid costume, which, predictably, was identical to the uniforms the waitresses were wearing at the cactus show.

You're one sick puppy, Salinger, she told her host as she located a pair of black stilettos. If she had to kick anyone in those open-toed beauties, it was going to hurt. On the other hand, she could probably put someone's eye out with one of the spiky heels.

She knew that at any moment the Axe might send someone to check on her and Mike, so she quickly replaced her long, red curls with a short, sassy black wig, then stuffed the original into the liner of a nearby wastebasket, along with the rest of her Melissa O'Hara ensemble, the bodyguard's Glock and the cell phone. Then she made a pit stop for some slick red lipstick at a well-stocked dressing table in Salinger's bedroom, where she also applied makeup to her breasts to hide abrasions caused by the shards of glass. Then she popped out her emerald contact lenses and applied some navy eyeliner to bring out the denim blue of her natural eye color. After tossing the lenses into the trash bag from a receptacle under the dressing table, she pulled that bag out and tied the top into a knot, adding it to her collection.

You're just a maid taking out a couple of trash bags, she told herself. *No one's even going to notice you. Just four more minutes, and it's all over.*

Squaring her shoulders, she stepped into the hall, listening and scanning for signs of life.

There was no one around and she was tempted to just duck into another room and hide, but she knew it was smarter to find the back staircase that led directly to the kitchen. From there, she could exit into the crowd and head for the service driveway, which was almost certainly where Jane Smith and her fully armed team would make their appearance.

It was difficult to stroll down the hall when she really wanted to kick off the stilettos and run for her life, but she forced herself to take long, unhurried steps, swinging the trash bags at her sides as though she had nothing better in the world to do.

Just taking out the trash, taking out the trash, taking out the trash...

In sharp contrast to the circular staircase she had climbed with the bodyguard, she discovered that the service stairway was a boxy, practical affair, with no gleaming brass rail and no windows. Still, to Kristie, it was a haven, and again she was tempted to just stay put. Sinking onto the fourth step from the bottom, she pulled out the Glock and practiced aiming it, first toward the top of the stairs, then toward the bottom. Then with a sigh she stuffed it back into the trash bag, stood up and smoothed her skimpy uniform into place. This was no time to wimp out.

From the kitchen came sounds of dishes rattling and people scurrying around and chattering nervously. Then a gruff male voice rang out, silencing the rest. "Listen up! The guests are getting restless. Get your pretty little asses out there and keep them happy. I want to see a glass of champagne in every hand. *Now!*"

When a flurry of activity ensued, Kristie used the opportunity to sneak into the kitchen. Five other young women were scurrying around in high heels, and the spinner was sure she wouldn't be noticed as she headed for the back door, but a frustrated roar stopped her in her tracks. "What do you think *you're* doing?"

She spun toward the voice and was relieved to see that while the man was clearly dangerous, he wasn't one of the guards whom she had previously encountered and who could possibly recognize her. Without bothering to appear confident, she explained, "I'm taking out the trash."

"Screw the trash!" He yanked both bags from her hands and tossed them into a corner. "Didn't you hear what I said? Get out there and spread some freaking sunshine. Make those bigwigs wanna stay, since we're not gonna let 'em leave until the burglars are apprehended. Is that clear?"

"Yes, sir." She snatched a heavy silver tray loaded with half-filled champagne flutes from a nearby table, flashed a tremulous smile and headed for the back door.

It was all worth it when she stepped into the hot, bright Palm Springs afternoon and saw dozens and dozens of well-dressed, harmless people murmuring to one another in small groups. It all seemed so normal. So perfectly reasonable. These people were concerned but not frantic, because they knew they were fundamentally safe. Undoubtedly they had been told there had been a burglary, but that Salinger's security team was there to protect them, and the authorities were on their way to apprehend the evildoers. Then the guests could go home safely, and as a bonus, they would have exciting stories to tell at their next cocktail parties.

Kristie suspected that the scene in the front yard near the metal detector was a bit wilder. The less-trusting people would be gathering there, clamoring to leave. And reporters, eager for details, would be making a nuisance of themselves.

But here in the back, things seemed civilized, despite the fact that everyone in sight was a virtual captive.

It's your job to make these lovely guests feel at home, Kristie told herself with wry a smile. *Especially that group near the edge of the driveway. It can't be more than twenty steps away, so just keep it together. Jane'll be here in a minute or two.*

Using elementary visualization techniques, she was able to imagine that she was already there, serving drinks, out of harm's way. A dozen squad cars would pull up, sirens blaring. Jane Smith and a horde of operatives would surround her, ensuring her safety. All she had to do was hold her head high and sashay over to that thirsty-looking group of cactus lovers.

But before she could execute this final step, she saw another group, dominated by a huge man in a dark suit, and her heart sank. It was the Axe, and she was sure he was looking for her. If he knew she had knocked out Mike the guard, he'd also realize she could be wearing a disguise and a wig from the closet. If she tried to cross the lawn to the driveway, he'd be on her in seconds.

Then she realized it wasn't so. She was the last thing on the Axe's mind. Instead, his attention was focused on a fair-haired man in a white polo shirt and khakis who was talking a mile a minute, a nervous smile pasted on his insincere face.

Pritchert!

As she watched in dismay, the Axe threw the CIA operative against a wall, then shoved a poorly concealed pistol into his ribs while a second man frisked him.

Kristie's heart began to beat at twice its normal rate. She had come so close, gone through so much. Now *this?*

"Darn you, Pritch!" she muttered under her breath. "In what universe am *I* supposed to take care of *you?*"

But there was no escape—not from the logic, nor from the irony. And so, with a last, longing glance toward the safety of the driveway, she set out to rescue her baby-sitter.

Chapter 8

Stopping along the way to serve other guests, Kristie mentally reviewed the information she had about Axel Holt, aka the Axe. From what she knew of him from the file and their brief encounter, he was ruthless and sadistic. And not particularly susceptible to feminine wiles. His sole focus was amassing wealth and power for Salinger's cartel while destroying anyone that tried to get in their way.

Of course, Kristie now knew the information supplied to her had been incomplete, painting the Axe as Salinger's lunatic minion when in fact he was secretly the dominant figure in the enterprise. The fact that he could keep his secret from his day-to-day associates told the spinner a lot about the Axe's intelligence and sophistication. And the fact that he had kept it from *her*—that she hadn't caught even a glimpse of it while poring over his file—was positively unnerving.

With enough time and better intel, she was confident she could devise a strategy to outwit this opponent. But there was no time. No definitive intel. And hence, no strategy at all, not even a tentative one.

With a new respect for field operatives and a new appreciation for her cubicle, she balanced her heavy silver tray on one hand and sauntered over to her target group, which consisted now of Pritchert, whose open palms were raised to shoulder level, the Axe, who was pressing a weapon into the agent's ribs through his coat pocket, and a small, stocky accomplice who also appeared to be training a concealed pistol on their prisoner. On the ground lay several pieces of white plastic—remnants of the weapon Pritchert had smuggled through the metal detector.

Apparently, they had searched the guests—or at least the ones who looked as if they could be players—and had decided Pritchert was involved in the burglary. Or maybe Pritch had tried to dispose of the incriminating evidence when the alarm first sounded, and one of the guards had noticed. In any case, he was in trouble because of Kristie, and she had to get him out of it, preferably without getting herself killed in the process.

Approaching them, she called out in a flirtatious voice, "You boys look kinda thirsty."

The Axe shot her a disgusted look. "Get lost."

At least he didn't recognize you, she told herself. *But the bad news is, Pritch doesn't seem to either!*

"We get a bonus if we get a drink into every guest's hand," she explained to the Axe, then she turned to Pritchert and said, "You look like more of a martini guy yourself," hoping he'd remember making that very comment to her earlier that afternoon. "But this is the best I can do."

It was subtle—just a flicker in his gray eyes—but she

knew he was on board, and her confidence returned in a rush.

"Get this bitch out of here," the Axe told his accomplice through clenched teeth. The man obeyed immediately, pulling his gun hand out of his pocket and taking a step toward Kristie.

It would be easy to bring this smaller man down, she suspected. But if she did that, the Axe would shoot Pritchert, so she exhaled slowly, then pushed past the accomplice and stepped right between the Axe and the CIA agent, insisting with a pout, "Don't be such a big grouch! This is a party, silly."

As the Axe roared in disbelief, Pritchert took advantage of the cover provided by Kristie's body and grabbed the accomplice by the neck, jerking him backward, then throwing him to the ground, immobilizing him and confiscating his gun in one fluid movement.

Terrified, Kristie lowered the silver serving tray into place as a shield just as the Axe fired his weapon. The bullet ricocheted away, but the impact on the tray knocked the spinner to the ground, vibrating her knuckles wildly in the process. Pritchert yanked her back to her feet, and while she was shaky, she was still gripping the tray with frozen-in-place fingers.

Then to her shock, Pritchert grappled her in front of himself so that she and her tray functioned as his own personal shield. Only then did he commence firing at the Axe, who immediately took cover behind a barbecue and began to return fire.

Pritchert took the opportunity to sprint toward a low stucco wall, dragging Kristie behind him. Meanwhile, the guests went wild, screaming as they dropped to the ground or scattered for cover. The spinner was shrieking, too, as a second bullet hit her tray, sending it hurtling into the yard. "Pritchert, you jackass!"

"Come on!"

They dived behind the three-foot-high wall, upsetting a huge metal garbage can in the process, just as a cacophony of gunfire filled the air. "He's got reinforcements," Pritchert muttered, raising himself up to shoot a volley of bullets over the top of the wall, then ducking down as shots whizzed over their heads.

You almost got me killed! You used me!"

"Stay down," he ordered her. "Listen for a second, will you? Hear that? Sounds like the cavalry's here."

Kristie forced herself to focus, and realized it was true. In the distance, tires were screeching on the gravel driveway, and then a woman's voice blared over a bullhorn, ordering the crowd to freeze, drop any weapons and show their hands.

"Just in time," Pritchert murmured. "Are you okay, Kristie?"

She came completely unglued. "If I am, it's no thanks to you! You used me like a freaking human shield!"

"Yeah, thanks." He winked. "I take back everything I ever said about you and your useless agency."

She wanted to strangle him, but the sight and sound of black vans and squad cars roaring right up onto the lawn, offloading swarms of armed men and women in uniform, distracted her, and she decided to take her complaint—and her sincere thanks for the rescue—to Jane Smith instead.

She hadn't expected to be treated like a hero, but also hadn't anticipated being discarded like an unimportant detail. Two hours later, as she paced the floor of her hotel suite, she could still remember being shoved into the back seat of a van by Jane Smith with instructions to return to

Palm Springs proper, get cleaned up and be ready to be debriefed. Then the door had slammed shut and the vehicle had sped away from Salinger's estate, leaving Jane and Pritchert behind, presumably to reap all the glory.

The spinner had no idea what had happened at the scene thereafter. Did they find the disks? Arrest Salinger? Was Salinger even alive after that whooping blow Kristie had inflicted on his skull?

And what about the Axe? She imagined he was screaming for her head right about now, so she prayed he was cuffed and under triple guard somewhere miles and miles away.

It was small comfort to know that she would eventually be debriefed. Would Jane Smith confirm that the Axe was actually the mastermind of the Salinger cartel? Had Kristie earned that courtesy, if nothing else, by putting her ass on the line for the ungrateful CIA bitch? Or would the debrief be a one-way street?

"She'd better admit it went pretty well, all things considered," Kristie told herself in disgust. "And she'd better not start with the lecturing. Sheesh, Ray's gonna give you enough of that!"

Fear of that lecture had kept her from phoning her supervisor the moment she returned to her hotel. Instead, she had jumped into a hot shower, anxious to wash away the prickly coating of blue and white splinters—not to mention the blood—that stubbornly clung to her body.

Now swathed in a thick white robe supplied by the hotel, she found herself growing more agitated by the moment. "They'd better return your stuff to you, that's all I have to say. That wig cost a lot of money! And they've still got your cell phone, too. What if someone tries to reach you? Aunt Jess and Uncle Matt? Or Justin? Or—"

Her thoughts veered toward Will McGregor, and for a moment her anger morphed into excitement. How much would she love to tell him about all this? He'd be impressed. And now that she was safe, he wouldn't waste time lecturing her—she was almost sure of that. He'd be on her side, one hundred percent. Maybe he'd even offer to kill Pritchert. Or better still, to teach her to do it herself!

She sent a longing glance in the direction of the hotel phone. Did she dare? It broke Ray's number-one rule, but he'd never know. And given the fact that the government had practically stolen her cell phone from her, she almost *had* to use the unmonitored line.

It was a crazy idea. If she thought about it for too long, she'd change her mind. So she decided to just do it.

Tingling with anticipation and leftover adrenaline, she sat on the edge of the bed, steadied her voice, then picked up the receiver and dialed 0. A nasal voice informed her she could charge a long-distance call to any major credit card, so she rattled off her account number from memory, followed by McGregor's cell-phone number, also from memory.

It rang once, then again, and she reminded herself it was Saturday night. He was probably on a date. What if he even had a woman at his house? Kristie would be mortified!

This is a bad idea. Hang up while you have the chance—

"Will McGregor."

"McGregor? Hi. Sorry to bother you on a Saturday night."

"Hey, Goldie! Nice surprise. I figured I wouldn't hear from you until Monday at least."

She forced herself to inhale and exhale slowly and completely in hopes of managing a breezy tone. "Actually, I just wanted to warn you that you can't reach me at the number I gave you. Not that I thought you'd call. But just in case, I wanted you to know I don't have my cell with me at the moment. It might be lost. So…" She cursed herself silently for sounding scattered. Then she finished with a shaky, "If you need to get in touch with me, just leave a message on my SPIN line. I'll check it every few hours. And I should be home by tomorrow, so—"

"Are you okay?" he demanded.

"Sure. Why do you ask?"

"You sound different."

"Well, I had a different sort of day. Kind of wild, actually."

"Yeah? Tell me about it."

She hesitated, but only for a moment. "I was part of a reconnaissance team. We went to a party at a suspect's house in preparation for a future op. But we got an irresistible window of opportunity, and we took it. I actually cracked a safe. Can you believe that?"

McGregor chuckled. "Sounds like fun. I'm a little surprised you're telling me about it, though."

"Because of the monitors? Well, like I said, I lost my cell. And I'm out of town, so I had to call you on an unmonitored line." She laughed lightly at the sound of her own babble. "I'm still pretty wound up, I guess. It was quite an experience. And I went dressed as Melissa, which is always an adventure."

McGregor was silent for a moment, then murmured, "Dressed as Melissa?"

"Yes."

"And this line isn't monitored?"

"Right."

"So." He cleared his throat. "What's Melissa wearing now?"

She laughed again, wondering what he'd say if she told him the truth—that she was naked except for a hotel robe. Deciding that discretion was the better part of ardor, she told him teasingly, "Just because this line isn't monitored doesn't mean I'm going to embarrass myself. I have a reputation to protect, too, you know."

"A reputation as who? S-3? Goldie? Melissa?" His voice warmed. "Tell me your real name."

"I can't, McGregor. You know that."

"Then at least tell me about that picture of Melissa. Which parts are you?"

"This was a bad idea," she whispered, mostly to herself.

"No. This was a great idea. And I've got a good one, too."

"I'm almost afraid to ask."

He cleared his throat. "You've told me all about my first date with Melissa. Why not let me tell you about ours?"

"*Our* first date?" She bit her lip, charmed that he was willing to admit so freely that their relationship was changing—growing—and had the potential for flesh-and-blood romance.

"Right. It'll start with flowers delivered to your front door. Roses. Lots of 'em."

"I like roses," she admitted.

"Then I'm gonna pick you up in a blue Mustang convertible and take you to a place I know that serves the best lobster on the planet."

"I love lobster. You sound like a fun date."

"Yeah, so do you." His tone grew husky. "We're gonna talk and talk for hours at the restaurant. Then I'm gonna take you home and we'll talk some more."

Kristie settled back into the pillows and sighed as he continued to tell her about their dream date in words so seductive—so mind-numbingly tender—they almost put her into a trance.

By the time he began describing their first kiss, she craved him so illogically she blurted out, "I wish you were here, McGregor."

"Believe me, I'm there," he reassured her. "And I'm going to take good care of you. Starting right now."

To her hazy delight, he then began to walk her through a slow, sexy fantasy, step by step, his words teasing her. Arousing her. Touching her in places she never knew a voice could go. And she knew she should interrupt him, but he was *so* good at this.

So good that she heard her own voice answering him, murmuring his name in a soft, slow rhythm until the syllables blended together in a soft, luxurious moan that resonated through her as her body tightened and trembled.

When she could finally speak, she whispered hesitantly, "McGregor?"

"Yeah, I'm good. Thanks."

His tone was so matter-of-fact, she knew she should be mortified, but instead she burst into laughter. "Glad I could help."

His chuckle rumbled over the phone line. "Does this officially count as our first date?"

"Absolutely not. It was fun, though. I'll probably be mortified in the morning, but for now…"

"Yeah, for now, it was pretty damn good."

Neither spoke for a moment, but the silence was comfortable. Affectionate. Reassuring.

Then a loud knocking on her hotel-room door ruined the mood, and she called out, "Just a minute!" in her most annoyed voice before informing McGregor, "I have to go. It's time for my debriefing."

"Do you want me to stay on the line until you verify who that is?"

She loved his instinctive desire to protect her, especially in light of Pritchert's ungallant behavior that afternoon. "I could have used you today when bad guys were firing at me. But I think I'm pretty safe now. Thanks, though."

"*Firing* at you? You forgot to mention that. What's Ortega's problem? You're not a field agent—"

"I've got to go," she repeated firmly. "Sweet dreams, McGregor. Thanks for the date."

Another round of knocking at the door sent her scurrying toward her suitcase for something to wear other than a bathrobe. Calling out "Give me a second!" she studied her options with perverse amusement.

One side of the case was packed with Melissa in mind, from impractical undergarments to provocative tube tops and shorts.

McGregor would love it, she told herself wistfully. But she was dressing for Jane Smith, so she turned to the Kristie pile of clothing, selecting jeans and a clean-cut UCLA T-shirt, similar to the outfit she'd been wearing just fourteen hours earlier, when the CIA had picked her up at her apartment. Freshly scrubbed, no-frills, down to earth. Innocent.

Since then, she had rendered two men senseless after letting one of them kiss her, had fired a pistol for the first time in her life and had had phone sex with a man she had never met.

All in all, not so innocent. Nor was her outfit very professional. But she reminded herself that Jane hadn't been very professional herself, banishing the spinner the way she had without even bothering to ask if she needed medical attention.

Kristie's anger over her mistreatment resurfaced, and she forced herself not to rush. The CIA had made her wait, and now it was their turn. Once dressed, she didn't bother to run a brush through her hair or otherwise double-check her appearance before throwing open the door, a defiant glare on her face.

"Hey, blondie." Pritchert grinned. "I was wondering which one of you would answer."

She folded her arms over her chest. "Where's Jane?"

"She's not back yet. This is a social call." He held up a martini shaker. "Find us a couple of glasses."

"You've got to be kidding." Kristie stepped closer to him, hoping he could read the disgust in her eyes. "First you insult me, then you use me as a human shield, then you expect me to drink with you?"

"Actually, I was hoping to drink with the redhead, but you'll have to do." He was clearly unrepentant. "Can I come in?"

"No."

"Chill out," he advised. "You're still pumped, right? That's how it is after an op, especially a wild one like today's. I'm here to help you unwind. Whatever you need," he added, his gaze roving over her suggestively.

"Yuck."

"You need to release that pent-up energy—"

"Pent-up anger, you mean. Toward *you.*"

He laughed as he pushed past her, closing the door behind himself. "Because I used you? Aren't you forgetting who put me in danger in the first place? You were supposed to sketch the house, not rob it."

"I saved you."

"Yeah, and *I* saved *you*. We're even." He rummaged in a cabinet above the wet bar until he found two crystal tumblers. "I used you for a shield because I knew you could handle it. It was a compliment."

"Go away."

He sat himself down at a small round table near the doorway to her balcony, then pushed a chair toward her with his foot. "Come on, Kristie. One little drink. I've got a feeling you need it."

"What I need is for you to get out." She swung open the door to the hallway and was startled to see Jane Smith standing there. "Oh. Hi, Jane."

Pritchert sprang to his feet. "Hey, boss! I'm glad you're here. We were just starting to deconstruct the op."

"Really?" She eyed the martini shaker with disdain, then asked Kristie, "May I come in?"

When the spinner stepped aside without answering, Jane strode to the center of the room, her eyes searching out details. Then she arched an eyebrow in Kristie's direction. "Do you need a drink?"

The spinner shook her head.

"Good. Pritch, I'd like to talk to Kristie alone."

"Sure, Jane. No problem."

Kristie waited until the male operative had exited into the hall, then she said bluntly, "Your boy there almost got me killed."

"Looks like you survived."

"Barely." The spinner scowled. "Just tell me you've got the disks."

"We've got them. Dusty but informative." The agent's voice warmed. "You did a great job."

The sentiment surprised Kristie. Given the agent's demeanor, she had expected to hear a catalog of transgressions. "Thank you."

Jane walked over to the open suitcase and picked up a lacy white tube top. "Melissa has provocative taste."

Again, Kristie was surprised at the agent's suddenly friendly attitude. She even suspected Jane was confusing her on purpose as part of some squirrely debriefing strategy. If so, the spinner needed to reassert control. This was her room, after all. And she worked for SPIN, not the CIA.

Gesturing toward the table and chairs, she murmured, "Shall we?"

"Thanks." The agent stretched as she sat down. "That feels good. I've been on the go for hours."

"How's Salinger?"

"They're holding him overnight for observation at a secure facility. A concussion but no fracture. He still can't see straight. Nice work."

"How about the guard? His name was Mike something-or-other."

"Fractured jaw."

"And the Axe?"

"He took two bullets, but he'll be fine." She eyed Kristie intently. "Ray says he gave you some classified information, based on your need to know."

"I needed it from the start, actually. You almost got me killed by withholding it."

"You were just supposed to be planning a backup strategy," Jane reminded her with a smile. "And you didn't have clearance. Now you do, by the way."

"Huh?"

"As of this evening, you've got high-level access. The same as Pritch, actually. You earned that with what you did." Leaning forward, she murmured, "We pieced most of it together, but I'd like to hear the details from your point of view if you don't mind."

Kristie hesitated, then gave her shoulders a slight shrug. "It all happened pretty quickly. Salinger approached me in the garden and we started talking. About art in general and his house in particular. The next thing I knew, he was offering to show me the gallery. I couldn't resist, because I was hot to figure out which painting he hid the safe behind. Purely research. But when we got there, he told the guards to turn off the room alarm and the closed-circuit cameras, and then he surprised me by turning off the secondary system that protected the paintings themselves—"

"Wait!" Jane leaned forward again. "Why would Salinger do that?"

Kristie rubbed her eyes as she remembered the pivotal moment. "There was a painting of a woman—a dying woman. He showed me how her handprint was embedded in part of the painting, and I reached out to touch it. He stopped me, of course, but he could see that I was honestly moved by the image, so he turned off the second alarm system so I could touch the handprint. It was such an incredible stroke of luck, Jane. And all I could think was, we might never get another chance like that."

Jane nodded. "And so?"

"And so I squirted him with the toxic lipstick." She waited until the agent had stopped laughing, then admitted sheepishly, "I figured I was home free at that point. I opened the safe, found the disks, then pointed Salinger's gun at his head, figuring I could just sit there and wait to be rescued. That's when I called Ray and found out Salinger wasn't the top dog, which sort of screwed up my plan. Suddenly, I had to get out of that room."

"So you made it look as though a team of burglars broke through the skylight, tied you and Salinger up, and robbed the place."

"Right."

"It was brilliant. But I still don't see how you got out of the room. How did you convince the Axe to let you go upstairs to Salinger's room?"

Kristie blushed. "I took my top off—"

"What?" Jane burst into laughter again. "I thought you said the Axe wouldn't fall for a ploy like that."

Kristie laughed, too. "I took it off before I broke the skylight. So it would get covered with glass slivers. I made sure my bra was filled with slivers, too. I figured they'd agree to let me use a bathroom at the very least. But in the back of my mind, I was hoping for Salinger's closet."

"Which is where you got the maid's outfit? After you neutralized the guard?"

"Right. After that, it was all downhill, or so I thought."

"Until you realized they were interrogating Pritch?"

"Or as I like to call him—Prick."

Jane was clearly struggling not to smile. "He's grateful to you. He knows you could have just hidden and waited for us to get there."

"Whatever."

"I'm grateful to you, too. For the whole operation. It was a great piece of work."

"You wouldn't know it from the way you got rid of me so fast. Without even a simple thank you."

Jane shrugged her shoulders. "I gave Ray my word I'd have you out of there in five minutes or less."

"Oh. That makes sense, I guess," Kristie admitted.

"One final question. Were you scared?"

"Of course. Who wouldn't be?"

The agent eyed her intently. "Most people would be so terrified, they couldn't think straight. But you plotted a complicated, high-stakes strategy on the fly. No panic. No mistakes, except the ones caused by faulty intel. And even then, you compensated brilliantly. So…" She leaned forward. "Tell me the truth. Were you scared?"

"I almost panicked a couple of times, but the plan was so solid. In some ways, it was almost an intellectual exercise," Kristie admitted. "Like I was back in my cubicle at SPIN, safe and sound—"

"While Melissa took all the chances?"

Kristie smiled in delight. "You're pretty perceptive, Jane. That's exactly what it was like."

Jane leaned back and folded her arms across her chest. "You'd make a great addition to my team. I want you to think about that."

"About working for you? Permanently?" Kristie's cheeks warmed. "That's really flattering. But I'm happy where I am. Thanks, though."

"SPIN was a good entry-level opportunity for you," Jane agreed. "Ray's one of the best profilers in the business, not to mention a brilliant strategist. But you've gotten all you need from him. You're ready for the big leagues now. Higher stakes. And we need you. Your country needs you. And it *really* needs Melissa."

"Huh?"

Jane hunched forward eagerly. "I see what's going on with you two, and it's amazing. *You* supply the rational, methodical objectivity, the quiet strength, the creativity. But *she's* got the guts and the passion—passion that would get in the way, blur your thinking, if you didn't know how to keep it in reserve for the moments when all else has failed. It's fascinating, really," she added with a dazzling smile. "Alone, either of you is a great find. Together, you're dynamite."

Kristie stared for a long moment, then burst into laughter. "Are you kidding me? You act like Melissa's a real person."

"No, *you* act like she's real." Jane arched an eyebrow. "Haven't you ever wondered where she came from?"

"I know exactly where she came from. Ray Ortega's vision of an ideal woman."

"Pardon?"

Kristie smiled sheepishly. "I invented Melissa for one reason—to get a job at SPIN. I figured the best way to impress Ray was to design a fake identity for myself that was so flawless, it could fool an expert like him. But because he was such an expert, I knew I had to keep him off his game a little. So I did some research on his taste in women, and came up with Melissa. Then I invented a wild résumé—mountain climbing, karate, et cetera. The opposite of the real me. The point was to show that I could create a believable undercover identity."

Jane nodded. "Obviously, you were successful."

"Right. After that, it just made sense to keep using that basic profile when I needed to create a fictitious female. Like on a recent assignment, when an operative needed an old girlfriend to brag about in a bar with a bunch of guys."

"Or like the night you called that fourteen-year-old boy in the detention center about his missing sister?"

"Exactly."

Jane's eyes began to twinkle. "Explain to me why you needed Melissa for that."

"Hmm?"

"It was you making the call, wasn't it?"

"Sure. But I couldn't use my own name."

The agent pursed her lips, then recited, "I'm six feet tall with flaming-red hair and I've saved hundreds of little girls. And—" her tone grew rich with approval "—I'm not afraid of anything. Isn't that what Melissa told that boy?"

"She needed to make him feel safe. And inspired."

"*She* did? Don't you mean, *you* did?"

"Whatever." Kristie glared. "How do you know what we said anyway? That call wasn't taped."

"The boy told the cops. It's in the police report." Jane gave her a sympathetic smile, then repeated, "She's six feet tall with flaming-red hair and she's not afraid of anything. Do you really think she's going to be satisfied sitting in a cubicle for the rest of her life while the field operatives have all the fun?"

"Okay, reality check. I'm me. I love my cubicle. I don't ever want to have another day like today. It's a miracle it went as well as it did. A fluke."

Kristie paused for a moment, then added grudgingly, "I'm glad it happened. It'll be a great memory for me. Something I can draw on when I'm planning future assignments. But believe me, I have no desire to ever go through that kind of craziness again. I'm not trained for it—"

"We'll get you all the training you need." The CIA agent held up a hand as though warding off further argument. "You don't need to decide tonight. Get some rest. Enjoy the amenities of a five-star hotel—one of the perks of working for me. My team travels in style. Speaking of which, our plane leaves at ten sharp tomorrow morning."

And you'll be recruiting me during the entire flight? Kristie shook her head. "Thanks anyway, but I'll make my own arrangements. Like you said, this is a minivacation for me. I might go home by way of Los Angeles. Just for the fun of it."

"What's there? Or should I say, who's there?"

Refusing to acknowledge, even to herself, that McGregor was the best attraction L.A. currently had to offer, the spinner gestured to the logo on her T-shirt. "I went to school there. Undergraduate. I'd like to see how much it's changed since then."

"You definitely deserve a vacation. But I promised Ray I'd deliver you home tomorrow. Safe and sound. I got the impression he'll be meeting our plane in person."

Kristie exhaled slowly, admitting to herself that a side trip to Los Angeles was a crazy idea. What could she hope to accomplish? To catch a glimpse of her phone lover? She'd seen enough photographs and video to know how good-looking he was. The true test would be a face-to-face meeting, and she wasn't ready for that yet, was she?

And even if she were, she couldn't just spring it on the guy unilaterally. It affected *his* career, too. As much as he might claim to want to break the rules with her, he had a spotless reputation. More important, he liked having Kristie as his spinner. If they openly acknowledged a personal relationship, Ray would have no choice but to permanently reassign them, assuming he didn't fire her on the spot.

"Kristie?"

She grimaced. "Sorry, Jane. I guess I'm more tired than I thought."

"We'll have plenty of time to visit on the jet tomorrow. Get some sleep. Shall I have Pritch bring you some food?"

"I'll order room service myself if that's okay."

"It's on us, and the sky's the limit. I'll make sure the front desk knows to put it on my tab."

Kristie nodded, making a mental note to check with the clerk to ensure her phone call to McGregor stayed on her personal credit card. The last thing she needed was an official government record of *that* conversation.

"Which reminds me, Jane. My cell phone and my Melissa outfit—"

"You'll get everything back tomorrow. We're having the wig cleaned—it had a rough day."

"Tell me about it." Kristie stood and stretched.

The agent took the hint, heading immediately for the door, where she turned and offered what appeared to be a truly genuine smile. "I've been looking for someone like you for a long time, Kristie. You're unique. A true phenomenon. And you're wasted at SPIN. Promise me you'll keep an open mind?"

"I love spinning for Ray. It's my dream job. But I'll listen to the rest of your pitch tomorrow, since I don't think I have a choice. Right?"

"I can be very, *very* persuasive," Jane said, arching an eyebrow for emphasis. "It's my best—and worst—quality."

"Thanks for the warning."

Jane laughed. "See you in the morning."

As soon as the agent was gone, Kristie's gaze settled on the unmonitored phone. Did she dare call McGregor again? Not for more funny business, but just to connect—to take this rare opportunity to talk about where their relationship was headed, if anywhere.

Almost immediately she was disgusted with herself. "Didn't you just tell Jane that spinning is your dream job? The last time I checked, there was a rule against personal contact with operatives."

Stepping onto the balcony, she forced herself to concentrate on her spectacular surroundings. The setting sun was casting red highlights over the landscape, accentuating the contrast between miles of lush green golf courses and the stark mountains beyond. It reminded her that this was indeed her first vacation in a very long time. Maybe she should just go for a swim in the Olympic-size pool and eat lobster on the CIA's tab.

Or she could call her aunt and uncle and arrange a real vacation. They had begged her to join them in Italy where their most recent carbon-dating project was under way. Even on her shoestring budget she could afford the flight as long as they could put her up.

Or she could call Justin. Talking to him was always a treat, with no danger of things going too far.

Or you can start acting like a professional and call Ray. Get it over with! Let him yell and threaten and call you a screwup. Then you can vow not to break the rules again, ever, and this time, you'd better mean it. Or your next paycheck will be from the CIA.

Returning to the room, she sat cross-legged on the bed and pulled the hotel phone into her lap, trying not to picture her boss's piercing, accusatory glare. Then she summoned her most contrite mood and dialed 0.

This was one call for which she would gladly let the CIA pay.

Chapter 9

By Monday morning Kristie was pretty sure she had already lost her spinning job—it was just that no one had bothered to tell her yet.

The first sensation of trouble had come during her call to Ray from Palm Springs. He had surprised her by congratulating her warmly, inquiring politely as to her health and state of mind, and then basically advising her to get some rest. His subdued attitude would have completely unnerved her had he not mentioned that they'd discuss "the matter" more fully in person when he picked her up at the airport.

That was the Ray Ortega she knew. He wanted to do this in person. To wave his arms and pound things—to let her see the golden flash of exasperation in his brown eyes. And she had to admit she was looking forward to it, too. Not just because it would help cleanse her guilty conscience, but because she knew that at some point, the fiery diatribe would morph into a passionate exaltation of the history and purpose of SPIN. Ray would wax poetic on such SPIN-like qualities as honor, patriotism, discipline, imagination and innovation. She loved those lectures, and had truly craved a rousing one.

In the meantime, her renewed commitment to her dream job had proven useful during her next encounter with Jane Smith, who had freely employed her own brand of inspirational rhetoric on Sunday's flight back to the East Coast.

According to the agent, Kristie's refusal to consider the CIA's offer was not only indefensible, it was unpatriotic. And irrational. Jane had plied the spinner with incentives—the lure of travel to exotic locales, access to top governmental secrets, technology that civilians didn't even dream existed yet, challenges that only the most creative minds in the country could possibly tackle.

But Kristie had been steadfast, focusing instead on the moment when the jet would land, and she would be picked up—and chewed out—by Ray Ortega.

Unfortunately, Ray hadn't met her plane as promised. Instead, he sent his second-in-command, David Wong, who explained that their boss had been called to the White House unexpectedly, but would see Kristie first thing in the morning at SPIN headquarters.

Now it *was* "first thing in the morning," and she wasn't about to go down without a fight, so she dressed the part of a reborn professional in a smartly tailored black suit and ivory silk shell complemented by sensible black heels and a no-nonsense briefcase. With any luck, her boss would be impressed, or at least mollified.

But when she arrived at SPIN, Ray's secretary informed

her that he hadn't even come in yet, and her panic became official.

"I'll just wait in his office if that's okay," Kristie murmured, not willing to be distracted by pleasant banter with David or piles of telephone messages. Not even messages from Agent Will McGregor.

Pulling the door closed behind her, she sank into a chair near his desk and began to worry. It wasn't like Ray to be late, especially when he had a lecture scheduled. Could he possibly be so angry—so completely disappointed and frustrated—that he simply couldn't expend the time and emotion to guide her any longer? Was he going to advise her to take the CIA's offer?

By the time his office door finally opened, she was ready to throw herself at his feet and plead for another chance. But it was Colonel Ulysses S. Payton, not Ray, who stood in front of her, a huge grin on his ruddy face.

"So, there's the heroine of the hour!" He slammed the door shut behind himself, then strode over to Kristie, grabbed her by the shoulders and beamed into her face. "How does it feel to be a star?"

Stunned, she couldn't do anything for a moment but stare back at him. Finally her equilibrium returned and she pulled free—politely but firmly. Then she stood and backed a judicious distance away.

This isn't good, her instincts told her. *You'd better hope Ray gets here soon. At least he'll have someone else to get mad at when he does.*

She hadn't had much interaction with Payton since her interview six months earlier. It had been clear that day that he was championing her candidacy. Equally clear had been the tension between the colonel and the SPIN director, so much so that she had feared Payton's support might hurt her chances rather than help them. Luckily, the Melissa Daniels charade had impressed Ray enough to counteract any adverse influence by Payton.

Thereafter, Kristie's suspicions about the relationship between Ray and Payton had been confirmed again and again. In response, she had done her best to avoid the interloper, waving to him from a distance when he visited SPIN headquarters, then ducking down in her cubicle and pretending to be on the phone whenever the colonel had attempted to engage her in conversation.

But there was no ducking him now, so she reminded herself that he had tried to be helpful—and he was the president's best friend and adviser, and thus was in a position to either support or hurt SPIN—so she gave him a gracious smile. "You heard about Palm Springs?"

"I know everything that goes on around here, especially when it has to do with you. My favorite pet project."

Pet project? Kristie winced. *What a jerk....*

Aloud, she murmured, "I have to get back to work. Ray should be here soon—"

"I'm here to see you, not him."

"Oh?"

He grinned again. "Say thank you."

"Pardon?"

His eyes twinkled. "I'm the one who recommended you to Jane Smith for that assignment."

"Really?"

"That's right. I told her all about you. Bragged about you to the president, too."

"Well, then…" Kristie grimaced. "Thanks, Colonel."

"There's more where that came from. Have a seat and I'll tell you about it."

"I'm fine standing." She looked directly into his eyes.

"I appreciate your interest in my career, Colonel Payton. But I don't really need anything more than I already have. The trip to Palm Springs was exciting, but not really my thing. I like it here, behind the scenes. So—" she allowed her voice to take on a hint of defiance "—please don't feel the need to do me any more favors."

"I'd say it's your turn to do me a favor or two," he countered her gruffly.

"What does that mean?"

He gave her a playful wink. "Let's just say I'd like to be your friend. Your very good friend. If you're smart, you'll want that, too. And don't worry about the age difference. I guarantee you I can keep up."

She glared in disgust. "Okay, two things. First of all, this has nothing to do with your age. Second of all, yuck." Her voice grew bolder. "I can't believe you're hitting on me. Don't do it again."

"Or what?"

"Didn't you claim to know all about Palm Springs? Where I broke one man's jaw and gave another one a concussion?"

Payton stuck a finger to within inches of her nose. "You'd better watch yourself—"

"Or what?" she demanded, echoing his challenge. "You'll tell the president I threatened you? Don't you think he'll wonder why I felt the need to do that? He might even wonder what you were doing alone in a room with me. You don't work here, you know. This is Ray Ortega's office, not yours, and if you're smart, you'll walk away now. And you'll stay away!"

"You're an ungrateful bitch!" he shouted, his face scarlet, his features contorted, his finger now trembling with undisguised rage. "I made you—"

"Bullshit. You didn't get me this job, and I don't believe you got me the assignment with the CIA either. And even if you did, I couldn't care less. So stop waving that finger in my face before I break it off and mail it to the White House."

She thought he was actually going to attack her, and part of her couldn't wait, but at that moment the door flew open and Ray charged into the room, his face every bit as apoplectic as the colonel's.

"Dammit, Payton! Since when do you talk to my staff—in my office!—without my permission?" Without waiting for a response, he turned to Kristie. "Are you okay?"

"I'm fine."

He surveyed her quickly, then instructed, "Excuse us then. I'd like to talk to the colonel alone."

She could see his white-hot anger, and knew it could damage his career if he unleashed it in Payton's direction. So she replied softly, "I'd like to stay. It concerns me, too."

"It doesn't have a damn thing to do with you," Ray corrected her. "This is between me and him."

"You'd better watch yourself, Ortega," Payton said with a sneer. "And just for the record, I didn't lay a hand on your wiseass girlfriend there."

"She's not—" Ray visibly reined himself in. "Just get the hell out of here. And stay out. I don't want to catch you anywhere near SPIN—or my spinners—again. Is that clear?"

Payton seemed about to protest, then he turned abruptly and walked to the door, muttering under his breath, "Say goodbye to your career. *Both* your careers, in fact."

Striding past Beth's desk into the hall, the colonel disappeared in the direction of the elevators.

"Sorry, Ray," Kristie murmured as she studied her supervisor's tortured profile. He was stressed to his breaking point, and she knew she had contributed to the phenomenon.

"Huh?" He looked over at her as though he'd forgotten she was there. Then he crossed to her in two long strides and grabbed her by the shoulders, just as Payton had done. "Are you okay?"

She nodded. "I'm just sorry I got him so angry."

"Forget about him." A reluctant smile lit his face. "You're really something, you know that?"

"So are you." She felt herself fully relax for the first time in more than a day. "Am I fired?"

"Do you *want* to be fired?" He moved to his side of the desk, then motioned toward the chair facing him. "Have a seat. We've got a lot to talk about."

"Let me guess, a new list of infractions?" she said, daring to tease him as relief coursed through her. He wasn't angry with her. That was a start. And she was apparently still a spinner. That was a miracle.

He smiled grimly. "First let me just repeat what I told you Saturday night. I'm proud of you. We all are."

"I know I broke some rules—"

"You exploited that opportunity like a seasoned professional. I don't have any criticisms or complaints. I just want to figure out what's going on."

She sat up straight. "I can tell you what *I've* figured out, if that helps. These crazy forays—first with Justin Russo, and now Salinger—have totally reaffirmed for me how much I love spinning. This is where I'm meant to be. Behind the scenes. Planning, plotting, strategizing here. With you. When it comes to executing the plan, I'll gladly let someone else take over."

He studied her in silence.

"Really, Ray. I know Jane thinks I belong in the field—"

"Who cares what Jane thinks? The point is, you've shown an aptitude for fieldwork. And an interest in it."

"You think I should work for the CIA?"

He blanched. "Don't be ridiculous. I was thinking of the Bureau. They'd kill for someone like you." His eyes narrowed. "She offered you a job?"

"You didn't know?" Kristie gave him a halfhearted smile. "I turned it down, of course. And I don't want to work for the Bureau either. I want to work for you. Period. If you'll still have me."

He was silent for a moment again. Then he surprised her by asking, "Do you know what I did on Saturday? Once I knew you were safe?"

"What?"

"I did what I should have done before I hired you. A thorough background check."

Kristie cocked her head to the side, confused. "Didn't you do that before you hired me?"

"I did a thorough one on Melissa Daniels. But just a cursory one on Kristie Hennessy." His smile was rueful. "You blew me away with that charade of yours. The mountain-climbing, Olympic athlete who spoke six languages and had a black belt."

"But then you found out the truth. That I was really an academic. From UCLA and Berkeley, not Yale and Stanford. You checked all that out. And since I had no personal life to speak of, there wasn't much else to do."

When Ray shrugged, she arched an eyebrow. "You're saying you discovered something dark and mysterious in my background on Saturday night?"

"Actually, I found something illuminating. About your parents, to be specific."

"I've told you all about them. Dozens of times. They were perfectly normal, well-adjusted, wonderful-hyphen-boring people. After they died in a plane crash when I was ten, I went to live with an even more normal-hyphen-boring couple, my aunt and uncle. College professors whose idea of interior design was floor-to-ceiling bookshelves." She eyed him grimly. "Are you trying to tell me my parents *didn't* die in a plane crash?"

His eyes widened. "No, nothing like that."

"Good. Because I thought for a minute you were starting to take this spy stuff a little too seriously."

Ray scowled. "Payton's right about you. You are a wiseass."

"Sorry, I couldn't resist." Kristie leaned forward and gave him an encouraging smile. "So? What's the big revelation?"

"You've always told me your father was a travel agent and your mother was a photographer."

"And you're saying they weren't?"

"Your father ran the Safari Express Travel Agency, specializing in trips to the jungles of Africa and South America, led by him personally."

"Right."

"He met your mother when she was preparing for a photo spread in *National Geographic* by living with a family of orangutans."

"Right."

Ray gave a rueful laugh. "The very fact that that seems normal-hyphen-boring to you is a dead giveaway. It's in your blood, Kris. And if I had bothered to look past the labels, I would have seen that."

"You mean, because they liked adventure? I guess that's true," she admitted with a shrug. "Although orangutans hardly qualify as dangerous, Ray. We practically raised one at our house and he was a sweetheart. And the safaris were just for the visual feast, not for hunting or anything like that."

When her boss arched an eyebrow, she raised her hands in playful surrender. "Okay, okay. They were thrill seekers in their own way. But I didn't inherit that quality, which is why I fit in perfectly when I went to live with my aunt and uncle. You're not going to accuse *them* of being exciting, are you?"

He laced his fingers behind his neck and rocked back in his chair. "I'm not pretending to know exactly what happened in your childhood to make you the person you are today. I'm just saying there's a part of you I didn't know about. I don't think *you* even knew about it. If we'd known, we would have seen this coming. The question now is, what do we do about it?"

Kristie bit back a smile. "You think my aunt and uncle stifled my wild adventurous urges? That's hilarious, Ray. And wrong. They begged me to go outside and play, to take chances, all that stuff. I'm the one who chose to stick my nose in a book and barely come up for air. Really."

"I'm sure they did their best."

She shook her head, frustrated but also amused. First Jane. Now Ray. Everyone seemed to think Kristie Hennessy had a wild side. "This is about Melissa, right?"

"Is it?"

She laughed at the tactical response. "You just said it yourself—it was a charade! I intentionally made her my exact opposite. I guess it worked too well, because Jane wants to hire her, and *you* want to—" She caught herself and flushed. "Well, let's just say, you think she's my parents' long-lost daughter."

He studied her for a moment, then surprised her by suggesting, "Maybe it's time we started being honest with one another."

"Honest?" Her thoughts shifted in the direction of her unmonitored phone call to McGregor.

The price of a guilty conscience, she told herself quickly. *Ray can't possibly know about that.*

"I'll start." He licked his lips, then gave her a pained smile. "I'm sure it won't surprise you to hear that I'm attracted to you."

Oh no...

"I hope it's mutual, but obviously, as long as I'm your supervisor, it's not something we can appropriately explore."

Kristie stared in dismay. "You want me to go work for the Bureau so we can start dating?"

"Did I say that?" he complained, his voice bordering on a growl. "I *knew* you'd make this impossible."

"Ray—"

"Let me finish." He exhaled, then insisted, "I don't want you to go work for the Bureau. I want you to stay here. I'm the one who's going to leave."

"What?"

He flushed. "Not because of you. It's just something I've been thinking about for a while now. And there's an opportunity that might come up sooner than later. So I thought you'd want to know."

"You can't leave SPIN. It's your baby."

"Babies grow up," Ray countered. "And don't worry. If and when it happens, I'll leave it in good hands. I've already picked out my replacement, and I can pretty much guarantee you'll approve."

Which means it's David Wong, she told herself, knowing that David would do a fine job, but sad nevertheless at the thought of Ray leaving SPIN. "This is so weird. I can't imagine this place without you."

"I'll stay involved. With SPIN. And with you. Which is my point, remember?"

"What kind of opportunity is it?"

"What difference does it make?" His eyes flashed. "Pay attention, Kris. I'm pouring my heart out to you here, and all you care about is the job. Try to focus, would you?"

He exhaled sharply. "Sorry, I didn't mean to raise my voice. I actually wanted this to be—well, a tender moment. So much for that, huh?"

"It was actually pretty romantic," she admitted. "Now it's my turn to be honest, right?"

"Right."

Employing her most understanding tone, she told him, "I didn't know until recently that you had this little crush on Melissa, and—"

"This *what?*"

She had to bite her lip to keep from smiling at the confounded expression on his face. "I'm the one who created this situation, and I take complete responsibility for it. I designed Melissa to appeal to your—well, your primitive urges. I guess it worked too well. I'm really sorry, Ray."

The muscles of his jaw tensed visibly. "Cut it out, Kris."

"You psychoanalyzed me a minute ago—inaccurately, I might add. Now it's my turn." She gave him an encouraging smile. "Think about it. Melissa's hair is just like your ex-wife's was when you met her. I saw that in a college-yearbook picture. I found it on the Internet, by the way. She was gorgeous, and you were smitten."

"This is nuts."

"Is it? Remember how Melissa was dressed? Just like Suzy Eberhardt, that sexy congresswoman from Ohio. I don't need to tell you why I used her as an example of your taste in women, do I?"

His response was a murderous glare.

"You know it's true, Ray. Melissa got to you. She was supposed to get to you. What I didn't realize was that you'd transfer all that to me. I thought we were becoming friends. I was being Kristie, but you were seeing Melissa."

"This conversation is over."

"No, it isn't." Kristie folded her arms across her chest. "I want to hear about this new job of yours."

"Again with the job?" He shook his head. "It's nothing definite. Just an opportunity I'm considering. Now more than ever," he added sarcastically.

"You can't get away from me that easily," she said, teasing. "We're going to be friends for the rest of our lives, Mr. Ortega. Whether you like it or not."

His eyes narrowed. "There's no attraction at all?"

"You're a total hunk. I'm sure if I hadn't spent so much time deconstructing your libido to prepare for my interview, I probably would have fallen for you. But by the time I actually met you, I knew what kind of girl you liked, so I guess I never entertained the possibility."

"So? What about now?"

"I love you like the grouchy brother I never had."

He winced, then nodded. "Fair enough."

She got up and walked around to his side of the desk, where she leaned down and kissed his cheek. "Are you okay?"

"I'll survive," he grumbled. "Get back to work. And watch your step."

"Okay, boss." She moved away, pausing in the doorway

to study him for a quick moment. Definitely a hunk. And one who clearly needed a girlfriend. The sooner he got over Melissa and found himself someone real, the better. And now that he understood what was really going on, she was sure that he would do just that.

Nice job crushing the poor guy's spirit, Melissa, she griped at her alter ego. *You may have gotten me this job in the first place, but these days, you're nothing but trouble. Maybe it's time for you to retire.*

She was only half-serious. After all, she didn't put much stock in Jane Smith's theory, nor in Ray's. They were highly trained operatives with excellent training and instincts, but neither of them was a trained psychologist. Not like Dr. Kristie Hennessy.

Still, she acknowledged things had gotten a little out of control lately. Not because she was a repressed thrill seeker, but because she was too invested in the success of her operations, which made her identify too completely with the field agents. That was counterproductive and would have to stop, especially if a new director took over.

She stole a glance at David Wong as she walked past his cubicle. He probably didn't want to be in charge, since he hated playing politics, and scrupulously protected the nine-to-five schedule that allowed him to spend time with his wife and three young children. But he'd do it for Ray.

And he'd probably run the place differently. Fewer rules. More laid-back. He was a licensed psychologist, just like Kristie. That was bound to affect his approach.

On impulse she stopped beside his desk. "Hi, David."

"Hey." He glanced toward Ray's office. "How'd it go?"

"Pretty well, considering that it was the second time in forty-eight hours that an amateur tried to psychoanalyze me. So I thought I'd check in with a professional."

"The good news is, you're nuts but you're not crazy," he quipped.

"That *is* good news. Be sure to send your bill to my home address."

"Hey, wait a minute." He seemed to be regretting his remark, and before she could stop him, he had grabbed a file and jumped to his feet. "Let's use one of the sound-proof rooms for this."

"For what?" she asked, but he was already heading for a glass-walled conference room on the far side of the office, so she trailed after him, insisting, "David, I was kidding."

"Come in and have a seat." He waited for her to enter, then closed the door behind her and motioned toward the room's rectangular table and comfortable chairs.

"This is silly. Ray's going to wonder—"

"That's why I brought this." He emptied the contents of the file onto the table. "No big deal, right? Just two colleagues conferring, like we've done a million times. So…" He settled into a chair, then leaned back and gave her an encouraging smile. "Talk to me."

Kristie hesitated, but the truth was, she really did want a professional opinion, so she selected a chair across from him. "Like I said, I'm tired of amateurs. First Jane Smith. Now Ray. They both seem to think I've repressed some wild side of my nature, and it's coming out in Melissa. Jane thinks it's great, by the way," she added dryly. "Two agents for the price of one, or something like that."

"And what do *you* think?"

Kristie arched an eyebrow. "Let's skip to the diagnosis, okay, Doc? I already had the mandatory eighteen months of therapy required to earn my Ph.D."

"Fair enough," he reassured her. "Tell me about Ray's theory. What wild side, and why did you repress it?"

Mollified, she explained. "My parents were moderately adventuresome, and as you know, it ended badly. In a fiery plane crash when I was ten. Then I went to live with an aunt and uncle who had chosen not to have kids. So the theory is that I inherited a wild side from Mom and Dad, but I repressed it, either from fear I'd die young and violently, or fear that I'd be a burden. According to Jane and Ray, that repressed personality—Melissa—is now clawing her way out."

"I can see at least two flaws in that theory."

Kristie smiled in relief. "The first being that if I were going to form multiple personalities, I'd have done it at a much younger age?"

"Correct. And as far as fear of dying young, or fear of being a burden, or fear of anything goes, I'd say that's completely off base. You're probably the most fearless person I've ever met."

"Me?"

"It's your defining quality," he insisted. "If someone asked me to describe you, do you know what I'd say?"

"What?"

"You're a great friend. One of the kindest and most considerate people I know. You're funny and sweet. You're a genius—I didn't need to see your test scores to know that, but I *have* seen the scores, and they're amazing. Still, the thing that makes you unique is your fearlessness. At least to me."

She bit her lip, touched and amazed by the tribute.

David smiled and continued. "I'll never forget your interview. A twenty-six-year-old professional student who'd never had a real job in her whole life. But you went toe-to-toe with Ray Ortega and Ulysses Payton. Beat them at their own game and had fun doing it. And don't tell me that was Melissa, because I see it every day. You open red folders that would make me cringe, but all you see is the challenge. The tougher the case, the better. You got that from Mom and Dad apparently. Zero fear of failure."

"That's so sweet, David." She stood and gave him a grateful smile. "Thanks."

"Wait." He motioned for her to sit back down. "Don't you want to hear my theory about Melissa?"

"You have a theory?" Kristie winced. "Since when?"

"Since last week."

"When I used Melissa for the Lizzie Rodriguez case?"

"When you told me you weren't attracted to Ray." He laughed ruefully. "That was the second time Melissa made a monkey out of me, and I didn't like it. And yes," he added more solemnly, "the Rodriguez case was provocative to say the least. So I've been giving it some thought. And assuming Melissa isn't conning me again, I think I'm making some progress with it."

"I love the way everyone talks about her like she really exists, but *I'm* the one who's crazy," Kristie complained. When David laughed without apology, she arched her eyebrow and suggested, "Let's just hear your theory."

"Okay, here goes." His tone softened. "You had a lot of options growing up. You were unusually intelligent and creative, obviously you were good-looking and, apparently, you had a fair amount of athletic ability. You could have chosen any of a number of careers, some of them physically demanding, some of them more intellectual. You chose to become a studious, charming, moderately fit psychologist, rather than, let's say, a mountain-climbing, sharpshooting world traveler. But you didn't repress your so-called wilder urges. You did what any healthy person does—you satisfied them vicariously, through books and movies. And since you were a voracious reader and intellectually acquisitive, you really fed those interests."

"In a healthy way."

"Correct. Then you heard about the perfect job for a psychologist who loves to analyze and solve problems while living vicariously through others. But a funny thing happened on the way to the interview."

Kristie laughed in delight. "Melissa Daniels."

"Right. You found a loophole. You didn't just live vicariously through someone else that day. You actually *were* someone else. It was fun. Exhilarating. And surprisingly easy for a person with your brains and creativity."

"And it worked. I never could have gotten this job as myself," Kristie reminded him. "Ray specifically recruited candidates with practical experience as well as excellent credentials. He never would have interviewed Kristie Hennessy. By posing as a thirty-year old Ph.D. from Yale who had worked as a profiler for three years, I got myself an interview and the job."

"Or as you like to say, Melissa got you the job."

Kristie winced. "When I say that, I'm just kidding. Honest, David. I *know* Melissa is me."

"Who saved Lizzie Rodriguez? You or Melissa?"

"I did. There's not a doubt in my mind about that. But it was the same situation. Just like Ray wouldn't have hired someone like me, Randy wouldn't have trusted Kristie Hennessy. I had to offer them Melissa. Someone with the experience I lacked. That's how I convinced them to listen to me."

"And when you were all alone in the gallery in Palm Springs? Who were you convincing then?" When Kristie winced, David laughed and patted her hand. "Don't worry. I think it's great. Just don't overdo it."

"How so?"

"Overconfidence can get a person killed. You can invent all the credentials and experiences for Melissa you want, but at some point, you have to acknowledge—internally at least—that your limits are her limits."

Kristie nodded. "That makes sense."

"And don't use her as a way to avoid taking personal risks, particularly in your social life. And by social life, I mean love life," he added with a teasing smile. "Don't delegate *that* to Melissa. Some things weren't meant to be experienced vicariously."

Or over the phone? Kristie mused wistfully. "I agree."

He sat back and smiled. "You've been through a lot this last week, Kris. Give yourself a break. I have a feeling your relationship with Melissa will play itself out on its own eventually. Or morph into something else."

"If she doesn't get me killed first? It's funny that you should say that," Kristie admitted, "because in a way, that's what almost happened in Palm Springs."

"Really? It sounded to me like she saved your life."

"I thought so, too, at the time," she agreed. "But think about it. When I called Ray from the gallery, he gave me a very simple, very direct way of getting out alive. That was the advice of a seasoned field agent. But I went for a more flamboyant—more reckless—solution, à la Melissa. Shattering skylights and playing dress-up." She sighed. "Maybe you're right. She's going to get me killed."

David shook his head. "You're forgetting why you made those choices in the first place. Not because you liked playing dress-up. Because you couldn't shoot those men in cold blood."

Kristie nodded ruefully. "That's true."

"If you'd done what Ray told you to do, we'd be sitting in here for a different reason. To talk about the nightmares you were having. The guilt. The images of Salinger's brains splattered on the carpet." David eyed her sternly. "Don't sell Melissa short. She probably *did* save your life that day, emotionally speaking."

"You're doing it again," Kristie told him with a fond smile. "Talking about her like she's a real person."

"Real or not, you're going to need her for a while longer if you're going to keep getting yourself into dangerous situations."

"Don't worry, I'm out of the field-agent business," she assured him.

"Good." He started gathering up the scattered papers. "We'll talk again in a few weeks, okay? Just to see how my theory's holding up."

"Okay." She walked to the doorway, then turned and said softly, "Everyone's been telling me this week how good I am at my job. I hope someone's telling you that, too, because you're really something."

He flushed. "Thanks. That means a lot coming from you."

She was smiling as she walked across the office toward her cubicle. David's theories about Melissa were fairly encouraging. Like Kristie, he saw the whole thing as a healthy, relatively harmless fantasy.

As long as that fantasy didn't get her killed, which wasn't likely to happen. She had been serious about retiring from fieldwork. And this talk with David—such a gifted psychologist and spinner—had inspired her further to concentrate on her chosen profession. It had also confirmed for her that he'd in fact be a wonderful boss.

Sheesh, you've already got Ray moved out of his office! How about a little loyalty? Or better yet, a little work! It's almost nine o'clock and you haven't even cracked a file.

Settling down at her desk, she checked her messages and was surprised to find one from McGregor, claiming that he needed to update her on the string of arrests that had resulted from Manny Mannington's information.

It pleased her that he had found such a tactful way to make the first contact since their phone-sex call. She had wanted to do it herself, but had been concerned it would make her seem needy. Or slutty. And if he hadn't ever called again, she would have felt dumped—a record, considering that she'd never even met the guy!

She should have known McGregor would handle it well. If nothing else, the man had proven he had good timing and great phone sense.

Dialing quickly, she sat back and enjoyed the sound of his usual, "Will McGregor."

"Hello, Agent McGregor. This is S-3 returning your call."

"Hi." He cleared his throat. "Thanks for getting back to me so quickly. I figured you'd want to know that they served the last of the arrest warrants today."

"That's great."

"Yeah. But this thing has been pretty tough on Manny."

"Oh?"

"I visited him yesterday at the jail. He really misses his wife. She's all he can think about. It's pretty rough when a guy is hung up on a woman he can't see or touch."

The spinner's cheeks warmed as she realized what he was really saying. "I'm sure Manny's wife thinks about him a lot, too."

"Yeah? That's good to hear. He was worried she might be mad at him."

"Really?"

"Yeah. I mean, it's bad enough that *he* broke the rules and got himself arrested. But he didn't want it to adversely affect *her*. Or her standing in the community. Not that he wouldn't do it again in a minute," he added hastily. "But he knows it put her in an awkward position."

Kristie sighed. McGregor was a classy guy to worry about her this way. And she had to admit, she wasn't sure how to handle their flirtation, given her new resolution to adhere strictly to Ray's rules. "I guess they both have some thinking to do."

"Yeah. Especially her. She's the one with the most at stake. And she's got to be asking herself how well she even knows this guy. Does she want to put her whole life on the line for a virtual stranger?" Before Kristie could respond, McGregor answered for her. "She needs to take it slow."

"I guess you're right."

"On the other hand, she needs to know Manny isn't going anywhere. That's the beauty of him being in prison, and her being free. When she's ready for Visiting Day, she'll know just where to find him."

She tried to think of something to say but failed.

"Talk to you later, S-3. Thanks for being there."

"Goodbye, Agent McGregor. Take care of yourself."

Once the click on the other end of the line confirmed that the conversation had ended, Kristie pretended to focus on her files. But in her mind—and heart—she was thinking about McGregor's romantic words of wisdom.

Visiting Day…the day she and McGregor would meet. A day of *her* choosing.

And she had almost chosen wrong. If she had flown from Palm Springs to Los Angeles and surprised him with a visit, the stakes would have been too high.

But when she was ready for Visiting Day, McGregor would be waiting. *That* was the most incredible part of his message.

For the next forty-eight hours she was courted. But not by Special Agent Will McGregor. Not even by Ray Ortega. It was Jane Smith who was determined to win the fair spinner with any and every inducement she could imagine. And Kristie had to give the CIA recruiter credit. She seemed to know her every weakness.

Books, for instance. Big juicy reference works. Modest little first editions. Signed autobiographies. There was a big package on Kristie's doorstep each evening when she got home. There was always a note, too, reminding the spinner that these were the sorts of "resources" that were virtually unlimited with a budget the size of the CIA's.

Jane called at least three times a day to share tantalizing tidbits about the international intrigue in which she and her team were currently embroiled. "All this can be yours, and a lot more money and freedom, too," was the parting shot to every conversation. "Think about it."

Kristie wondered what Jane would do if she knew about her crush on Will McGregor. She'd probably deliver him right to her doorstep naked, after ordering him to service the spinner as part of his patriotic duty!

And that might just work, she admitted to herself, pulling out a photograph she kept locked in the top drawer of her desk. It was a five-by-seven of McGregor, dressed in black jeans and a gray striped dress shirt, his sleeves rolled up, his collar open. She had been salivating over that image for two days straight. Two days and two nights.

Patience, Goldie. Some things are worth waiting for.

But enough was enough. She was tired of being patient. And she had a feeling McGregor was, too.

It was definitely time for Visiting Day.

Chapter 10

Kristie's plan was to call McGregor from a pay phone on her lunch hour so that they could brainstorm where and when they should have their first face-to-face meeting. The next step would be the tough one—informing Ray that, through no fault of her own, she had developed a social relationship with a field agent, that she intended to pursue it and that she and McGregor both understood the ramifications and were formally requesting reassignment of his cases from that point forward.

That part still bothered Kristie. McGregor's projects were some of the most challenging she had faced professionally. And now that she had feelings for him—in theory at least— it would be difficult to entrust his safety to someone else. But Ray was right about objectivity, and if she and McGregor actually started seeing one another, she simply wouldn't be able to trust her instincts where he was concerned.

On the other hand, if the affair stalled, either because of a lack of in-person chemistry or simple geography, what then? She and the agent would probably form a solid friendship, but that shouldn't preclude her working on his cases. After all, she was friends with Justin Russo, wasn't she?

You're getting a little ahead of yourself, aren't you? You've got the affair with McGregor going south before it even begins! How about looking forward to the first kiss or something?

Her operative line began to ring and she bit her lip, wondering if it might be her virtual boyfriend himself. He had implied he would wait for her to make the next move. But then again, he had phenomenal instincts. So…

Reminding herself to keep the nerdy anticipation out of her voice, she picked up the receiver and said crisply, "This is S-3. Please identify yourself."

"Hey, Goldie, it's me. Do you have a minute?"

"Of course, Agent McGregor. How can I help you?"

"I've got a question about your training."

"My training?" She settled back into her chair, intrigued. If this was going to turn into a mischievous, what-is-Melissa-wearing kind of call, he was doing a good job of hiding it from the monitors. His voice sounded almost depressed.

"I know all you spinners are psychologists, right?"

"Most of us, yes."

"So, did you only study the hard-core criminal stuff? Or did you take courses about regular problems and regular people? I mean, are you a full-fledged shrink, or just a profiler?"

She was about to remind him, for the benefit of the monitors, that she wasn't allowed to reveal personal information about herself or her background, when he explained, "We talked about my sister once before, remember? She really hit rock bottom last night, and I'm running out of ideas on how to help her."

"Oh, McGregor, I'm sorry. What happened?"

"She called me from a street corner in the middle of nowhere, with no idea where she was or how she got there. It took forever just to locate her, and when I did, she was pretty out of it. It's a miracle she's survived this long, Goldie, the way she runs around."

Kristie pulled his file from a nearby shelf and located a publicity shot of twenty-three-year-old Ellie, a beautiful girl with dark curls and a winsome smile.

The spinner gave a sympathetic sigh. "You mentioned drugs. Was that a factor last night?"

"No. Her recreational medium of choice was booze."

"Well, at least she called you."

"Yeah. And what if I'd been away on assignment? She'd be dead. Or worse." He exhaled sharply. "The problem is, she's fine during the day. So I probably can't have her committed. Right?"

"That would be a little extreme," Kristie assured him gently. "Is she seeing anyone professionally?"

"Yeah. There's been a string of them. Obviously they suck. No offense."

"It's okay."

"I'm sure they're terrific. But they can't do any good if she doesn't cooperate, right?"

"Does she keep her appointments?"

"Yeah, I think so."

"And she calls you when she needs you?"

"Yeah."

"And she's okay in the daytime. So it sounds like she

wants to cooperate." Kristie opened her computer-based address book. "I know a professor. At UCLA. She has some very innovative techniques. If you want, I could call her and get an appointment for Ellie."

"Man, that would be great."

"I'll have her get in touch with you. If she can't take Ellie herself, she'll recommend someone just as good. She'll understand that you won't know my name, et cetera, so there won't be any confusion about that. And McGregor? As good as Professor Ramirez is, it's going to take time. You understand that, right?"

"Absolutely. You're incredible, Goldie."

"And you're such a good big brother. Ellie's lucky to have you." She bit her lip. "I'm so sorry you had such a rough night, Will. You should have called me right away."

"I thought about it. I knew just the sound of your voice would help. But this doctor—that's such a great bonus, Goldie."

Her other line began to flash red, and she grimaced, suspecting it was the CIA with more ridiculous inducements. But she couldn't just ignore it, so she murmured, "I've got to go, McGregor. Hang in there. We'll talk again this afternoon, okay?"

"Sure. Thanks again."

"My pleasure. Bye."

She could barely concentrate on the call, which did in fact turn out to be Jane inviting her to lunch. Kristie turned down the invitation, but ended up talking to the agent for over an hour about her current prey, a Peruvian terrorist who had kidnapped an American businesswoman. Ordinarily Kristie would have been tempted to offer assistance— another temporary loan from SPIN, assuming Ray approved—but her thoughts were on the FBI, not the CIA.

She knew now that McGregor needed to concentrate on his sister for the indefinite future. As much as Kristie wanted to meet him face-to-face, the timing was wrong, at least for the moment. In the coming months, that might change. But for now, the best thing she could do for either of them was put him in touch with Professor Jacqueline Ramirez as soon as possible.

And in the meantime, Kristie could indulge in a little informal therapy of her own with David on the provocative subject of Melissa.

When she finally managed to extricate herself from Jane's tele-clutches, she put in the call to UCLA and left a message on Professor Ramirez's answering machine, briefly outlining the situation with Ellie and requesting a callback. She had tremendous confidence in this woman, and even before she hung up the phone, she was feeling hopeful that McGregor's situation would be improving quickly.

"Kristie?"

"Oh, Beth!" Kristie smiled at Ray's secretary over the top of her cubicle. "I didn't even realize you were standing there."

"He wants to see you."

"Okay." The spinner eyed Beth intently. "Is everything okay?"

The secretary shook her head. "Just be ready. He's mad again. He's mad all the time these days."

"He's got a lot going on."

"I know, but…" Beth shrugged. "Remember how you guys used to hang out together on breaks and joke around? I think he misses that. Not that I blame you. He's been such a bear. Speaking of which, you'd better get in there."

"Hey." Kristie jumped up and squeezed Beth's shoulders. "It's fine. He'll yell, he'll feel better—problem solved. Don't worry about him."

"I'm worried about *you*," Beth admitted. "You're not going to take that other job, are you? With that awful woman?"

"Do I look crazy? Don't answer that." Kristie gave Beth's shoulders a final squeeze, then strode over to Ray's office, trying to imagine what was setting him off now. Probably something to do with Jane. Or it could be Payton again. There were so many sources of stress in the poor guy's life.

But when she approached his desk and saw the shiny reel-to-reel tape recorder waiting for her, she had an uneasy feeling she couldn't blame this one on anyone but herself.

"So…?" She managed a weak smile. "Everything okay?"

"You tell me."

Closing the door, she settled quietly into the chair facing him. This was a new Ray—completely calm. And very scary.

At least it can't be the phone-sex call, she assured herself. *It's got to be something else. One of the flirtatious ones from the first weeks with McGregor. Maybe this is the push you need to break the news to him.*

She gave her boss another, warmer smile. "I'm really sorry, Ray."

"Are you?" His tone was soft with disbelief. "You have a lot of friends here, you know. Me. Beth. David. The whole staff, really, including the monitors. Nameless, faceless jokes to you, of course—"

"That's not true!"

"Isn't it?" He stood and began to pace. "They're dedicated professionals. And they're crazy about you. You should hear how they talk—reveling in your progress. Your success. They've been so completely charmed by you, they let this—this *shit*—go on for way, way too long."

"You mean McGregor?"

"Yeah," he drawled. "I mean McGregor."

"Ray, I'm sorry. I know how you feel about me, or at least, how you think you feel—"

"Screw that!" His voice was now a full-fledged roar. "Here's a news flash for you—you're not the first woman to turn me down and you won't be the last. So do me a favor and don't mention it again. Is that clear?"

"Yes."

He sank into his chair. "It isn't about that anyway. All that stupid flirting—I knew about that, more or less. It's your style, or so I told myself. With Russo in particular. I'm surprised to hear that someone of Will McGregor's caliber participated in it, but that's your talent, right? Anonymous seduction?"

"That isn't fair."

He shrugged. "I want the flirting to stop. That goes without saying. But with McGregor, it's gone way past that stage, hasn't it?"

The spinner cringed.

"Well, at least you seem to know it's wrong," Ray said, almost sneering. "That's a start. Now we just have to figure out what to do about it."

She waited, silent and apprehensive.

Then he reached for the recorder and pushed the Play button, and she heard McGregor's soft, rumbling voice.

We talked about my sister once before, remember? She really hit rock bottom last night, and I'm running out of ideas on how to help her.

Kristie squirmed as she heard her own voice, warm with affection, reassuring the agent. Then McGregor was speaking again.

She called me from a street corner in the middle of nowhere, with no idea where she was or how she got there. It took forever just to locate her, and when I did, she was pretty out of it. It's a miracle she's survived this long, Goldie, the way she runs around.

"Ray—"

"Just listen." He punched Play, and again Kristie was talking, her voice so choked with feeling it was almost unrecognizable.

I'm so sorry you had such a rough night, Will. You should have called me right away.

I thought about it. I knew just the sound of your voice would help...

Finally the conversation ended, and Ray turned off the machine. Then he stared at Kristie, accusation in his golden-brown eyes.

And for a moment she was unable to respond. Not because he seemed so angry, but because of the way she had sounded on the tape. So tender. So intimate. So completely absorbed in Will McGregor's dilemma.

And the FBI agent had been the same way. Talking to her as though they were the only two people on earth.

No wonder Ray was so upset.

"What were you thinking?" he demanded finally.

"I don't know. I can see why you're concerned—"

"Concerned? I'm *way* past that. To the point of wondering whether you can handle this type of work at all without getting personally involved."

"I don't blame you." She nodded pensively. "I guess even I didn't realize until right now how far it had gone."

"Well," he muttered. "Thank you for that at least."

She nodded again.

"The monitors feel like shit for ratting you out, by the way."

"I'm sorry. Can you tell them that for me? Or better yet, can I tell them myself?"

"Sure. In fact, why don't you do it right now?"

"Pardon?"

He turned on his speakerphone and pressed a preprogrammed button. A series of quick tones sounded, followed by three rings. Then the call connected.

This is Will McGregor. Leave a message and I'll get back to you.

"Oh!" Kristie stared up at Ray, surprised and confused. She had been ready to apologize to the monitors directly, but not like this. And definitely not with a message left on an answering machine.

Ray motioned for her to talk, and she gulped, searching for the right words.

"Hi, Agent McGregor. This is S-3. I'm sorry we missed you. I'm here with Director Ortega. We—well, we wanted you to know I've been officially reprimanded for the conversation you and I had this morning about your sister."

She glanced up at Ray, who nodded for her to continue.

"Anyway, I've listened to the tape and I see now that we—or at least, I—really did cross a line. My behavior wasn't fair to you or to the people I work with, whom I truly, *truly* respect. I take full responsibility, and I'm sorry—"

"Agent McGregor, this is Ortega," Ray interrupted, his tone clipped to the point of dismissal. "We just wanted to let you know you won't be talking to S-3 anymore unless you have an active assignment with her. Which won't be happening anytime soon, believe me. Consider the matter closed. No need to return the call. Goodbye."

When the connection had been ended, Kristie stared down at her hands in her lap, humiliated. And while she knew Ray was within his rights, she still couldn't forgive him for forcing her to make such a painful call in so embarrassing a way.

What would McGregor think when he heard that awful message? Not that she could afford to care about that too much at the moment. Her job itself was on the line.

And at the moment, she wasn't entirely sure she cared.

"We're not as boutique-y as you and Pritchert think, Jane. At last count, SPIN had forty-five employees, plus a bunch of subcontractors." Kristie spread a pat of butter on a warm, crusty roll and gave her dinner companion an apologetic smile. "Sorry, I didn't mean to come on so strong. It's just that you guys always seem to assume we're such a joke."

"If you were a joke, would I be recruiting you?"

Kristie turned her attention back to her food, which was her excuse for being there in the first place. She hadn't eaten a bite since breakfast, mostly because she had lost her appetite after the showdown with Ray.

She had half expected him to make peace with her before she went home for the night, and when he hadn't, her already low spirits had taken a nosedive. All she had wanted to do after work was trudge home, crawl into bed and pull the covers over her head, blotting out the world.

Then steps away from her apartment, a black SUV had pulled in front of her, cutting her off. The passenger window had descended noiselessly, allowing Jane Smith to proffer a dinner invitation.

At any other time, Kristie would have turned Jane down. But suddenly, she was hungry—not only for food, but also for a little professional appreciation. And while it had seemed unwise to dine with a recruiter on the same day her boss had reprimanded her, she had decided to take the risk.

Jane was oozing with uncharacteristic charm. "You were saying? Forty-five employees? At SPIN? That's hard to believe."

"Most of them are in the field crews—they do advance work on-site for us. Then when it's over—or things go wrong—they do the cleanup."

"We have people like that, too."

Kristie savored a mouthful of ravioli, then continued. "There's the support staff, too—they're terrific, especially Ray's secretary. And the monitors. And of course, there are the spinners."

"Four of you in addition to Ray, right?"

"Yes. Two in the office, two off site and three backups who take care of our cases when we're asleep or out of town. All of them have some spin-type experience. For various reasons—babies, health, burnout, retirement—they have special needs, and Ray values each of them so much, he tailors the job to suit them. That's the beauty of a small agency. He can fine-tune it—make it almost perfect."

"In other words, he can obsessively control every detail?" Jane grinned. "Don't forget, I worked with him. I know how he is."

Kristie felt a telltale warmth redden her cheeks. "He's a perfectionist. And a visionary. And a good friend." *Most of the time, at least,* she added to herself.

"I agree. But it's his way or the highway. Correct?"

"I guess."

"Quite a paradox, don't you think? He surrounds himself with innovative, creative thinkers, then wants to tell them how to think and act. For example, this rule he has against spinners ever going into the field. It's fine in general, but occasionally—as you yourself have recently proved—exceptions should be made. Sometimes the spinner is the only one who can see what needs to be done and do it quickly. Correct?"

Kristie nodded, but it felt disloyal, so she quickly refocused on her ravioli.

Jane was undaunted. "On an educational level—well, you said it yourself in Palm Springs. You'll be able to draw on your experience in the Salinger case to make your future spinning that much more effective. More proof that you're right to take chances occasionally."

"Where do you come up with these ideas? First the split-personality theory in Palm Springs. Now this one." Kristie grinned reluctantly. "Tell me the truth. You don't really think Melissa and I are two distinct people trapped in the same body, do you?"

"Do *you*?"

"No. But you made me think it through. I even consulted a fellow psychologist about it."

"And what did this doctor say?"

"He's pretty sure it's just good clean fun. But we're going to explore it a little more, just to make extra sure I don't need an exorcism or something."

Jane's skin had taken on an ashen tone. "What?"

"I'm kidding! Sheesh, Jane. Lighten up." Kristie gave her an apologetic smile. "We'd better stay off the subject of Melissa, huh?"

"Don't sell her short. She's what makes you so unique," Jane insisted. "Therapy can only destroy that."

When Kristie stared at the recruiter, disquieted by the remark, Jane gave an embarrassed laugh. "Apparently I'm the only person who really appreciates your gift. Another reason why you should work for me."

Kristie shrugged. "Ray appreciates me, too, most of the time. If I'm a good spinner, it's because of him, not Melissa."

"He did a good job training you," Jane agreed. Then she leaned forward, her eyes flashing with challenge. "Do you think it's a coincidence that all your rule-breaking started in the last couple of weeks? I disagree. I think you spent your first six months learning. Following the rules scrupulously, like any great student should. But now that you've mastered the basics, it's time for you to put your own— well, your own spin on them. A synergy between raw talent and time-honored techniques."

Sitting back, Jane added bluntly, "I predict you're going to break the rules more and more often as time goes on. Either Ray's going to learn to accommodate that, or you'll have to find a job where you can spin to your heart's content, and do it *your* way. The way that works best for your unique set of gifts."

Kristie felt a wave of panic, mostly because Jane's words had echoed the thoughts *she'd* been having for hours. "I never really felt comfortable in the field. I didn't even like it. But I did it because—well, like you said, the opportunity presented itself and I felt I had to exploit it.

"It was exhilarating, sure. But believe me, the most exhilarating part of my job is when I'm studying a file, playing with possibilities, and it just doesn't seem to work, then suddenly..."

"Then suddenly, inspiration strikes?"

Kristie nodded enthusiastically. "Yes. Everything falls into place, and it's such a rush."

"You can get that rush on my team," Jane promised. "As much of it as you want. Believe me, I don't intend to make a full-time field agent out of you. What would be the point? They're a dime a dozen." She leaned forward eagerly. "You'll still be spinning, Kristie. I promise you that. But on those occasions when you can't trust anyone but yourself to execute your scenario—or when there's just no time to explain it to someone else—when you want to go for it, you can. The best of both worlds. And in the place of Ray's rules, I only have one."

Kristie cocked her head to the side and waited.

"You have to keep me informed. You can do what you want otherwise. I don't control my people. As long as I get results, I'm hands-off. All I ask is that you keep me in the loop."

"Where would I live? Where do *you* live?"

"I have an apartment here, and one on the West Coast. Most of my people have a place here, but it's not required." Her smile was infectious. "You can live wherever you want, and when we need you, we'll put you up in a five-star hotel, like we did in Palm Springs."

"That was pretty swanky," Kristie admitted.

"If you could live anywhere—anywhere in the world— where would it be?"

Kristie's immediate thought—Los Angeles—made her groan inwardly. Was she crazy?

In fact, this whole conversation was beginning to seem a little crazy.

Or rather, it was subversive. Which of course was just what Jane wanted. To drive a wedge between Ray and Kristie, which was pretty easy to do these days.

Just look at her, the spinner advised herself. *Do you want to end up like that? A dead sea turtle has more warmth! And she can say what she wants about Ray's rules, but they're there for your protection and the protection of the field agents. She just told you she couldn't care less about any of that. She wants results at any price, human or otherwise.*

Wasn't that the point? The CIA was a job, and a heartless one at that. SPIN was special because it had heart. Ray's heart, to be specific. Into which Kristie had been doing a good job of twisting a knife lately.

But to be fair, he had twisted a fairly good-size dagger into hers as well, hadn't he?

"I need to use the ladies' room," she told Jane abruptly. Without waiting for a reply, she grabbed her purse and dashed past the other tables until she found the rest area.

Her head was swimming, and she finally understood all of the cooling-off laws she had heard about over the years. Jane was a great saleswoman. And Ray was a lousy salesman. But for whom would she rather work?

Is this about McGregor? she challenged herself. *A guy you've never even met? Get real! Or better yet, grow up. If you can't handle Ray's controlling personality, then quit SPIN. But don't jump into the CIA because of it. And don't run to California to meet a guy who already has one crazy female on his plate.*

Of all the scattered thoughts and urges she had had over the last few hours, this was the only useful one. She had to divest herself of thoughts of McGregor. Then maybe she could deal with the rest.

And fortunately, the ladies' room had what she needed—a monitor-free pay phone. Dialing rapidly, she was thwarted by his message, delivered in a voice that could still confuse her with its sexy potential.

But she was on a mission, so she told his answering

machine, "Hi, McGregor. Sorry I missed you. I just wanted to tell you—well, you could probably sense from that crummy message we left you that I was a little upset earlier today. But I'm fine now, so don't worry. I mean, obviously I have some thinking to do about this job—but not because of you or anything like that. So don't worry. That's the theme of this call, by the way—that you shouldn't worry. This is *my* problem, not yours. You didn't get me in trouble or anything like that.

"So that's it for now. We both have a lot on our minds, but maybe once we've sorted through our various issues— you about Ellie, me about Ray and SPIN—well, it would be really nice to meet you someday. Just a nice, no-pressure get-together. Or not. Don't worry about *that* either. Sheesh, now I sound like a stalker!" She laughed sadly. "I just wanted to say goodbye for now. We won't be talking for a while, but I'll be thinking about you—in a nonstalking way. And I've made arrangements for Ellie's appointment, so you should be hearing about that soon. I'll keep my fingers crossed. And in the meantime, take care, okay? Bye."

Even after she heard McGregor's machine hang up, Kristie was reluctant to place the receiver back in the cradle, thereby officially ending their phone flirtation for the indefinite future.

It seemed like such a shame—such a nice, innocent phenomenon gone wrong. Or maybe she had just outgrown it, the way she had outgrown SPIN.

"Kristie? Is everything okay?"

She turned toward Jane Smith's voice. "I didn't hear you come in. I guess that's one of your specialties, right?"

Jane motioned toward the receiver in Kristie's hand. "Do you need to make a call?"

"No." She set it back in its holder and murmured, "I'm done with phones. All they do is get me into trouble."

"Another reason to come and work for me."

Kristie shrugged her shoulders.

"You're actually thinking about it, aren't you?"

"I'm too tired to think. I'm just going to grab a cab and head home if you don't mind. Thanks for dinner."

"I'll drop you. Come on." Jane held open the door, and when the spinner hesitated, she told her softly, "No more pressure, Kristie. I promise. I'm officially backing off for a while. You've heard all the pros and cons. Now it's up to you."

Kristie nodded. It *was* up to her. That was obvious. But in a sense, it was also up to Ray. She only hoped he was astute enough—or cared enough—to recognize it in time.

Chapter 11

"Kris! Kristie! Open up! It's me."

Ray?

Turning down the flame under a pot of canned soup she had been warming, Kristie sprinted for the front door of her apartment, alarmed by his wild pounding. It seemed impossible—or at least ridiculous—that he had chosen Sunday at noon to finally have this talk, after ignoring her completely all day Friday at SPIN headquarters.

And while she hoped it meant her boss had decided to throw himself at her feet and beg her forgiveness, she knew it wasn't exactly Ray Ortega's style. And if he were feeling humble, would he be yelling? More likely, he had found out about some other infraction. If so, this routine was getting pretty stale.

Reminding herself that the best defense was a good offense, she threw open the door and fixed her boss with a reproving glare. "Is the building on fire?"

But she immediately regretted the quip. His expression was tortured, and he clearly hadn't slept.

"Ray? You look terrible."

"Yeah, I know. Can I come in?"

"Of course." She stepped aside, resisting an urge to give him a hug. "There's soup. And a fresh pot of coffee. Want some?"

"Coffee sounds great if you don't mind. Make it fast, though. We need to talk."

"No one's dead, are they?"

He hesitated, then nodded. "Ulysses Payton was killed last night in his Malibu beach place."

"Uh-oh." She headed for the kitchen, instructing over her shoulder, "I'm listening. Who killed him?"

"We don't know yet," Ray called back to her. "All indications are he surprised an intruder. An altercation ensued, and he got his head smashed in."

She returned with two mugs—one black for him, one with extra cream. While he sipped appreciatively, she said, "So? How do you feel about it?"

"Like crap," he admitted. "You know how it was between him and me. I must have wished the guy dead a hundred times."

"But you didn't mean dead-dead. Just, get-lost-dead."

"Exactly."

"It's perfectly natural for you to feel conflicted," she told him, motioning for him to join her on the couch. "I'm glad you came to see me about this."

"I'm not here for a therapy session. I'm here to tell you you're gonna get a phone call." He pulled his cell phone out of his belt clip, checked the display and predicted, "Any second now, actually."

"A phone call? From whom?"

"The president wants you to investigate Payton's murder. Personally."

"Me?" She scanned his eyes for signs of teasing, but he was apparently serious.

Then the phone rang, and when Ray flipped it open, he surprised her by handing it directly to her. "Show time."

She gulped. "Hello?"

"Hello, Kristie. This is Jonathan Standish."

There was no mistaking the president's distinctive drawl, made famous during a series of contentious debates in his first campaign. Now he was in his second term, but that steady, reassuring voice hadn't changed a bit. Kristie had voted for him both times, not just because of what he said, but how he said it.

Inspired, she was able to reply with a crisp, "Good afternoon, Mr. President."

"Did Ray fill you in?"

"A little. I'm so sorry to hear about your friend, sir."

"Thank you. It's a great loss to the country. And to me personally."

"Yes, sir."

"I've asked Ray to drop everything and take over the investigation. I'm asking you to do the same. I want to know who murdered Yuley, and I want to know now."

"Yes, sir. We'll do our best. But you know we aren't crime scene experts."

"You'll get all the help you want from the Bureau and the local cops. I've arranged for SPIN to coordinate the effort." The president sighed. "Yuley was a big fan of yours. Did you know that?"

"Yes, sir."

"He was a great patriot. Not afraid to have an opinion. I think that's why they killed him, Kristie. To silence him."

She winced. "They?"

"Foreign agents. That's what my gut tells me. Assassins."

"Well…"

"I know what Ray thinks—that it was a burglary gone wrong. But Yuley had a sixth sense for danger. Had it since we were kids. He wouldn't walk right into something like that."

"I see."

"That's why I want SPIN out there. Build me a profile of that killer, Kristie."

"I will, sir."

"If it was an assassination, the country should know about it." His voice rang with conviction. "I want everyone to understand he died for his beliefs. And I want to punish the bastards who did it."

"Yes, sir. Absolutely."

"And if it was just—well, just a stupid, meaningless crime—" he choked back a sob "—I need to know that, too."

Kristie's heart ached for him. "We'll find out what happened, Mr. President. I promise."

"Thank you, Kristie. He'll rest easier, knowing you're on the case. And so will I. So…" His tone grew commanding. "Get on out there and do what you do. Spare no expense. If you need anything, Ray knows how to get ahold of me, day or night."

"Okay, Mr. President. Take care. We'll be in touch."

Within an hour the two spinners had boarded a chartered jet, which they proceeded to turn into a research center, complete with computers, files and a huge white wipe-off board. Kristie quickly mapped out the sequence of events.

"These golfing buddies got to his place at approximately 8:00 a.m. Pacific time?"

"Right." Ray glanced up from his monitor. "They had a standing Saturday-morning tee time of eight-thirty, at a course about ten minutes away."

"Do we know much about them?"

"Pillars of the law-enforcement community, which was good, because they were smart enough not to touch anything—or at least, that's the impression the crew got. I hope they're right."

She nodded, still amazed that the crime scene was sitting there, relatively undisturbed, awaiting the arrival of the SPIN director. Apparently, the authorities had known how close Payton was to the president, and had played this one carefully, contacting the White House before making another move. She imagined they hadn't been too happy to hear that they should just secure the premises and wait for SPIN, but with the exception of a cursory evaluation by the medical examiner, the site was apparently pristine, with the understanding that once SPIN had done its inspection, the case would be turned over to the local authorities to conduct a traditional investigation.

"The president is so sure it was an assassination."

Ray nodded. "That's how he saw Payton—as a statesman. A patriot. He never understood that to the rest of us the guy was just a nuisance."

She pursed her lips. "He had a lot of influence with the president, though. You said it yourself the other day. Is it possible someone mistook that for something more?"

"Anything's possible. We definitely have to rule it out. Except for the meddling—which was getting out of hand, true, but wasn't actually controversial—he was just a pain in the ass. Fairly hawkish, especially for this administration, but not something the international community was taking note of as far as I know. We'll put some feelers out though. Just to be sure."

He rubbed his eyes. "I may try to grab a nap while you get up to speed on Payton's background, if that's okay with you. I'm familiar with all that, and I'd like to be fresh when we land. It's gonna be a zoo."

"Go ahead."

He walked over to her and patted her shoulder. "Don't you want to ask me something first?"

"Hmm?"

He laughed fondly. "Come on, Kris. I'll be disappointed in you if you don't."

She shook her head, honestly stumped.

His smile faded. "There was bad blood between me and the victim. You know that better than anyone."

"Oh." It was Kristie's turn to laugh. "Okay, fine. Did you murder him for interfering in SPIN business, harassing your employees and just generally being a Neanderthal loser?"

"No."

"Okay. Go get some sleep."

"I have an alibi."

"Whew, that's a relief." When he didn't smile, she murmured, "Don't do this to yourself, Ray. No one suspects you. The president himself asked you to head up the investigation."

"He asked for you, too."

"Because I was Payton's quote-unquote pet project. Not because he suspects any involvement on your part." She reached up and patted his cheek. "I've never seen you like this."

"There were so many times I wanted to punch his lights out. It's bizarre that someone really did it."

"Want some advice?"

"Definitely."

"You'll be briefing the press before the day is out. And the president's going to want a report. And who knows who else you'll be talking to. You really need that nap. You can't be charming in this condition." Smiling fondly, she insisted, "You're a little off balance because of your history with Payton. Who wouldn't be? But you've got to pull yourself together and be the confidence-inspiring Ray Ortega we all know and love. Got it?"

"Thanks, Kris." He surprised her by kissing the top of her head, then he turned abruptly and headed for the back of the jet, where he hunkered down under a blanket, his face turned to the window.

Be nice to him from now on, she scolded herself. *Look at what a sweetheart he is, deep down inside. Sure, he's got a few rules. Okay, more than a few. But you can work with that. Think of all he's done for you.*

For the first time since her dinner with Jane Smith, she felt certain she wasn't going to leave SPIN, and that knowledge brought with it a rush of energy that allowed her to attack the eight-inch file on Ulysses Payton that Ray had spread onto a tabletop. Maybe by the time he awoke, she'd find something useful.

Or maybe it was just a simple burglary, in which case, she knew the president would be disappointed. Not that she wanted to find an assassin—that would raise a whole new series of problems the country didn't need. But a nice fat motive for murder by an old army buddy or an ex-girlfriend—*that* would be fine. The president would get some needed closure, and Ray would be intrigued, like any good spinner in the face of a challenging case.

And in light of Kristie's recent experience with the lascivious colonel, her money was on the ex-girlfriend.

"I'm sorry he's dead, but he couldn't have chosen a more beautiful spot for it. Look at this place! It's gorgeous." Spreading her arms out to encompass the view of white sand and blue surf, Kristie leaned against the railing of Payton's balcony. "I think I see a whale!"

"Get back to work," Ray advised from the living room.

She laughed. "I *am* working. Two separate messages on the hot line reported seeing a strange man with a golden retriever jogging past this spot around nine-thirty last night. Just around the time the assassins would have arrived."

Ray chuckled. "Enough with the assassins." Stepping out onto the balcony, he sat on the edge of a raised redwood hot tub. "So? Was there anything useful at all on the hot-line tape?"

"Not so far. The usual hilarity. UFOs, that sort of thing. And neighbors accusing neighbors. All anonymous, of course."

"But in person, none of the neighbors admitted seeing anything?"

"Correct. That was before I heard about the man with the dog, though. I'm going back tomorrow to ask them each about that."

Ray shook his head. "I've seen dozens of men with dogs since we got here. Sounds like a red herring to me."

"All of the herrings in this case are red. I'm determined to exhaust every one of them anyway."

With a last longing glance toward the blue-green surf, she strolled back into the house to study the crime scene for the umpteenth time.

Based on findings by the medical examiner, it seemed indisputable that Payton had hit—or been hit on—his head, and that the blow had been the cause of death. Signs of a brief struggle were present at the scene, and after conducting separate analyses, each spinner had arrived at the same tentative conclusion—that Payton had entered the house during a burglary, had fought with the intruder or intruders, had fallen or been shoved backward and had struck the back of his skull on the white brick fireplace next to the balcony doorway. Thereafter, it appeared that the intruder or intruders had tried to clean up the mess, wiping away prints and planting evidence to make it seem as though Payton had slipped on melted ice from a spilled drink.

To Kristie, that was the most fascinating aspect of the scene. It was definitely staged—she and Ray agreed on that point. And the most reasonable assumption was that a burglar had tried to stage an accident. But what if the president was correct? What if assassins had been waiting for Payton, and had thereafter staged both a botched burglary *and* an accident?

Ray had scoffed at the suggestion, pointing to the many nonprofessional touches in the staging attempts and also reminding her that Payton, while brimming with influence, hadn't had the sort of ideological prominence to attract foreign agents. Or even domestic ones.

Kristie secretly agreed with her boss, but also knew the president was going to quiz her on the assassination theory the next time they spoke, so she wanted to be certain she was ready.

"He knew a lot of important people," she murmured, moving to the far wall of the room, which was covered with framed photos of Payton and various celebrities, politicians and dignitaries. "Here he is with the first lady. What did she think of him?"

"Not much. But she's probably wracked with guilt about it today."

"Let's hope not. Hey!" Kristie tapped a photo of five men dressed in parkas and boots, standing in front of a picturesque ski lodge. "That's you!"

"I was wondering when you'd finally notice that. Yeah, that's me."

"And the president and Payton. And Director Oakes of the FBI, right? And who's the fifth guy?"

"He's CIA. That was taken after a very successful joint op about two years ago. SPIN really started coming into its own after that, which is why Payton started taking a personal interest in it." Ray studied the picture wistfully. "He seemed pretty harmless back then. I wonder what Oakes thinks about all this."

"Do you mean, because the president asked SPIN to investigate instead of the FBI?"

Ray shrugged. "Actually, I meant because Oakes knows I hated Payton's guts."

"That again? No one suspects you, Ray. You're above reproach. You earned that status."

"Still…" He folded his arms across his chest and leaned against the edge of Payton's dining table. "Remember that job opportunity I told you about?"

Kristie nodded.

"Oakes is having health problems. That's a secret, by the way. He wants to step down, and he recommended me as his replacement."

"Oh!" Kristie clapped in delight. "That's so amazing. No wonder you're considering it. Director of the FBI! It's such an honor."

"Right. Anyway, Payton was openly opposed to the appointment. I think the buffoon actually wanted the job for himself. We had a series of heated meetings, with Oakes in attendance. And that argument we had last week in my office didn't help matters much either, I'm sure."

"Uh-oh." Kristie winced. "I hope I didn't make things worse. I'm pretty sure I called him a jackass, and I *know* I threatened to break his finger off."

"Maybe I should be checking out *your* alibi," Ray said, arching an eyebrow to tease her. "Anyway, we'll see if the job offer is still on the table after this."

"Of course it is. The very fact that the president asked you to conduct the investigation proves that."

"Yeah. That surprised me. I guess it's a good sign, although—" he arched an eyebrow again "—he sent you along to keep an eye on me. So maybe you ought to start doing your job. Starting with this," he added, turning to pick a package up off the table, then handing it to Kristie.

She studied the label. "When did this come?"

"About an hour ago, while you were interviewing one of the neighbors. I had a messenger bring it straight here."

"It feels like a videotape."

"Right. Depending on how clear it is, it should corroborate my alibi."

Kristie glared. "Stop talking like that."

"Do your job," he repeated simply. "You haven't asked me even one question about it. If you're willing to investigate every crackpot message from the hot line, you ought to rule out suspects who have had public fights with the victim in the last few weeks."

She shrugged. "I'll bet lots of guys—and women—fit that description."

"But you know about me."

"Fine!" She put her hands on her hips and challenged him with feigned ferocity. "Where were you last night at midnight Eastern time?"

"On a date."

"Oh." She wasn't sure why it surprised her, but it did. "Really?"

"Yeah."

"And you videotaped it? That's a little yucky."

Ray scowled. "Her building has security cameras. I sent David over to take a look, hoping there were some shots of me arriving or leaving. From what he told me on the phone, it's embarrassingly definitive."

"Really?"

"Before you watch it—"

"I'm not going to watch it. I'll take David's word for it."

"Before you watch it—and you will—you should know something about this particular female."

"Oh no." Kristie felt a sinking sensation in the pit of her stomach. "Jane Smith, right?"

"No!" Ray seemed appalled at the thought. "Geez, Kristie, don't even joke about that."

"Whew." She swiped her forehead with the back of her hand in exaggerated relief. "Okay, fire away. But as long as Madame X had a pulse and was with you at midnight last night, she's good enough for me."

"Sit down. And be serious for a minute, will you?"

She plopped into one of the dining chairs. "I'm listening."

He cleared his throat. "Let me start by saying, there may be a grain of truth to your theory about me and Melissa. About the crush, I mean."

"Because?"

"Because this particular woman has that look. More or less. Mostly more. The hair, the legs, the attitude. I just wanted you to know that before you watched the tape."

Kristie was charmed by the hint of a blush under his tanned cheeks. "I'm not going to watch the tape, Ray. But I'm glad you told me about it. When did you meet her?"

"Last week. It's not serious—just a mutual pickup in a bar. But it's pretty interesting, given your theory about me."

"Because she fits the profile, so to speak?"

"Yeah. And because the sex is unbelievable."

"Hookay, then." Kristie pretended to cover her ears. "Too much information, Mr. Ortega. Let's just drop it."

"I'm trying to tell you something," Ray insisted.

Kristie sighed. "So? It's really that good?"

"The truth? I thought I was past that stage. Then this girl comes along and I'm completely blown away."

"What's her name?"

"It's Miranda. Take my word for it, nothing's going to come of it. It's just a fling. But it taught me something."

"That I was right?" she asked teasingly.

"You're such a brat."

Kristie laughed, enjoying the return of their bantering, bickering, twins-separated-at-birth relationship. "I've loved working with you today, Ray. It reminded me of why I took this job. I hope it reminded you of why you hired me."

"I've missed the way it used to be between us." To Kristie's surprise, he seemed to be choosing his words carefully. "I'm just not sure we can go back to that."

"Not back. Forward. Together." She took his hands in her own. "If you go to the FBI—well, that's tremendous. But you'll still have an influence on SPIN—not just because you founded it, but an active, ongoing influence. It's part of you. And it's part of me, too. Right?"

"Is it?"

She drew back, hurt, but reminded herself to be fair. She *had* been considering Jane Smith's offer. Which meant she herself had questioned whether SPIN was the right place for her. Why shouldn't Ray be allowed the same privilege?

"I've given it a lot of thought, Ray, and I've honestly come to appreciate your rules. That's what this is about, isn't it?"

He nodded.

"Well, I'm ready to admit they apply ninety-nine percent of the time."

"Ninety-nine percent?"

"Right. You can give me *that,* can't you?" she asked with a hopeful smile. "One percent to cover unique situations. Times when the rules need to be flexed."

He shrugged. "I'll admit there should be exceptions for extraordinary situations. All I've ever asked is that you run it by me *before* taking action, to determine if the exception should be made. If you'd done that in Palm Springs, I could have told you about the Axe before you put yourself in jeopardy."

"But—"

"But it all worked out in the end?" he finished for her, his tone caustic.

Kristie folded her arms across her chest. "So that's that? It's your call in one hundred percent of situations? Even if there's no time to consult before taking action? That's pretty controlling, Ray. I think I've earned more latitude than that."

"And I think I've given you tons of latitude. More than you deserved in some cases."

"Wow." She struggled to find a steady voice. "I guess we'd better get back to work."

Ray seemed about to reassure her, then he murmured instead, "Let's just wrap things up for the night. I'll take you out to dinner. You must know some great places from your UCLA days."

"I'm not hungry."

"We'll just go back to the hotel then. We could both use some rest. And if you get hungry later, we can order room service."

"The CIA bought me lobster in Palm Springs," she told him coolly.

"That's definitely something to consider."

"Huh?"

He shrugged. "There are pluses and minuses to each job. For them, the huge budget and unlimited resources are definitely pluses. SPIN can't usually compete with that. But I'll be happy to buy you lobster, or anything else you want, on this particular assignment. President's orders."

She stared, ignoring most of his words, while a few echoed harshly in her ears. "You want me to think about the CIA?"

He winced. "I didn't say that. But I wouldn't be much of a friend if I didn't encourage you—"

"Don't bother. I'm miles ahead of you." She stuffed her notes and charts into her briefcase, then looked up at him defiantly. "I'll be in the car when you're ready."

Chapter 12

Two of the FBI's best crime-scene reconstruction experts had been sent to Los Angeles to assist SPIN's investigation, courtesy of Director Oakes. To Kristie, the best part of that assistance was the way the agents occupied Ray's attention in the living room, allowing her to easily avoid him by concentrating on the rest of Payton's beach house.

Ray seemed to understand and gave her a wide berth. But at noon he appeared in the doorway of the master bedroom and cleared his throat. "Almost done in here? We're ready to dazzle you in the other room."

Kristie looked up from the stacks of papers and photographs she had piled in the middle of Payton's king-size bed. "You can't open a drawer around here without finding another motive for murdering this creep."

"What's all this?"

"See for yourself." She shoved a handful of X-rated pictures in his direction.

Ray took a quick glance, then said firmly, "All the more reason to wrap things up. Why stare at this junk when you can be enjoying your hotel suite?" He flashed a charming smile. "The president got us some cool digs, didn't you think? High-definition TVs. Sunken tubs. Full-size, fully stocked refrigerators. Why not work from there for the rest of the investigation?"

Kristie shrugged, wondering what Ray would say if she told him that, to her, the best feature of her luxury suite had been the unmonitored telephone. It had beckoned to her all night long, tempting her to call Will McGregor and flirt. And perhaps cry on his shoulder a little.

The only thing stopping her had been the certainty that it would sound the death knell for her career at SPIN. Even if Ray never found out, even if he apologized for pushing her away, and tried to tempt her back, she would never again be able to claim she was willing to follow the rules. It was bad enough that she had tucked the black wig from Salinger's closet into Melissa's side of her suitcase along with some false identification, just in case she decided to pay McGregor a visit.

"I'll be out in a minute," she told him, turning her attention to her latest find, a cache of photographs from Payton's nightstand. The colonel had apparently taken the shots himself on some sort of time-delayed camera so that he could pose with the nubile young women who had fallen into his clutches. The girls were usually in the hot tub, naked and smiling, or occasionally sprawled out on the bed. "I hate this guy," she muttered.

"Well, he's dead, so let it go."

"Look at these faces. So sweet. So young."

"Underage?"

"No." She glared at her boss for implying that these twenty-somethings deserved what they got. "Not underage. But still victims."

"Looks pretty consensual to me."

She glared again, imagining the incentives a wealthy, well-connected older man could offer naive girls who were hoping to become movie stars or famous models. Consensual? Perhaps, but that didn't make Payton any less a predator.

Ellie McGregor is lucky to have a big brother in this crazy town to protect her, Kristie decided. She suspected most of Payton's "girlfriends" were hundreds of miles away from their families and thus vulnerable in ways Ellie would never be.

Throwing the pictures into a heap, she left the bed and followed Ray, who had already rejoined his associates in the next room. Smiling at the pair of agents—a man and woman, both in their midthirties—Kristie said, "I hear I'm about to be dazzled."

"Not likely," Special Agent Carl Ewing replied, returning the smile. "You and Ray called it yourself. It's fairly routine, actually, except for the victim. Anyway…" His tone grew matter-of-fact. "We believe a single burglar entered from the balcony. It doesn't look like that lock put up much of a fight. Anyone standing on the beach could get a clear look at Payton's collection of medals through the undraped sliding door. We figure our guy was an amateur, lured by the bright, shiny medals, which actually aren't worth all that much. He intended to make it quick—"

"You're sure it was a guy?" Kristie interrupted.

Carl's partner, Special Agent Eve Monroe, nodded.

"There aren't any prints, but whoever smashed Payton in the mouth had a big fist." She clenched her own fingers into a ball to demonstrate. "Twice the size of mine, at least."

"Okay. Go on. The burglar was burgling…? And…?"

"And Payton came in unexpectedly," Carl continued. "He probably jumped the intruder right about here, causing him to drop the medals. They struggled. Payton landed at least one good punch—his right hand showed abrasions consistent with that. Then the burglar hit Payton square in the jaw. Payton goes backward, in this direction—" the agent pretended to fall back toward the brick hearth "—hits his head, and it's *adios* for him. The burglar gathers up the medals and puts them in a box on the washing machine, hoping it will look like Payton was doing some spring-cleaning. Then he spilled a glass of ice water here, and tried to make a skid mark with Payton's boot, right along here."

The agent dragged his own foot lightly across the floor, then looked up and shrugged. "Not a bad idea, but poorly executed. Finally he exited by the balcony, making sure to obliterate his footprints in the sand—not that we'd have much luck with that, considering the hundreds of prints out there."

"In other words," Eve Monroe said with a smile, "pretty much what you and Ray deduced yesterday."

"But with much more detail. It gives us the comfort level we need," Ray replied. "We appreciate the quick response. I know the president does, too."

"We're hoping the guy was stupid enough to take one or two of the medals, believing no one would notice they were missing. That's pretty common in these botched attempts."

"We'll have the local cops follow up on that," Ray said with a nod. "They're hot to get on this guy's trail as soon as we turn the case back over to them."

"That's the plan?"

Ray nodded. "The president wanted us to rule out other possibilities. But if it's a burglary, he understands the cops can and should take over."

"Well…" Carl smiled. "It's safe to say it was a burglary."

Ray turned to Kristie. "Do you have any questions for these guys before they head out?"

"No." She exhaled slowly. "It all makes sense, I guess."

"Except something still bothers you?" Eve seemed genuinely intrigued. "Tell us. We don't pretend to be infallible, and we definitely want to get this one right."

"Go on, Kris," Ray urged. "That's what they're here for."

"It's nothing." The spinner grimaced apologetically. "I just keep wondering about the odds of this happening."

"The odds of a burglary? In this neighborhood? Pretty good," Carl assured her.

"I was thinking about Payton, not the neighborhood," Kristie admitted. "This was a guy with so many enemies, you couldn't count them on fingers, toes and an abacus combined. But when he finally got punched in the mouth, it was by a stranger who didn't mean anything personal by it. What are the odds of that?"

The female agent cocked her head to the side. "We heard he was annoying—"

"Try disgusting. Offensive. Predatory. He ticked some people off in the administration, but there's more. People with much more personal motives. Men whose starlet daughters he exploited. Or whose wives cheated with him. That sort of thing."

"Well, at least you've dropped the assassination theory," Ray said, his smile tinged with frustration. "Looks like we're not done here yet, guys. What do you think?"

"It still fits," Eve murmured. "Instead of a burglar, an irate husband was waiting for him when he got home. Maybe just to punch him in the nose, but it went a little too far. So the husband panicked..." Her voice trailed off.

"That's where it doesn't work," her partner insisted. "If the irate husband wanted to make it look like a burglary, he would have taken something—something noticeable—like a TV or VCR. Why bother disturbing the medals, and then just leaving them behind?"

"Is it possible Payton really was doing spring-cleaning, and put the box of medals on the washing machine himself? Oh!" Kristie corrected herself with a sheepish laugh. "Those fresh scratches on the floor—those were made when the burglar dropped the box of medals?"

"As opposed to the toenails of your mysterious golden retriever," Ray confirmed, adding for the agents' benefit, "There was an anonymous tip about a guy on the beach with a dog."

"And you thought the dog made the scratches? They aren't consistent with that," Eve assured her.

Kristie laughed. "I had a feeling it was too good to be true. Okay, I'm ninety-nine percent sold."

Ray glanced at her, and she flushed, remembering the other "ninety-nine percent" over which they had argued the night before.

Then he turned to the agents. "You guys can take off. But it looks like Kris and I are gonna stay for a while longer. Ninety-nine percent isn't bad for routine cases, but given the president's interest in this one, I want Kristie to be completely convinced."

"The sooner the local cops start working the case, the better your chances are of catching the culprit," Eve warned. "Maybe you should put the whole investigation on a dual track. Have them work it as a burglary *and* as an irate father's attack. See what they come up with."

"Except the president might not like us smearing Payton's reputation unless we're very sure that's what happened," her partner objected. "Killed by a burglar—that's a senseless tragedy. But if the press ever thought the suspect was the father of some twenty-year-old starlet…"

"Instant scandal. Good point, Carl." Eve gave Kristie a sympathetic smile. "If there are as many potential suspects as you think, it could take quite a while to rule them all out."

"Assuming we could even identify them in the first place, which is unlikely," Ray said, nodding. "We have the girls' pictures—some of them, at least. I suppose we could contact a few of the talent agencies here. But we'd have to do it discreetly."

"And we're convinced the perp was a burglar." Carl was clearly frustrated. "I hate to see you go to all that trouble and risk smearing the president's buddy for nothing."

"That's Kristie's call," Ray told him with a dismissive shrug.

The spinner shot her boss a grateful glance, surprised that he would take her side so completely, given his diminished confidence in her.

"We're gonna take off then," the agent said, offering Ray a quick handshake. Then he assured Kristie, "We've heard some amazing things about you from your boss here. I wish my supervisor was half as impressed with me."

She flushed and shook hands with him, then with his partner. When the pair had departed, she turned to Ray and murmured, "That was interesting. Thanks for backing me up."

"I meant what I said. This isn't over until you say it's over."

"Are you talking about the investigation?"

"Sure. What else?"

"Never mind." She smiled sadly. "Just give me a few minutes to think about it, okay? And I want to listen to any new messages on the hot-line tape. Then we can go back to the hotel and brainstorm a little. That's probably all I really need."

"Take your time. I'll nose around outside one last time. See if I can find any chatty kids."

"Okay. I'll make it quick." She watched him disappear onto the front porch, then she walked back to Payton's bedroom, pausing in the doorway to survey the mess she'd made with her haphazard piles of photographs.

They're right, you know. Too many suspects is as bad as none at all. There have got to be twenty different girls in the pictures you've found so far, and that's just the tip of the iceberg. And what about all the men he offended in other ways, like interfering in their business the way he did with Ray? You can't investigate everyone who hated this man or it'll be the only case you ever work on!

And wasn't Ray correct about the scandal angle? Unless Kristie was dead sure about that, why drag Payton's name through the mud when all it would do is damage the president's reputation? And for what? The best in the business said this was a burglary gone wrong. Who was she to argue?

A comfort level. That's what Ray had called it, and maybe he was right. She just needed to mull it over a bit more.

And you need to stop looking at these horrible pictures,
she told herself, scooping up a handful to stick back into
the nightstand. Then one particular dark-eyed girl stared
up at her from the swirling bubbles of Payton's hot tub,
and the spinner winced.

It was so much like the picture of Ellie McGregor in
her SPIN file, it could have been her twin sister.

Or it could be her...

Or your mind could be playing tricks on you, she coun-
seled herself sternly.

Trying to keep her imagination from going wild, she
sorted through the rest of that batch of pictures, knowing
from experience that Payton usually took at least two shots
of every victim. She found it quickly—the bed shot—and
now there was no doubt in her mind. It was Ellie, her eyes
glassy, her smile winsome. Her dignity hopelessly compro-
mised.

Shaken to the core, Kristie shoved the two photos into
her briefcase, then locked it quickly, as though hiding the
pictures away would make them untrue.

"Kris?"

She spun toward Ray's voice. "Hi."

"Are you okay?"

"Yes. I'm actually ready to go back to the hotel, if you
are."

He cocked his head to the side, studying her. "Are you
mad at me?"

"Huh? No, of course not."

He sighed and settled onto the foot of the bed. "We'll
talk it out eventually, I promise. Just not right away. Let's
get this case wrapped up and go home first, okay?"

"That's fine." She tried to seem nonchalant. "Have you
talked to the president yet today?"

"Twice. You're the one he really wants to talk to, though. When you think you're ready."

"Okay."

He smiled encouragingly. "Anything I can do?"

"No. I just need to let all the information percolate in my brain for a few hours."

"That always helps me, too. And I was thinking we could do some follow-up on those starlets if you think it's important."

"Pardon?"

He shrugged. "It's your call. As long as we're discreet, we could talk to a few of the girls. Get a sense of how exploitative the situation really was. That might tell us whether an irate father or boyfriend is a likelihood we need to pursue."

"If it got out, it would cause a scandal. You and Carl were right about that," she insisted, trying not to hear the screams of protest from her guilty conscience. "It would hurt the president, and it would hurt all the girls, too."

"Or it might be liberating for them. To know he got what he deserved."

"No, Ray. That kind of publicity…" She bit her lip, remembering what McGregor had said: that even if the theater director had never laid a hand on Ellie, the publicity over the case had done so much damage, she might never recover. Ten years later she was still hurting inside. Hurting herself, while her loved ones stood by in helpless despair.

The thought that another young woman might go through that—or worse, that Ellie's pictures would come to light, and more scandal would haunt the already fragile girl—made Kristie's heart pound with confusion.

"Think about it," Ray told her, squeezing her arm. "Like

I said, it's your call. You're the objective one here. That's why the president trusts your instincts for this one. And for the record, so do I. I know I've been hard on you these last few days—"

"Not now, Ray. Okay?"

He looked surprised. Then hurt. Then he shrugged his shoulders as if to say, *You had your chance.*

But Kristie couldn't afford to care about that.

Wearing a black wig and fidgeting with a wisp of lace on the bodice of her green-and-white sundress, Kristie sat in a rented car in front of Will McGregor's bungalow-style house, trying to tell herself she was doing the right thing. Or at least, the closest thing to right, given the circumstances.

The last two hours had been agony as she weighed and reweighed her options, her loyalties and her professional responsibilities. She still couldn't quite believe she had removed evidence from a crime scene, even for a few hours. What if Ray found out? And even if he didn't, what was her plan? To keep it from him forever? To tell him she had decided the burglary theory was ironclad, and they could all go home?

Maybe you are cut out for the CIA after all, she had taunted herself. *Stealing evidence. Being glad the victim's dead.*

She knew her emotions were teetering on some indefinable precipice, ready to tumble. The only thing keeping her safe was her need to help the McGregors, and even that was a minefield. It would upset the agent to see the photos. Then he'd be enraged and want to punch someone, but of course, the "someone" was dead. So where would all that anger and frustration go?

And poor Ellie. Her brother would confront her—tenderly, Kristie hoped—but still, it would be painful.

You have to do it, she told herself now. *If this ever gets out, the publicity could put McGregor's sister right over the edge. He needs to be ready—to take her out of town for a few months if necessary—so that she can weather this. After that, Professor Ramirez can help them. You just have to avoid the kind of major setback the publicity might cause Ellie.*

This was really a job for Melissa, but Kristie hadn't dared bring the red wig on this trip, given Ray's crush.

Now as she exited the rental car and walked toward McGregor's porch, she lamented her last fantasy of her first meeting with him. It was supposed to be so romantic, so perfectly orchestrated. Now it was going to be grueling for both of them.

"Can I help you?" a familiar voice called from the driveway, and she spun toward it, her pulse racing.

She had been so busy deciding how to break the news to him about Ellie, she hadn't thought about how she was going to introduce herself. Or even how to explain why she was wearing a wig.

The disguise was functional, but also pretty, and Kristie had to admit, that was something she had definitely given some thought to.

Because even if this conversation was a disaster, even if she and McGregor never spoke to one another again, she wanted to leave a searing impression on the FBI agent's brain. So she had worn something from the Melissa side of her wardrobe—a sexy sundress and sexier taupe heels. And if the car-rental guy's reaction had been any indication, she had succeeded in making herself presentable.

She walked around the corner of the house and saw that McGregor was cleaning his hands on a rag, his attention trained in her direction, his blue eyes vibrant and arresting. None of the photographs had done those eyes justice. But everything else was just as she'd known it would be— the blue-black, collar-length wavy hair, square jaw, broad shoulders, lean build. Even in faded jeans and a ragged black T-shirt, he was more handsome than any man she'd ever seen.

"Hi," she said softly.

His mouth opened slightly, as though he was having trouble finding the right reply, so she prompted him with, "You're working on your car?"

"Yeah."

She admired the blue convertible out of the corner of her eye. "It's a classic."

"Not exactly cherry, but I'm trying to scrounge enough parts at the junkyard to build a decent ride. I just bought it last week."

Walking right up to him, she dared to ask, "Any significance in the fact that it's a 1969 Mustang?"

He stared into her eyes, then finally murmured, "Goldie?"

She felt her cheeks begin to burn. "Hi, McGregor."

A huge grin spread across his features. "Well, look at you."

"Look at *you*," she replied, breathless to the point of silliness.

He leaned forward, and she wasn't sure if he was going to actually kiss her, or just wanted to study her more closely. "You look so great. I don't want to get grease on you—come on inside and I'll get washed up."

"Okay."

He grabbed a clean rag, then rested it on her bare shoulder so that he could guide her toward the back porch and through the laundry room, where he quickly scrubbed his hands in an oversize sink. "Go on in. I'll get us something to drink in a minute."

She was enjoying the sensation of his nearness so much, she didn't want to move away from him. "I'll wait."

He dried his hands on a towel, then clapped them onto both her shoulders and pulled her to within inches of his body. "I can't believe you're here. What's going on?" A slight frown marred his features. "You didn't quit your job, did you?"

"No. Not yet, at least."

He exhaled in relief. "Your last message had me worried. I wanted to call back, but you said not to."

She nodded.

"Now here you are, just like you promised. Nonstalking me."

She laughed in embarrassed delight. "I forgot I said that."

"Yeah? Well, I remember every word." His gaze softened and he leaned down to her again, so close she could feel his breath on her face. "You've been on my mind. A lot. I've listened to that last tape *way* too often. And I have that beat-up picture of you in my wallet. Never figured you for a brunette, though."

"It's a wig."

"Yeah?" His eyes were sparkling again. "I like it."

She melted under his playful scrutiny. "I should have called first."

"No way. This is great. Come on." He propelled her through the kitchen, pausing only to grab two bottles of beer from the refrigerator. "Let's go in the living room.

Pardon the mess. Here." He scooped a pile of haphazardly folded towels off the couch and motioned for her to sit down. Then he threw the laundry on the nearby dining table and joined her.

He was grinning again, and it was so infectious, she couldn't think of anything to say, so she just smiled back, enjoying the sight of him, and laughing at herself for having feared there might not be enough chemistry between them in person.

McGregor's arm was resting on the couch behind her, and now he edged closer, mischief in his eyes. "I've been imagining this moment. A lot."

"Me, too. I figured we'd either just fizzle out, or we'd be tearing each other's clothes off. This is so much better."

"Yeah, let's enjoy the whole ride. Starting with this." He slid his hand behind her head, then he covered her mouth with his, tasting with gentle appreciation. When the kiss deepened, she twined her arms around his neck, pulling him against her as she groaned his name.

"I can't believe you're here," he told her again when they finally came up for air.

"I had to come. We have to talk about something, Mc-Gregor. Something serious."

"Don't quit your job. We'll work this out." His hand stroked her cheek. "I've been looking for a new position anyway. Out of the undercover game."

"Oh, no. You're so good at it."

"Ten years is enough."

"I don't want you to quit for me."

"You're just the frosting on the cake," he said teasingly. "I want to keep a closer eye on Ellie. Be around more. She likes the new shrink by the way. Your usual perfect solution to every problem."

Before Kristie could interrupt, he added bluntly, "You need to patch things up with Ortega. I tried to help. Did he tell you?"

"You talked to Ray?"

McGregor nodded. "Just a quick call. I didn't want him to get suspicious, so I just told him how you consistently reminded me about the rules. And I consistently bent them. I said I had only called because I was worried about Ellie. Not quite true, but he seemed to buy my story."

"He's convinced I'm some sort of maverick. And maybe he's right." She bit her lip, then admitted, "I've got another job offer. From the CIA. Basically doing the same thing I do at SPIN, but for them."

"I hope you're joking." McGregor scowled. "The CIA isn't anything like SPIN. Or the Bureau. We're the good guys. Not that they're all bad," he explained quickly. "But they've got an ends-justify-the-means philosophy that you'd never be able to live with."

Kristie nodded, remembering how Jane Smith had said she didn't care how her people got results as long as they got them.

"Stay away from them, Goldie. Make peace with Ortega. You've got a great job there, and you're terrific at it."

"It's not that simple."

"Hey." He cupped her chin in his rough hand. "Let's see that smile again."

When Kristie obliged him, he nodded with relief. "I was having the worst day of my life a few minutes ago. Now here you are, making things perfect." Caressing her cheek with his thumb, he added slyly, "Do you like your car?"

"It's for me?"

"Who else?" He flashed a dazzling smile. "I figured if I

just went and worked on it every time I got the urge to call you, I'd have it done by the time we finally met face-to-face."

"I don't have anything for you."

"Wanna bet?" He arched an eyebrow as his gaze swept over her provocative outfit.

She felt her cheeks burn with delight. "Well, I love the car. But I'm sorry you were having such a bad day. Would it help to talk about it?"

"No. Just more grief from my sister."

Startled, she pulled free, remembering why she was there. "I have to talk to you, McGregor."

"Sure." His mood grew serious. "Are you here undercover? Is that why you're wearing the wig?"

"More or less." She took a deep breath, then told him, "I'm investigating the death of Ulysses Payton. You heard about that, I'm sure."

His blue eyes darkened with instant and unmistakable hatred. "That bastard."

Kristie drew back, alarmed. "You knew him?"

The agent's face relaxed, and he was suddenly unreadable. "No. Never met him. Just heard enough to know the world's better off without him."

Confused, the spinner bit her lip. It hadn't occurred to her that McGregor might already know about Payton's seduction of Ellie. Had she made a stupid mistake?

Thankful that she had left the photographs in the car for the time being, she decided to buy herself time to think by changing the subject. Then a convenient interruption presented itself in the form of a ruckus that broke out on the front porch, with children laughing and shouting, "Hey, Will! We're back!"

McGregor gave her a rueful smile. "Give me a second.

That's the neighbor boys returning my dog. Don't go anywhere."

"Your dog?"

"Yeah. They take him to the park and run him for me. Works for everyone. Stay put."

As McGregor exchanged booming pleasantries with the children, then playfully ordered them to go away, Kristie closed her eyes and tried to calm her nerves. So what if he hated Payton? So what if he had a dog? So what if he was a perfect stranger? None of that meant anything.

"Come on, Nugget," she heard him announce. "You're gonna meet someone special. Don't slobber on her."

Nugget? Kristie's heart began to pound, and even before the golden-haired animal lumbered into view, she knew it would be a retriever.

And even when the adorable creature sat himself down at her feet and offered her his paw in friendship, she could barely manage to breathe, much less to respond.

"You're not afraid of animals, are you?" McGregor asked.

"No. I love them." She steadied herself and leaned down to the dog, shaking his hand, then ruffling his lustrous coat. "Hi, Nugget. Nice to meet you. Uh-oh... We're tangled up..."

She sent McGregor an apologetic grimace as she disengaged her watchband from the dog's fur. Then she murmured, "It's hard to believe you called me Goldie with a beautiful blonde like this in the house."

McGregor laughed. "I still haven't seen any proof of your alleged blondeness."

That laugh, coupled with his teasing comment, brought a lump of confusion to her throat. She had dreamed of this so often. It was so perfect. So perfect, but also so wrong.

Forcing herself to smile, she stood to face him. "I've really got to go, or Ray will start asking questions."

McGregor frowned. "Don't let the dog ruin the mood. He's usually outside—"

"It's not him. He's darling. Really." She stooped to pet the animal again, careful not to use her watch hand. Then she grabbed her purse and edged toward the door. "I'll call you later this evening from my hotel room. Will you be home?"

"Hey." He caught her by the arm and pulled her against himself. "Don't run off."

"I have to. Really." She stroked his jaw with her fingertips and couldn't help but murmur, as they'd done when they first laid eyes on each other, "Look at you."

"Look at *you*," he answered, then he kissed her gently.

She wanted to relax and enjoy the feel of his lips on hers, but she had a feeling she'd never relax until she had a chance to think. Alone. To shake off these silly coincidences. Or if she couldn't, to share them with Ray so that he could help her decide what to do next.

"You've got to eat sometime," McGregor was saying with a seductive smile. "Can I take you to dinner? I could wear a disguise, too, if that helps."

She sighed and admitted, "That sounds like so much fun. But probably not tonight. I'm meeting Ray, and we've got a lot of work ahead of us."

"Right." His scowl returned. "Payton's murder."

"Right." She pulled free, unnerved once again by his clear animosity at the mere mention of the colonel's name.

Afraid McGregor might read too much into her expression, she forced herself to smile and peck him on the cheek with pursed lips. Then she turned and hurried to the door, insisting over her shoulder, "I'll call you tonight. I promise."

He was still scowling, and as she escaped onto the porch and ran to her car, she tried to convince herself it was just disappointment over their aborted date. But in her gut, she knew something much more serious was bothering him.

She only hoped she was wrong about what it was.

Chapter 13

She didn't want to be alone and would have gone straight to the hotel bar after returning the rental-car keys to the lobby, but Ray might be there and she didn't want to explain the black wig. Once back in her room, she gladly shed the sexy sundress and heels as well, trading them for white jeans, a pink silk tee and comfortable sling sandals. Then she unpinned her hair and gave it a quick brushing. As she did so, she studied herself in the mirror.

What are you going to do now?

It was the question she'd been asking herself again and again since her abrupt departure from McGregor's house. She had weighed and reweighed the evidence, confusing herself completely. The only thing she knew for sure was she couldn't keep this to herself forever. Even if it meant nothing, it had to be disclosed. Didn't it?

Ray had labeled the hot-line reports of a man with a

golden retriever a red herring. Would he still think so if he knew what Kristie knew?

And what about the crime-scene reconstruction team? Would they be so completely convinced that a burglar had killed Payton if they knew a highly trained FBI agent who lived in L.A. despised the colonel for abusing his sister?

They'd probably say it's all a coincidence. You're over-thinking it! You have been from the start. Two experts, plus Ray, are convinced it was a burglary because every-thing points to that, including the bumbling attempt to make it look as if Payton slipped. McGregor—or any other enemy of Payton's—would have taken a completely dif-ferent approach to covering it up. They would have stolen the VCR or something like that. Made it look like a sim-ple breaking and entering that went wrong.

As she set her hairbrush onto the vanity, she noticed a tuft of Nugget's fur entangled in her watchband. Pulling it loose, she was about to toss it in the wastebasket when she remembered that a team had done some cleanup both inside and around the beach house, and later still on the beach for twenty yards in every direction. Ray had scoffed at her when she'd instructed them to look for golden dog hair, and everyone had had a fairly lively laugh at her ex-pense when the beach sweep had turned up hair of every possible color and texture, a tribute to the fact that dozens of joggers every day had dogs with them, and fur from such animals could become embedded in the sand for weeks or months.

They were right to laugh at you. You're being ridicu-lous, she told herself. *Just throw the fur away and go get a big margarita. And stop trying to find evidence against the poor guy. You're supposed to be on his side!*

But she couldn't make herself dispose of the fur, so she

sealed it in a white envelope from the room's fully stocked desk, then paper-clipped it to the large manila envelope containing Ellie's photos. Just for the time being. If she ended up sharing the information with Ray, great. He could deal with the whole mess at that time.

And if she decided to keep all knowledge of the silly coincidences to herself, she'd dispose of the dog fur at that time. Then she'd sneak the photos back into the drawer of Payton's nightstand, where they'd sit with dozens of others, unrecognized, until the day Payton's relatives came to claim their inheritance, saw firsthand what a lecherous bastard their relative had been, and shredded all such mementos in mournful disgust.

Ray wasn't in the bar, which was practically deserted, and Kristie sat alone at a table overlooking the pool, wondering if she should call her supervisor's suite and ask him to join her. He had wanted to have their heart-to-heart talk earlier, hadn't he? Maybe now was the time. They could air their grievances and repair their friendship, then she'd avail herself of his years of experience and knowledge to work though the McGregor dilemma.

But first she'd explain that she had one of those "one percent" situations where the rules shouldn't apply. As much as she needed him to reassure her that the burglary theory was still ironclad, there simply was no reason to make the information about McGregor part of the official investigation record.

But he won't do that, she decided as she drained her drink, then sucked on a wedge of lime. *That's the whole crux of the problem. Ray has to do everything by the book. His book, of course. The one with a million rules in it.*

And even if he really were capable of making excep-

*tions, I don't think he'd start with McGregor. There's still
some tension there—right?—or he would have told you
last week that McGregor called to defend you. Ray may
not have a crush on you and Melissa anymore, thanks to
his hot new girlfriend, but there's still something going on
there. I can feel it.*

Ray was prejudiced against McGregor. And Kristie
wasn't impartial either. So she asked herself what David
Wong would do. How would an objective spinner approach the situation?

To her surprise, she was able to slip easily into an analytical mode, at least for the moment, and she felt a rush of
excitement as she reviewed the body of evidence one last
time.

Ellie McGregor had become involved with a powerful
older man. Her protective brother knew about it. Disap-
proved of it. Hated Payton because of it. That didn't mean
he acted on that hate, any more than a dozen other people
who openly hated Payton, including Ray and the first lady.
McGregor's career in law enforcement had been a stellar
one because he had self-control, integrity and respect for
the judicial process. Hadn't he said it that afternoon—the
ends did *not* justify the means in his philosophy.

If he were guilty, he wouldn't have allowed Kristie to
see how much he hated Payton. He knew she was investigating the killing, and he would have played it cool.

And if he had killed Payton, his law-enforcement background would have enabled him to stage an open-and-shut
burglary. He would have emptied Payton's wallet and
taken something else of value that was plainly detectable.
So once again, the facts seemed to mitigate against
McGregor as a suspect. David would react the same way
the reconstruction experts had reacted.

Nugget? A red herring, plain and simple.

David wouldn't believe for one second that McGregor killed Payton. But as a professional spinner, he would advise routine investigation, such as finding out if McGregor had an alibi.

Kristie smiled in relief. Wasn't that the answer? Just ask McGregor. He might not even have been back yet from San Diego on Saturday night. Or maybe he'd been home working on the Mustang in full view of his neighbors.

All you have to do is ask him. If he's got an ironclad alibi, you can just go to Ray and tell him you're a hundred percent convinced that Payton interrupted a burglary, just as everyone else says.

Or you could even tell him the whole story.

It was so simple. *If* McGregor had an alibi. But if he didn't…

"Is this seat taken?"

Kristie spun toward Jane Smith's voice, completely disoriented to see the agent in Los Angeles. "What…? Hi. This is a huge surprise. I didn't know you were in town."

"I'm not," the agent assured her with a wry smile. "Just a quick stopover on my way to South America."

"South America? Does that mean you figured out a way to rescue that businesswoman?"

"No. And since I'm pretty sure *you* could have come up with something by now, I'm very frustrated. That's why I'm here." Before Kristie could protest, Jane added quickly, "I agreed not to pressure you and I meant it. I'm not asking for your help on this one, although God knows we need it. My team's already in place, and we have a great negotiator available. So hopefully, we'll muddle through on our own. But this experience, plus the one in Palm Springs, has taught me something. I need someone like you. Preferably the original, but if you're really not going to come around, I need to start looking for someone else."

Kristie was surprised and pleased by Jane's attitude. The spinner had been truly concerned that an element of obsession had been present in the recruiter's efforts, and was relieved to see that her diagnosis had been inaccurate. "Jane—"

"It's fine, Kristie. Obviously, you aren't ready. I was just hoping we might be able to reach an understanding before I left the country."

"I'm right in the middle of an assignment."

"The Payton killing. Yes, I know." She signaled to a passing waitress and asked for two glasses of white wine. Then she said, "I heard the president requested you personally. Quite an honor."

The spinner nodded.

"You deserve the recognition. And the opportunity to work on these sorts of high-profile cases. But with honor comes responsibility, Kris. You could be serving your country every day, in more ways than you can imagine, if you came to work for me. You could save lives, like the woman's in South America." She took a deep breath. "I know you think our work is somehow less lofty—less pure—than your life at SPIN—"

"That's not true. But…" Kristie smiled to ease any possible insult. "There's more of a bright line at SPIN, I think. And I'm the kind of person who needs that. I'm not judging. I just know my own limits."

The agent pursed her lips, seeming to consider her next words carefully. "You're young. You have friends at SPIN. It's like a family. Safe, cozy, familiar. With my team, there's amazing camaraderie, but we're not going to be your support group. That's for sure. And yes, you'll have to make difficult choices sometimes. But the truth is, there *is* no bright line. It's a myth that works most of the time, but it's still a myth."

Arching an eyebrow, Jane went on to predict, "You're going to have to get your hands dirty someday, even if you stay at SPIN. It's called growing up."

The waitress arrived at that moment and set the drinks on the table. Jane tossed a twenty-dollar bill onto the woman's tray, and then, when they were alone again, raised her glass to Kristie. "To growing up. Let's hope it isn't too painful for you."

The spinner frowned. "I'd like to think I can keep my ideals and still make a positive, realistic contribution to the world around me."

"You can. But ideals are a lot like Ray's rules—you have to be willing to flex them for a good cause. Otherwise, you're elevating form over substance."

"In other words, the ends justify the means?" Kristie replied, echoing McGregor's earlier observation. "I'm just not there yet, I guess. And to tell you the truth, I hope I *never* get there."

Jane seemed surprised, then she shrugged and stood up. "My plane leaves at ten. If you change your mind, or just want to talk between now and then, call me on my cell. Otherwise, I'll be out of touch for a while."

"Thanks for the drink, Jane."

And good riddance, Kristie added silently as she watched the recruiter disappear into the lobby. *I don't ever want to end up like you. Manipulative. Cold. Working with pricks like Pritchert. And having a philosophy that sucks. I'll take Ray's rules over that anytime.*

Jane's right about one thing though, she reminded herself, pushing the second drink aside and gathering up her wallet and keycard. *SPIN is like a family. You need to take advantage of that. And the first step is to invite Ray to your room and dump this whole McGregor mess into his lap. He'll know what to do. And he won't hurt anyone in the process. That's what separates SPIN from the CIA.*

She was so intent on getting to the phone and calling Ray, she didn't actually see McGregor as she pushed open the door to her suite and stepped inside. But she sensed him, even before his angry voice mocked her, saying, "I was beginning to think you were going to spend all night in the bar."

"McGregor!" She instinctively tried to catch the door before it closed, but she failed, so she backed against it instead. "How did you get in?"

"I've been doing this for years, remember? It's my job."

"Right."

He stepped up to her, his eyes narrowed. "You took off in such a hurry this afternoon. I kept telling myself the dog spooked you, but that wasn't it, was it?"

"No."

"You're something else, Goldie. Pretending to pay me a social visit, when you were really investigating me. It's unbelievable."

She shook her head. "You're wrong, McGregor. I didn't suspect you of anything—"

"Don't lie to me!" he began, then he visibly reined in his temper. "Dammit, Goldie, what's going on? What's the connection between Payton's death and my sister? If you think she's involved—if you think *I'm* involved—just say so. Don't go sneaking around collecting dog hair and dirty pictures—"

"It wasn't like that, McGregor. I promise." Reaching

her hand out, she touched his cheek, repeating firmly, "It wasn't like that. Really."

He pulled away, but seemed mollified. "Go on."

Taking him by the hand, she led him to a small sofa. When they were seated, she explained, "As soon as I heard I was coming to Los Angeles to investigate Payton's death, I started fantasizing about visiting you. But I don't think I really would have—I'm in enough trouble with Ray these days. Then I found some pictures of Ellie in a drawer at Payton's beach house. I guess you've seen them by now, right?" she added, noting that the manila envelope was no longer on the desk where she had left it.

He nodded.

Kristie sighed. "There were lots of pictures of lots of girls. Similar poses. I kept thinking about all the fathers or husbands who had a motive to wring Payton's neck. But when I saw Ellie, all I could think about was what a disaster it would be if she got sucked into any negative publicity. I was afraid she couldn't emotionally survive another scandal like that."

"Yeah. I've been thinking that, too." He moistened his lips. "Tell me why you came to my house."

"To warn you, I guess. Prepare you—so you could prepare her—in case it ever hit the newspapers. But even if it didn't, I figured you probably needed to know what kind of trouble she was getting herself into."

"Yeah. Those pictures are pretty hard-core. I almost lost my mind when I saw them."

"I'm sorry, McGregor. I had them in the car when I visited you, but I was hoping you'd never actually have to see them."

"Except, I had *already* seen them." He studied her surprised reaction. "You really didn't know that?"

She shook her head.

Standing, he crossed to the bed and picked up two envelopes. Then he handed her the thicker of the two. "Imagine how I felt when I found this in my mailbox today."

Opening the package, she forced herself to look through half a dozen shots of Ellie, alone and with Payton. "Oh, McGregor. How awful for you. And for her."

"Yeah." He touched her arm. "You wanted to protect me from this? That's pretty sweet, Goldie. Or should I call you Kristie?" He grimaced as he admitted, "I went through your briefcase. After I broke into your hotel room. That's the thanks you get for trying to help me."

She smiled. "I shouldn't have run away from you like I did. It was silly of me. All we had to do was talk it through, like we're doing now."

"So? Why exactly did you take off like that?"

"Well, you were half-right. It was sort of Nugget's fault. Because—and this is just the most irrelevant detail in the world, but bear with me—we had reports that a man with a golden retriever was seen on the beach near Payton's house right around the time of death."

"Man…" McGregor pursed his lips. "That's one hell of a coincidence."

Kristie nodded. Then she turned the envelope over in her hands, noting the postmark. "Do you have any idea who sent this?"

"None. It's local, though."

"I see that. It just came today?"

He nodded. "That's what I meant when I told you at the house it was such a bad day. I didn't know what to think. About the pictures themselves, or the fact that someone sent them to me anonymously. I needed to calm down. To decide how to approach Ellie about it. So I worked on the car. And then you arrived, and the day got better."

"And then it got worse. But it's better again now, right?"

"Yeah."

She looked at the postmark again. "It's strange that it took ten days to get to you. Like you said, they were mailed locally."

"Yeah, that is strange." He shrugged. "It happens, though."

She nodded.

"I guess I'll always wonder what I would've done if I'd seen these pictures while that bastard was still alive. It added to the craziness of the day, seeing them so soon after he was murdered. It *was* murder, I assume?"

Kristie hesitated, then nodded again. "Ray thinks Payton interrupted a burglar and was killed in the ensuing struggle. Director Oakes sent the Bureau's reconstruction experts over, and they think so, too."

He tilted his head to the side. "And?"

"And I think so, too."

"But?"

She laughed nervously. "There's no but. Not really."

When he arched an eyebrow, she laughed again. "You know how I am, McGregor. Obsessed with the little details, almost to a fault. Definitely to a fault."

"Like, the man with the dog on the beach?"

"Yes," she admitted. "And the fact that Payton was so universally despised. So many people had a motive to kill him. It seems odd that when it finally happened, it wasn't personal at all."

"Either way, the guy deserved it."

She forced herself not to look at the postmark a third time. "You must have been so angry when you first saw these pictures."

"Believe it. I'm still pretty raw. But thanks to you, I'm feeling better. Strange, isn't it?" He played with a strand of her hair. "I like the blond look, by the way."

"Thanks," she murmured, ignoring the tingle caused by his fingertips.

"So? Sounds like you guys are ready to wrap up the investigation."

"Just about."

"Where does that leave us?" He slipped his arm around her waist. "Maybe we should just come clean with Ortega. Stop sneaking around. Now that we know—well, we know more than we did—I don't really want to go back to the way it was. Do you?"

She allowed his smile to warm her for a moment. It was such a nice idea. They'd tell Ray, who would have an absolute fit. Then he'd calm down and agree to permanently reassign Kristie to other cases so she could begin dating McGregor. It would still be a long-distance relationship, but at least, as he'd said, they wouldn't have to keep it a secret.

There was only one problem. Or rather, one last hurdle. But she had a feeling it was going to be a tough one. "I need to say something to you, Will. Something annoying. Please, just let me finish before you take it the wrong way."

"Okay. Shoot."

She took a deep breath. "Like I said, Ray thinks a burglar killed Payton. I personally think it was someone who knew him. But we all agree on one thing— it was definitely an accident."

McGregor frowned. "I'm not catching your drift."

"Payton fell and hit his head. We know that for a fact. So if it wasn't a burglar—if it was an acquaintance, for instance—then it's very possible no crime was committed at all. Payton was pugnacious by nature. Someone could have come to that house just to talk to him, maybe warn him to stay away from his wife or daughter, and Payton started a fight. And if the visitor—this husband or father—"

"Or brother?" McGregor stared, clearly stunned, then he jumped to his feet. "My God, you actually think I did it!"

She stood and tried to reach for him, but he backed away, so she just spread her arms in a gesture of abject apology. "I just had to say it. I had to make sure you knew—for your own peace of mind if nothing else—that the evidence clearly shows what happened. I just had to say it," she repeated unhappily. "I'm sorry, Will. Please? Now that I've said it, can we just let it go?"

"What a mess." He was shaking his head slowly. "Be straight with me, Gold—I mean, Kristie. Am I a suspect?"

"No. Absolutely not."

He took a deep breath and held it for a moment, then let the air out slowly. "We can put it behind us, then?"

"Yes. Like I said, Ray and the other experts are completely convinced it was a burglary. I don't think these photos—or some silly dog fur—is going to change their minds. Everything at the scene points in the other direction. So I'm sure Ray's going to just want to close the case. And I'm almost positive he'll agree not to put any of this in the official report—"

"You're going to tell Ortega about the pictures? Why?"

Kristie winced. "He's my boss. I have to tell him everything."

"Since when?" McGregor's light tone was tinged with frustration. "You've been breaking every rule in the place for weeks."

"*Temporarily* breaking them. There's a difference." She gave him an encouraging smile. "Ray has a really high opinion of you as a person and an agent. This won't go anywhere."

"Then why tell him? If you believe me—if you're really convinced I'm innocent—it doesn't accomplish anything. And it hurts Ellie."

His eyes blazed with concern for his sister. "If the press gets wind of Payton's affairs, Ellie's the one who will suffer. It won't matter whether or how fast I clear myself. Those pictures of all those girls, but especially Ellie, will take on a life of their own. You know how the media eats this stuff up."

"We'll explain that to Ray—"

"And he'll be sympathetic. But he'll also want to be thorough. If I were in his position, I'd do the same." McGregor cupped her chin in his hand. "If you have doubts about whether or not I killed Payton, that's a different story. Then you have to do what you have to do. I wouldn't respect you if you didn't. But if you're honestly convinced I'm innocent—"

"I honestly am," she murmured. "And I wouldn't hurt Ellie for the world. The whole reason I sneaked the pictures out of Payton's house in the first place was to give you some time to prepare her, in case they came to light."

"Prepare her? Do you really believe that's possible? In her fragile state?"

"No," Kristie admitted. "I guess not."

"I'm asking you then, don't tell Ortega. Don't take that chance."

The spinner looked deep into his blue eyes, remembering how sexy they had seemed that afternoon. Now they mesmerized her for another reason as they blazed with love for his sister. With his burning need to protect her.

"Okay."

He touched her cheek. "Really?"

She jerked free, then winced in apology. "Sorry, I'm a little—well, never mind. It's fine. It's the right thing to do. For Ellie."

McGregor seemed unconvinced. "You're sure?"

"Yes. Absolutely. We'll just keep all this—the photos from the house and the ones from the mail—between you and me."

"Between you and me," he echoed, touching her cheek again. "And you're sure you can handle it?"

"Yes." She forced herself not to pull away again. Instead, she tried to sound confident. "Ray was ready hours ago to endorse the burglary theory and turn this over to the local cops to complete the investigation. He's just waiting for me to get on board. In other words, it's my call."

"Good."

She nodded. "I'll let him know right away. He'll be relieved. You should probably go home for now," she added softly. "I'll give you a call as soon as I'm sure it's taken care of."

McGregor's jaw tensed. "I wouldn't ask this for myself—"

"I'm doing it for Ellie, not you. And only because it can't possibly affect the investigation."

"Okay, then." He hesitated, then leaned down, brushing his lips across hers. "I'll get going. Call me as soon as you're done."

"Right. Drive carefully. And don't worry about a thing."

He nodded then left without another word.

She wasn't surprised that he didn't try to kiss her again. It would have been like kissing cardboard. She knew that because that's just about how much sensation—or how little—the other brush of their lips had given her.

She sank onto the sofa, feeling more miserable and alone than at any other time in her life. Even after her parents' plane crash, there had been arms to hold her. People to care for her. But now, there was no one.

Especially not McGregor. She had no illusions about the future of their love affair. It had ended when he asked her to withhold evidence from an investigation.

And when she agreed to it, she lost everything else. Her relationship with Ray, with SPIN—her supposed family—and with the ideals about which she had bragged so confidently to Jane Smith a lifetime ago in the bar.

So much for a bright line between good and evil. You just crossed it, she taunted herself, unclipping the small white envelope of dog hair from the larger manila one that contained photos of Ellie McGregor. Striding into the bathroom, she flushed Nugget's beautiful golden fur down the toilet. Then she stepped back and stared at the swirling water, numbed by the enormity of her action.

She had just destroyed evidence. The fact that that evidence could be easily replaced didn't change the magnitude of the transgression, at least in the spinner's eyes.

Almost in a trance, she returned to the bedroom and located Jane Smith's business card. Then she sat on the edge of the bed and dialed the cell-phone number.

Jane answered on the first ring. "Kristie?"

"How did you know it was me?"

"It's my job to know these things," the agent reminded her.

"Right. I'm glad I caught you. If the job offer's still open, I'm ready to take it."

"Wonderful. What changed your mind?"

Swallowing a lump in her throat, Kristie admitted, "I guess I grew up."

The agent was silent for a few seconds. When she finally spoke, her voice was uncharacteristically warm. "Do you want to talk about it?"

"No thanks."

"Maybe when I get back—"

"I'm never going to want to talk about it. I assume that's not a problem?"

"Not at all. I'm just delighted you're joining the team. You won't regret it, I promise you. How soon can you start?"

Kristie felt a stinging behind her eyes, but reminded herself sharply that she was a CIA agent now, with no room for silly sentiment. "I'll talk to Ray tonight. But please keep this between you and me until you're back from South America, okay? Give me time to wrap up this Payton thing. I wouldn't want anyone to associate my leaving SPIN with this particular assignment. It could hurt Ray in the president's eyes, and that would be unfair, since he has nothing to do with my decision."

"I won't say a word to anyone," Jane promised. "Not even the rest of my team—*our* team—until I get the word from Ray that he's approving your transfer." Clearing her throat, she added, "He'll try to talk you out of it, you know."

"Actually, I don't think he will. He's been very—well, very supportive of the idea."

"Terrific. I wish I could talk longer, but they're announcing my flight—"

"I have to go, too. I've got a million things to do. Call me when you get back."

"I will. Goodbye, Kristie. Take care of yourself."

Hanging up the phone, Kristie forced herself to return to the desk, where the two envelopes filled with photos were awaiting her. She could call the front desk and ask if the hotel had a shredder. But what if Ray heard about it? It seemed safer to just stuff them in the bottom of her suitcase until she returned home.

But that could be two or three days away, and it would drive her crazy, knowing the pictures were lurking there, under her clothes. She even thought about burning the evidence in the sink or tub. But wasn't this a nonsmoking room? Maybe alarms would sound—*that* would be just her luck.

You're not very good at this spy game yet, are you? she taunted herself. *But at least you've got the mantra down— the ends justify the means. In this case, protecting Ellie.*

A chill had descended on the room, so she rummaged in her suitcase for something to cover her silk top.

Something from Melissa's wardrobe, she decided, but all of those garments were scanty, sexy, and reliant on a different sort of heat. So she pulled out a pink hooded sweatshirt and bundled herself into it, then began to bury the two envelopes under lacy lingerie.

As she did so, something caught her eye. The postmark on McGregor's envelope, or rather, the white sticker with the postmark on it. It had come loose at one corner of the package—so loose that it would be easy to just rip it off and shred it.

So easy. And prudent, too, given its incriminating nature.

That's the one piece of evidence that really makes it seem as though McGregor's a suspect, she told herself. *If Ray ever saw that, he'd have to do something. It would be his duty. His duty as a spinner.*

In contrast, Kristie had no such duty anymore. Because she wasn't a spinner anymore.

A wave of emotions—anger, frustration, humiliation—surged through her, and she stuffed the envelope back under her clothes, then picked up the whole suitcase and hurled it across the room, knocking over a lamp in the process.

"Okay, Melissa, you crazy bitch. You made this mess. I know you did! So why don't *you* clean it up? And while you're at it," she challenged her alter ego, "get rid of that postmark, too. It shouldn't be hard. You're the rule breaker, right? You're the one who stole the pictures from Payton's house in the first place. This is all your fault!"

The burst of emotion subsided, and she crossed to the suitcase to gather up her scattered belongings. When she finally picked up the thick package of photos, her gaze locked helplessly on the loose postmark that theoretically incriminated McGregor.

All she had to do was rip it off and tear it to bits.

But she couldn't do it. Couldn't destroy evidence. The dog fur had been an anomaly—gathered by Kristie by mistake, and eminently replaceable. Just like the photos that she had fully intended to return to the crime scene.

And Melissa Daniels couldn't do it either! That was a revelation, but true nevertheless. For all her wild antics, Melissa was fundamentally incapable of such behavior. Bending the rules? Absolutely. But dishonoring those rules, and the ideals behind them? That redhead would sooner die.

"There's your answer, David!" she announced proudly. "What are Melissa's limits? They're the same as mine! How far will she go? No farther than me."

"And do you know why? Because she *is* me."

Kristie laughed out loud at the thoughts playing in her head. It felt so good to know she was one of the good guys. And it had felt so bad to think—even for a few minutes—that she wasn't.

She didn't want Will McGregor to experience that terrible mix of guilt and despair. Not ever. But eventually, he would. Maybe not today, with his concern for Ellie in the forefront. But in the future, every time he thought about what he'd done—what he had asked Kristie to do—he'd have an ache in the pit of his stomach. A shiver running down the part of his spine where his confidence and ideals had once been. She knew that because she had felt that shiver—that ache—so recently herself.

Reaching for her purse and key card, she strode to the doorway, knowing she had to report her renaissance to McGregor, then convince him to come with her to confess their sins to Ray.

But when she flung open the door, she saw that it wasn't necessary. McGregor was standing right there.

Chapter 14

Unprepared, Kristie didn't hesitate, but simply blurted out, "I can't do it."

"Good, because I don't want you to."

"You don't?"

"We'll figure something else out." He pulled her hard against himself, then kissed her so deeply, she knew he was trying to banish the taste of cardboard from his mouth, once and for all. And it was working quite well, as waves of trust and hope washed over them, flooding their bodies with warmth.

With one last nip at her lips, he raised his head and gazed down at her, his blue eyes blazing. "I was halfway home when I realized it would never work."

"Tell me why."

He stroked her jawline with his thumb. "I'd like to say it's because I'm noble. Or upstanding. But actually—I just don't want this standing between us. I feel like shit for even suggesting it." He steered her into her suite and closed the door. "You didn't do anything drastic, did you?"

"You mean, like join the CIA?"

"Huh?"

"Never mind." She laughed ruefully. "I didn't shred the photos. I wanted to, but I couldn't. I flushed the dog hair though."

"There's plenty more where that came from. We can go get it right now if you want."

She took him by the hand and led him to the sofa. "Let's just talk for a minute. We need to decide what happens now."

"That's simple. We solve the murder. That's the only way you can know for sure I didn't do it."

"Will...." She touched his cheek. "I already know that. And solving the murder may not be that easy. It was a random burglary, and there aren't any prints or other solid leads. We'd need help. And Ray would want to know why you were involved."

"I'm not so convinced it was a burglary."

Kristie stared, certain she had misheard him. "Pardon?"

He flashed a disarming smile. "I had the whole ride back here to think about it, so for once, maybe I'm a little ahead of you." Then he gripped her by the shoulders and explained, "Someone mailed those photos to me. Someone who wanted me to stop Payton from bothering Ellie. That's a logical assumption, right? Maybe he figured I'd get the package in a day or so and take some sort of action. When a week went by with no response from me— well, what if he decided to take care of it himself?"

"It makes sense to find out who sent them," she said, her brain taking the bait. "But we can also work from the other end. Maybe ask your mail carrier if he or she remembers delivering the package today rather than last week. Right? That refutes the glitch with the postmark."

She stood and began to pace as she strategized. "I'm guessing you don't have an alibi for Saturday night, or you would have mentioned it by now. But still, couldn't we ask your neighbors? Check phone records? Find proof that you couldn't have been at Payton's at the time of death?"

McGregor nodded. "I'd like to spend the next twenty-four hours doing all that, preferably before we tell anyone else about the photos. Maybe we'll get lucky. But either way, it's a given that we're gonna come clean with Ortega. I'd like to try to clear my name first, but that's your call."

"Twenty-four hours." She nodded and rejoined him on the sofa. "No problem. Thanks."

He twirled a lock of her hair around his finger. "I like this look the best. Just like I imagined you."

She felt her cheeks warm. "I was afraid you might have unreasonable expectations from that computer-enhanced picture of Melissa. I wouldn't want to compete with her."

"Trust me, you'd win. She's not my type."

"Too bad," Kristie said with mock regret. "She had some interesting plans for you."

McGregor arched a mischievous eyebrow. "Okay. She can come out to play one night a week. But warn me first, because she scares the shit out of me."

Kristie laughed, then scooted onto his lap and gazed happily into his eyes. "You're so much fun, Will. I was worried it would be different in person. But it's just the same, only better."

"Yeah, definitely better," he murmured, lowering his mouth to hers, teasing lightly. Then his tongue parted her lips and the kiss deepened dramatically.

Kristie slipped one hand behind his neck, then buried the fingers of the other in his thick, wavy hair, sighing his name in blissful surrender. His hand worked its way under her sweatshirt, stroking her through her silky tee, teasing her already tingling body.

She was about to suggest they move to the bed, when he broke off the kiss and stared down at her, frustration and apology in his eyes. "We've got work to do, Goldie."

"Tonight?"

He nodded. "When we finally get down to business, I don't want anything between us."

"I agree. I just don't see what we can accomplish so late."

"We can talk to my sister."

Kristie sat back, impressed by his willingness to tackle their dilemma so logically. "I thought you'd want to save that for a last resort."

"If anyone knows who might have sent those pictures to me, it'd be her. Right?"

Kristie nodded.

"And I'm going to talk to her about them eventually anyway. That was my plan from the moment I first laid eyes on them. I just wasn't sure how to go about it. Now—" he squared his shoulders "—we'll just do it."

"Are you sure you want me to come with you?"

"Yeah. I need you there."

"Okay. There's something I have to do first, though. Just sit and look handsome for a minute."

She lingered for a moment, savoring his smile, then she crossed to the bed and dialed Jane Smith's number. After three rings, a message instructed, *I'm not available. Leave a name and number and I'll get back to you.*

Kristie hated giving bad news this way, but knew it had

to be done as soon as possible, so she spoke rapidly at the beep. "Hi, Jane. It's Kristie. I wanted to let you know right away that I'm not going to be taking the job after all. Thanks, though. It was a tremendous honor to be asked, but I guess I'm just a spinner at heart. I had a moment of— well, disillusionment. But I'm past it now, and I'm sure this is best for everyone. Anyway—" she paused for a deep breath "—I figured you'd want to know right away. So, that's that. I'm sorry. Good luck on the new mission. Bye."

McGregor was staring at her. "You really *did* join the CIA?"

"Just for a few minutes."

"Man, you're full of surprises."

"You have no idea," she assured him as she gathered up her key card and wallet and stuffed them into her purse. Then with a playful glare she demanded, "Do we have a crime to solve or not?"

"Are you sure your sister will still be up? I don't want to make a lousy first impression by showing up in the middle of the night uninvited."

"She's a night owl. Among other things. That's her place right there. Last condo on the left. See? The lights are blazing."

"What if she has company? She could be in the middle of a hot date."

"Bring it on," McGregor said with a scowl. "I've been wanting to kick someone's ass all day."

"You might want to take it down a notch there. We want to be reassuring and supportive, not judgmental."

They left McGregor's pickup in the driveway alongside Ellie's unit, then strolled hand in hand up the front walkway. Kristie knew she should focus on their business, but the last twenty minutes—riding next to McGregor, teasing and laughing—had been so perfect, it was tough to keep from smiling ear to ear.

He had quizzed her on the CIA connection, and had been so appalled by the story of her infiltration of Salinger's estate that he had sounded just like Ray. And when she had drawn that fact to his attention, he had been completely unrepentant, telling her to "listen to Ortega from now on."

"If I had listened to Ray, I never would have gotten to know you," she had reminded him with a mischievous smile.

"It would've taken a little longer, but it would've happened," he had corrected her. "I was pretty much hooked the first time I heard your voice. And then when you started telling me those Melissa stories—well, let's just say, I made up my mind that day I wanted to meet you. It was just a matter of time."

When they reached Ellie's front door, Kristie looped her arms around the agent's neck and kissed him lightly.

"What's that for?"

"Take a guess."

"The car?" He arched a playful eyebrow. "You can thank me as soon as we get this over with."

Kristie wanted to melt, but forced her attention back to the meeting with Ellie, noting that soft rock music was playing somewhere in the house. "It really does sound like she's on a date, Will. Do you think we should come back tomorrow?"

"Why? Her date's officially over." McGregor punctuated the prophecy by ringing the doorbell. When there wasn't an immediate response, he pounded the door until it rattled, ignoring Kristie's whispered protests.

Finally, the door inched open and a small, dark-haired young woman peeked at them. "Will? Wait a sec." She seemed a little shaky as she unhooked the chain, then opened the door wide.

She was wearing lightweight running shorts, a tube top and knee socks, and from her rumpled hair and pink cheeks it was obvious she had just woken up. Her McGregor-blue eyes were glassy, her pupils dilated, and the smile that played across her lips as she looked at Kristie was tinged with confusion. "Hi. Do I know you?"

"I'm sorry we woke you. I'm Kristie Hennessy. A friend—associate, actually—of Will's."

"And she's a shrink, thank God. It looks like we're just in time," McGregor said, his voice gruff with disapproval.

Kristie murmured, "McGregor, don't," then sent Ellie a reassuring smile. "I'm just here as a friend."

"Good, because I already have a new therapist, and she's really good," the sister told her defensively. "Come on in. Excuse the mess."

Ellie led them into a combination living–dining room that was strewn with papers, CDs and stuffed animals. Lowering the volume on the stereo, she offered, "Can I get you something to drink? Coffee? Beer?"

"This isn't a social call, Elle."

"Yes, it is," Kristie corrected McGregor. "But you don't have to wait on us, Ellie. Just sit and visit, okay? We have something we need to talk to you about."

The spinner moved to the dining table and took a seat, careful not to disturb the profusion of half-finished sketches that littered the surface. "I didn't know you were an artist."

"Neither did I. It's part of my new therapy."

McGregor wandered over to the table and examined the artwork. "What do you know? These are really good."

Ellie nodded, still defensive. "Dr. Ramirez thought so, too. *She* has faith in me."

"Kristie's the one who recommended her, you know."

Ellie turned surprised eyes to Kristie, then she crossed the room and told the spinner softly, "Thank you so much."

"I'm glad it's working out."

"Working out? Are you in the same universe I'm in?" McGregor complained. "Look at her eyes, Goldie. She's high as a kite. As usual."

Ellie gave her brother a furious look, then turned back to Kristie. "I've been having terrible nightmares the last two nights. Dr. Ramirez prescribed some pills to help me sleep."

"Are you sure you took the right dosage?" the spinner asked gently.

"Last night I took one pill, and it wasn't nearly enough. So I tried an extra one tonight, and obviously, it kicked in pretty hard. I didn't even make it to the bedroom." To her brother, she added unhappily, "I'm doing my best."

"That's all I ask," he replied, his voice still stern. "Just stick with it. At least we know you won't starve. These drawings really are great. A little dark, though, don't you think?"

"Dr. Ramirez wants me to draw my dreams. And my nightmares. And even my daydreams," Ellie explained, slipping into a seat across from Kristie.

When McGregor had settled into a chair at his sister's side, she continued. "Dr. Ramirez says drawing is the perfect complement to my career. Once I'm established as an actress, I might want to try directing. And that requires a strong visual sense. Which I guess I have." She arched an eyebrow as if to ward off any contradiction by her brother.

"I know, I know. I've got a long way to go. But it's good to have goals, right?"

"Right." McGregor cleared his throat. "I need to ask you something, Elle."

"Okay." She straightened in her chair. "What is it?"

"It's about Colonel Ulysses Payton."

"The dead guy on the news?" Ellie frowned. "What about him?"

"How well did you know him?"

"I didn't."

"You're sure?" His tone softened. "There've been a couple of times when you've been pretty out of it, right? Is it possible you met him at a party but were too doped up or drunk to remember?"

"McGregor!" Kristie shook her head.

Ellie's cheeks had turned bright red, but she didn't protest. Instead, she asked unhappily, "What makes you think I knew this colonel guy?"

"There are some photographs of you with him. I was hoping you'd remember when they were taken. And who might have been around at the time. Someone sent them to me, Elle," McGregor added, touching her shoulder. "They're pretty explicit."

"Uh-oh. Sorry, Will." Ellie's face fell. Then she spread her hands in a gesture of helplessness. "I really don't remember. Do you have the pictures with you?"

Kristie held her breath as McGregor reached into his briefcase for the package he had received in the mail. She knew it was difficult enough for him to look at the pictures himself, much less spread them on the table in front of his little sister's eyes as he was doing now.

Ellie cringed. "That's me all right. In the flesh, as they say."

We found other pictures like this, of other girls, at Payton's house. *Lots* of other girls," Kristie told her sympathetically.

"Do they jog your memory at all, Ellie?" McGregor asked.

She nodded. "I remember the hot tub. It's here somewhere, actually." She rummaged in the stack of sketches and produced an excellent likeness of Payton's balcony, hot tub and all. "And his face is vaguely familiar. He looks different here than on the news."

"There are a lot of pictures floating around on TV from early in his career," Kristie agreed. "But these are closer to how he looked last week when I saw him. Pudgier than in his better days."

"You knew him? But you didn't—well, *know* him, right?"

"No. Nothing like that."

McGregor took his sister's hands in his own. "Tell us what you remember."

"I really only remember what's in the drawing." She looked her brother right in the eye. "I really *have* been having terrible nightmares, Will. Sometimes I'm dancing under one of those big silver balls that reflects all the flashing lights. Then I'm in that hot tub. Then I'm someplace else completely. Like a car, or at the circus. It's all a jumble."

"So? There's no way of knowing when these were taken?"

"I haven't gone out partying since that awful night you picked me up in the middle of dregsville. So it was before then. Does that help?"

"Everything helps." He gave her an encouraging smile. "Do you have any idea who might have wanted to protect you by sending me the photos?"

"Protect me? More like get me into trouble," she said, rolling her huge blue eyes for emphasis. "But I can't think of anyone. Is it important?"

"I'm just trying to figure out who sent these to me. And why."

Ellie cocked her head to the side. "My bad lifestyle keeps biting you in the ass, doesn't it? I'm really sorry, Will. But maybe all that will change with Dr. Ramirez. She's so smart. And inspiring. And bossy as hell," she added, grimacing.

He chuckled. "Bossy is good. And the art therapy impresses me, too."

"And she has another cool technique. Wait!" Ellie sprinted into the kitchen.

Kristie gave McGregor a playful scowl. "Whatever she says, be supportive."

"I'm doing my best," he assured her. "And I definitely want to stay on your good side tonight."

She felt her cheeks heat up, and was glad when Ellie returned with a newspaper article mounted on a piece of white construction paper. "Part of my therapy is to read this every morning with my first cup of coffee. It's all about the trial."

"The trial?" McGregor's smile turned into an overprotective scowl as he grabbed the article from her hands and scanned it with condemning eyes. "You're supposed to be forgetting about this shit, not remembering it!"

"Dr. Ramirez says I need to know what motivates me, consciously and unconsciously. And actually, the article is pretty interesting. You should read it, too, Will."

"No, thanks," he muttered, but when Kristie arched an eyebrow in warning, he added grudgingly, "What's so interesting about it?"

"Well, for one thing…" Ellie gave a tremulous sigh. "I always thought it was all about me. In a bad way, I mean. But I'm really only in a couple of paragraphs. There's a lot more about the other girls. The ones who lied. And guess what?" She bit her lip, then blurted out, "Dr. Ramirez said *they're* the ones who probably won't ever be able to put the experience behind themselves, because *they* hurt an innocent man. They'll always be haunted by it.

"I'm the lucky one, see?" she continued proudly. "Because I told the truth under oath, even though it was hard to do. Dr. Ramirez says I have a lot of inner strength. Me! Can you believe that?"

McGregor cupped his sister's chin in his hand and stared into her eyes, as though needing the connection. Then he murmured, "Yeah, I can believe it."

He seemed about to say more, but instead he pushed his chair backward and announced, "I'm ready for that beer now."

After he had disappeared into the kitchen, Ellie turned to Kristie. "Who do you think he's mad at? Dr. Ramirez or me?"

"I don't think he's mad at anyone. I think he's happy," Kristie told her, imagining how McGregor was feeling at that moment. He had experienced so much heartache over the last ten years, due to his certainty that a lustful director had manhandled his baby sister, and that he hadn't done anything to prevent it. To find out that it probably wasn't so had to be such a relief. And to find out his sister hadn't been lying to him about it…

"Yeah, I'm happy," McGregor confirmed from the doorway. "But I feel like shit, too. And I'm trying to impress my new girlfriend with my macho toughness, so do me a favor and don't get me all choked up again."

Ellie gave him a rueful smile. "No lecture this time?"

"No lecture."

"And you really think the drawings are good?"

"Actually, I think they're incredible." Without warning, he strode over to Ellie and grappled her to his chest, then murmured over her head at Kristie, "It's official. You're a genius who can solve any problem."

"Except this one," the spinner reminded him, holding up a photo of Ellie and Payton.

Ellie turned in time to see the gesture. "What's the problem with those, exactly? I mean, other than the obvious."

"It's possible that they might come to light in the course of the murder investigation," her brother explained. "We don't think they will, but they could."

"How embarrassing." Ellie shivered with exaggerated intensity. "Not just for me, but for the other girls, too. And for you, too, of course."

McGregor seemed surprised. "Don't worry about me. Don't worry at all, in fact. We may be able to keep all this under wraps."

"You have to do your job," Ellie reminded him. "If it happens, I'll deal with it. And at least I look good in a couple of these pictures, don't you think?" She shot him a teasing smile. "Maybe I'll get an audition from all the publicity."

"What a brat," McGregor muttered. Then he slipped his arm around her shoulders.

Ellie immediately snuggled against him, loudly stifling a yawn.

And Kristie watched it all with a wistful smile, remembering how she'd told herself McGregor needed time to work things out with Ellie before he and Kristie could begin their affair. Clearly, these two had a long way to go. And apparently, Kristie was going along for the ride. With Professor Ramirez's help, she had a feeling it would all work out.

"Don't you think we should let Ellie get back to sleep, McGregor?" she suggested finally.

"Yeah. Go sleep it off," he said, giving his sister a playful shove. "But give me a call first thing in the morning. You can read that piece-of-shit article to me over the phone if you want."

Ellie laughed, then walked over to Kristie and gave her a sheepish embrace. "Will I see you again soon?"

"Yes."

"Good. You guys can let yourselves out. Just pull the door tight behind you. It'll lock automatically." With a wave in her brother's direction, she gave a full-bodied yawn and drifted up the staircase.

"She's sweet, Will," Kristie murmured.

"Glad you like her." McGregor's eyes twinkled. "Now let's go back to my place. I want to get you out of those clothes."

"So much for sentiment."

"I'm human. You're sexy. Do the math." He walked over to her and nuzzled her neck.

"Nice," she admitted. "Just give me a minute, okay?" Wriggling away, she began to shuffle the photographs of Ellie and Payton back into their packaging. Then she moved to the dining table to straighten up the piles of sketches. "It's interesting how Ellie concentrates so much on the setting of her nightmares, instead of the characters in them. Maybe she doesn't dream faces. Or can't draw them."

"She's pretty good at faces, too, actually." McGregor

scooped up a second pile of drawings from the coffee table and carried them to Kristie. "Look at these."

"Wow. They're amazing. A little scary, but so detailed." She glanced through the stack, noticing sadly that the men all seemed to be frowning or leering.

And then she gasped. Because one of those leering faces was a familiar one. And even though it was her business—and talent—to connect the dots, her mind could not accept that this face was connected to Ellie.

"What's wrong, Goldie?" McGregor demanded. "Did you find a sketch of Payton?"

"No," she whispered as chills shimmied up and down her spine. "This guy's CIA. And he's a prick—with a capital *P*."

Chapter 15

"CIA? You're sure?" McGregor took the sketch from Kristie and studied it with a confused scowl.

The spinner folded her arms across her chest, hugging away the waves of intuition that were now shuddering through her. "He's one of Jane Smith's men. The guy who used me as a human shield in Palm Springs. Remember? Oh God, McGregor, I have a bad feeling about this."

The agent pulled her over to the couch and sat her down next to him, wrapping his arm around her. "Try to relax. Try to think. Where would Ellie meet this guy?"

"Payton once told me he recommended me to the CIA for the job in Palm Springs. Maybe he was friends with Pritchert and Jane. And maybe Ellie met him through Payton."

"Except she doesn't even remember her night with Payton," McGregor reminded her. "That's a pretty tenuous connection."

Kristie nodded. "*I'm* the one with the clear connection to both Payton and Pritchert. I know it seems crazy, but… Well, remember what you told me? They aren't the good guys. They're the ends-justify-the-means guys. All I can think of is—" She looked deep into McGregor's blue eyes. "Jane wanted me on her team, right? That makes *me* the end. The goal. And Ellie was a way to get to me, through you."

"Get to you? How?"

"I have no idea." Kristie gave him a weak smile. "At least one mystery is cleared up. The stupid postmark. Now that we know Jane's team is involved, it's obvious. They would have the ability—not to mention the guts and the ruthlessness—to fake a postmark on a package."

"To make it look like I got the pictures ahead of the murder? So that I'd be a suspect?"

"Right. *You* know the package didn't arrive until after the murder. But objectively speaking, it looks like you knew about Payton and Ellie for at least a few days before the killing."

"You think these guys would go to all this trouble? Actually frame a federal agent for murder? Just to recruit you?" McGregor shook his head. "I know you're good at what you do, but still, that's nuts."

"I agree. It's crazy. But Jane has this wacky theory about me and Melissa. Almost a fixation, really. She sees us as two separate personalities who combine into a unique super-operative."

"That's nuts," McGregor repeated. "And it still doesn't explain where Ellie saw this creep's face. Or why it made such an impression on her."

"What can I say? I'm an impressive guy," a cheerful voice informed them from the kitchen doorway.

Kristie and McGregor turned to stare at Pritchert, who stepped into the room with his gun drawn. Right behind him was Jane Smith, who was holding a finger to her lips, shushing McGregor, while using her other hand to point up the stairs.

Toward Ellie.

"Oh no," Kristie whispered. "Just do what she says."

"Good instincts, as always," Jane told her dryly. "Pritch, frisk Agent McGregor."

Kristie could see McGregor's hand clench into a fist at his side, and she quickly grabbed it, reminding him, "We have to do what they say or they'll hurt Ellie. Do you hear me? They probably have someone upstairs with her right now, so just go along with them. Just for a while, till we sort all this out."

"Listen to her, buddy," said Pritchert, adding with a wink, "She hasn't steered you wrong yet, has she? Arms up now. Let's see what you've got."

McGregor shot the agent a furious glare, but stood still and raised his arms, allowing Pritchert to pat him down.

After confiscating McGregor's Beretta, Pritchert turned to Kristie. "Arms up, beautiful. I've *really* been looking forward to this."

"That's enough," Jane warned him.

As the agent's hands roamed over her, Kristie forced herself not to react. Instead, she fantasized about the moment when she'd get her hands on her purse, which contained the toxic lipstick they'd given her in Palm Springs.

But as usual, Jane Smith was one step ahead of her. The agent gathered up Kristie's purse, along with McGregor's briefcase and the sketch of Pritchert's face, and stuffed them into a duffel bag supplied by a third member of her team who had been hovering in the background.

"You're going to come with us now. Quiet like little mice. Is that understood?"

When the pair just stood and stared at her, Jane practically growled at them. "Let me make this painfully clear. Cooperate, and your sister will live. Give me one moment of grief, and she's dead."

"We'll cooperate," Kristie murmured. "But aren't you making too much of this? You can have the sketch and the postmark. Take everything. Just stop trying to frame McGregor and we'll let the rest of it go. You haven't really committed any crime yet, except maybe mail fraud. Why up the ante by kidnapping us?"

"You haven't figured it out yet," Jane explained with a shrug. "But when you do, you'll understand. For now, just take my word for it. We need to have a nice long talk, and we can't do it here. So go with Pritch to the van."

The van... Kristie didn't like the sound of that, but there really wasn't a choice. She just hoped McGregor knew that, too.

"Pritch, cuff them and put them in the back seat," Jane continued. "Make sure no one sees you. If they try anything—if they even sneeze—shoot Kristie first. That will be Mark's signal to strangle the actress."

"Okay, boss."

"Evan?" She turned to the other member of her team. "Take Agent McGregor's keys and follow us in his pickup. Be discreet. Send Gabe on those errands we talked about. And meanwhile, Mark will stay here with the sister. If we hit a snag, he can kill her. Is everyone clear on the procedure?"

Pritchert and Evan nodded, then Jane sent an inquiring look toward McGregor, who muttered his assent.

"And just in case you don't believe there *is* a Mark..."

Jane pulled a small walkie-talkie out of her blazer pocket and whispered, "Mark? Did you get all that?"

"Loud and clear, boss."

"How's the drama queen?"

"Out like a light. This girl loves her pills, God bless her. She loves her brother, too. There's a picture of him on her nightstand, with some middle-aged couple—must be the folks. Nice family."

Kristie reached for McGregor's hand and squeezed it just seconds before Pritchert cuffed her wrists in front of her. After he did the same to McGregor, he motioned for them to follow.

And because they had no choice, they did so without a struggle.

The van was dark gray inside and out, with a metal grid separating the front seats from the rear, which was where McGregor and Kristie sat, unbelted but unable to escape, thanks to an electronic locking system that was controlled from the front.

Pritchert was driving, while Jane Smith alternated between giving orders—some whispered, some not—to her other operatives on her cell phone, and offering reassurances to her prisoners that they "only wanted to talk."

Despite the glib promises, Kristie was almost certain they were going to be killed. And given the direction the van was taking, she suspected the murders were going to take place at McGregor's house.

"Let me guess," she told Jane finally. "You're going to make it look like I came to visit McGregor and confronted him with evidence of the photos and the golden retriever. He confessed to murdering Payton but used our relationship to try to convince me not to betray him. When I refused, he tried to shoot me, and in the struggle, we both got killed. Something like that, right?"

Jane frowned. "You're jumping to conclusions. All we want to do is talk. Just be quiet, and try not to worry. We'll be there soon."

Kristie met her gaze coolly. "What I can't figure out is, why? What does it get you? Did *you* kill Payton? Is that it? Or did you just capitalize on his accidental death to frame McGregor? To get him out of my life so I'd be more likely to accept your job offer?"

"Frame him?" Jane laughed contemptuously. "No jury in the country would convict a man on a few photos and some dog hair. Especially not an FBI agent with a spotless record. After all, dozens of other men had the same motive—the victim was a pig, the crime scene indicated a passionless burglary and no dog fur was ever found on the beach matching that of McGregor's dog."

Kristie winced. It was true. If Jane Smith had wanted to frame McGregor, she could have done something much more direct, like calling the hot line and reporting the license-plate number of his pickup truck. Why fool around with phony postmarks and nebulous descriptions of dogs?

"Then what was your plan?"

Jane licked her lips before admitting, "We knew you'd find the photos of his sister at Payton's house. And because of her traumatic childhood, you'd hide the photos from Ray until you had a chance to discuss them with McGregor. He'd ask you to suppress them. And because you were almost certain he was innocent, you'd agree."

Kristie nodded. "You knew that if the evidence had any weight at all to it, McGregor would never ask me to keep it from Ray. And even if he did, I'd never agree. So you intentionally made it weak. Just enough to pose a moral dilemma for me."

"A crossroads," Jane agreed. "You'd protect him, but it would be the end of your relationship. You couldn't love a man who asked you to do that for him. And he could never love you, because he'd know that you believed—in a tiny part of your soul—that he might be a murderer. It was perfect. I knew it was, because it happened once to me, long ago."

"Except, it didn't work this time," McGregor reminded her, his jaw jutting forward in defiance. "Because Kristie's nothing like you."

"Correction. She's simply not as attracted to you as I thought. After that phone-sex call, I was sure the two of you were rabid enough to do anything for each other, including lie and suppress evidence. My miscalculation."

Kristie's stomach twisted into a knot.

How could she have been so naive? Hadn't Ray warned her not to trust Jane? "You tapped my phone at the hotel in Palm Springs? Why?"

"We had to be sure you wouldn't do something stupid and jeopardize our operation. Instead, you got my agent all stirred up. Didn't she, Pritch?"

"Yeah," he confirmed with a wink in the rearview mirror. "I still listen to that tape every night before I go to sleep."

McGregor lunged out of his seat, aiming for Pritchert's neck, and rattled the grate ferociously with his bound hands, cursing and swearing with colorful specificity.

Kristie was right there with him in spirit, remembering in disgust how Pritchert had come to her room with martinis and sexual suggestions right after the call. What a creep.

When McGregor had settled back beside her, still cursing, Kristie pressed her knee against his in solidarity, then prompted Jane Smith to continue. "Okay, so you wanted to alienate me from McGregor so I'd be more inclined to accept your job offer."

"Correction. I wanted to alienate you from SPIN. And you were already halfway there. On the outs with Ray. But you were still starry-eyed about your precious bright line between right and wrong. You were convinced you couldn't possibly conceal or manipulate evidence. And McGregor was your hero—the poster boy for integrity."

"Then it all fell apart." Kristie closed her eyes, remembering that awful moment when she thought she had lost everyone and everything that mattered to her.

"It all fell apart," Jane echoed. "Right according to schedule. Although, you had me worried in the bar. But then the phone rang and…" Her voice softened. "I almost felt sorry for you. It was like you had just lost your best friend."

"It was brilliant. And it almost worked." Kristie leaned toward Jane. "But in the end, you lost. So why make it worse? At this point, we can't prove you did anything wrong. Obviously you phonied up the postmark and made the calls to the hot line about the golden retriever. But that's our word against yours. Plus, we know you're capable of hurting Ellie, so we'll just let it go. There's nothing for us to gain from getting into that kind of contest with you. At least, not over a little mail fraud."

"You'd just let it go?"

"Absolutely. It was a prank!" The spinner forced herself to chuckle. "Why make a federal case out of mail fraud, right? We'll keep our mouths shut, won't we, McGregor?"

She turned to the FBI agent, expecting him to play along. But instead, McGregor grasped her bound hands in his own. "Don't you see? They did a lot more than just mail fraud."

She eyed him warily. "You mean, abducting us like this? We can forgive that, can't we? For Ellie's sake?"

"Listen to your boyfriend," Jane advised. "He's got it all figured out."

Kristie winced. "McGregor?"

His eyes blazed with pain. "Ellie's been having nightmares for two nights straight. Ever since the night Payton was murdered. She dreams about hot tubs, and lights flashing, and car rides. And *this* bastard."

When Kristie just stared, not daring to understand, he explained gently. "Ellie never met Payton. These assholes took the pictures after he died and planted them at the crime scene for you to find. They must have known the colonel had a proclivity for young starlets. And they used that. To get to you through me, just like you said."

Bile rose to within millimeters of Kristie's mouth. "Oh no."

"This isn't something I can ever let go. And they know it. I'll kill them if they don't kill me first."

"Wait a minute." It was Pritchert's turn to shake his head in confusion. "We're not actually going to kill them, are we, Janie?"

Jane sent him a haughty glare. "Since when are you squeamish about killing?"

Kristie could see Pritchert's expression in the rearview mirror, and knew he hadn't really understood until now how obsessed his boss had become. How increasingly irrational Jane's decisions were becoming. Even with Kristie's training, she had noted, but dismissed, the danger signals.

If Pritchert were a stronger man, he might take action now to prevent actual bloodshed. But for all his bluster, he was a follower, not a leader. Ultimately he would do whatever Jane said.

"An FBI agent whose only crime is falling for a good-looking blonde? That's a new low even for us. The Bureau would be all over it." To McGregor, Pritchert added desperately, "We just want to have a long talk. To make sure you understand what we'll do to the little actress if you even think about coming after us."

"You're an idiot," McGregor told him. "But your boss isn't. Tell him the truth, *Janie*."

Jane's eyes locked with McGregor's, but she didn't respond.

"I agree with Pritchert," Kristie heard herself insisting. "No one has to get killed. We'll let it go. All of it. What you did to Ellie—trust me, you'll burn in hell for that, and I'll bring the marshmallows. But you'll get away with it in this life, because McGregor loves his sister too much to endanger her just to get revenge. Right, McGregor?"

"Nope. I'll hide Ellie somewhere—someplace they'll never be able to find her. And then I'll come after them and make sure they pay."

"McGregor!"

Jane was visibly fascinated. "I'm beginning to see what Kristie sees in you, Will. Balls of steel. They're going to get you killed, but at least you aren't wasting my time by pretending you'll just let it go."

"We can't kill the spinner either," Pritchert told Jane, his tone now frantic. "Ortega would gut me like a sturgeon. Remember that guy in Panama? He hung him by his own freaking intestines!"

"Shut up, Pritch!" Jane glared. "Not another word."

"That's right! What about Ray?" Kristie exhaled in sharp relief. "If I'm not back soon, he'll come looking for me. He'll see right through any staged killings at McGregor's house."

"You're so naive," Jane told her quietly. "It's almost humbling. You just can't see what's right before your eyes."

"You're *all* missing the point!" McGregor's growl was so scathing—so commanding—that everyone in the van snapped to attention, including Kristie.

When he spoke again, his voice was eerily calm. "You don't have to stage any killings. No one has to die. The perfect cover-up for any crimes you've committed up till now is right here in the van with you."

Jane eyed him suspiciously. "What are you talking about? What perfect cover-up?"

"I don't know. But I know *she* knows," he said, inclining his head toward Kristie as he spoke. "Or at least, if you give her a pencil, paper and five minutes, she can come up with it. It's what she does. And she's the best. Which means no one has to die tonight. Right, S-3?"

When Kristie just stared at him, McGregor gave her an encouraging smile. "Okay, so this one's a little different, because it's *your* life on the line. Not just some anonymous agent. But you pulled it off in Palm Springs, didn't you? There you were, stuck in a windowless room in the middle of nowhere with armed guards at the door, and you came up with a plan."

He turned back to Jane. "If you kill us, dozens of things could go wrong, starting with some foul-up by that clown next to you. Then you're suddenly charged with the abduction and premeditated murder of two federal agents. Believe me, there's no one—not even someone as good as

S-3—who'll be able to help you then. Take advantage of this opportunity and let her plan something for you before it gets any more out of hand. I guarantee you, she's a miracle worker."

Jane pursed her lips as though seriously considering the offer. "Kristie? Do you have any ideas?"

"I actually like the idea of Ray disemboweling Pritchert," she began, but when McGregor growled at her, she added quickly, "It'll take more than five minutes. And I'll need a lot more information. But yes, I think I can do it."

"Fine." Jane eyed them coolly. "We'll be at the house momentarily. After that, I'll give you one half hour to come up with a plan."

Kristie wasn't fooled. Jane was just playing along, hoping they would be less likely to try anything during the transfer from the van to McGregor's house if they thought they were safe. Once inside, she'd renege on their bargain and kill them.

Which seemed only fair, since Kristie fully intended to renege as well. She had no intention of designing a scenario to help Jane when she could use the time just as effectively to design one that would take her down.

And she suspected McGregor was miles ahead of her.

"I need every detail," the spinner reminded Jane. "I especially need to know who else knows what's been going on."

"Let me tell her," Pritchert asked his boss. When Jane nodded for him to proceed, he grinned into the rearview mirror. "Janie gets this call Saturday night. An old friend of hers says he went to Payton's house, just to talk. They got into a scuffle and the colonel hit his head. Dead as a doornail. So Jane's friend asks her to cover it up for him, for old times' sake. Me and Jane and the West Coast team—Mark, Evan and Gabriel—go to the beach house, wipe it down, then stage the burglary. No sweat.

"*Then* things started getting interesting. We found all those hot pictures of struggling starlets stashed all over the place. It made Jane think about McGregor here. About his sister. How he'd feel if his sister were one of them."

Kristie snuggled closer to McGregor, knowing this next part would be unbearable for him.

Pritchert's grin widened. "We did a good job, don't you think? Even a so-called genius like you never questioned them."

"Just give Kristie the facts. No editorializing," Jane suggested. "But for the record, Agent McGregor, your sister was treated with respect to the extent possible. I insisted on that."

McGregor didn't respond, but Kristie could see the muscles in his jaw working overtime. He was hating Pritchert for touching his sister, and hating himself for not questioning the authenticity of the photos—for just assuming Ellie had engaged in a night of semiconsensual depravity with Payton.

"Okay, just the facts," Pritchert continued. "I went and got her. She was already asleep and easy to drug. My kind of girl."

"You're such a pig," Kristie whispered.

"Stop baiting them," Jane agreed. "In fact, just get to the punch line."

The punch line. Kristie almost didn't want to hear it.

But Pritchert was on a roll. "While the West Coast team was cleaning up the crime scene and taking the photos, Jane's old friend—aka the colonel's killer—was whisked back home on Jane's private jet. To the East Coast. Where the rest of the team was waiting for him, ready to fake him an alibi."

"Jane's old friend lives on the East Coast?" Kristie swallowed a lump of dread that had formed low in her throat.

"Add it all up," Pritchert advised her. "Lives on the East Coast, hated Payton, was an old friend of Jane's, and came up with a very convenient alibi for Saturday night. Ring any bells, genius?"

"You're talking about Ray?"

"Bingo."

Jane was eyeing Kristie intently. "Do you remember telling me how you created Melissa to fit Ray's specifications for an ideal female? I have a new operative who really looks the part, as I'm sure you could see from the security video."

The tightness in Kristie's throat moved to her stomach. "I never watched it."

"Too bad. It was an amazing piece of work," Jane told her proudly. "Miranda lives in a secure building, so it was simple. She and Ray got hot and heavy in front of the security cameras in the lobby and the elevator. Then my team went in and changed the times and dates, so it would appear they'd had three dates that week, the last one on Saturday night." She paused for a breath.

"There was no doubt President Standish would involve Ray, to some extent, in the investigation of his best friend's murder. After all, he was going to appoint Ray as head of the FBI, which shows how much confidence he had in his law-enforcement ability. And Ray would naturally insist on involving *you,* because of his checkered relationship with Payton. He'd need your objectivity. At first, we just wanted you to bolster Ray's credibility, especially in regard to his alibi with the Melissa look-alike. But we caught a huge break when Standish actually made SPIN the lead agency."

"The Melissa look-alike," Kristie repeated softly.

"Right. We knew you'd be so charmed by the girl's resemblance to Melissa—so pleased that your theory about Ray's libido was correct—you'd be more easily lulled into believing it."

Kristie met Jane's eyes with her own challenging stare. "Do you expect me to believe Ray Ortega went along with all of this? Abducting an innocent girl and taking X rated pictures of her?"

"All he asked us to do was cover up his involvement in the killing," Jane admitted. "We found the porno shots after he'd already left the crime scene. So you're right. Technically, he didn't know. I saw an opportunity for further isolating you from SPIN. So I took it. And anyway—" she gave Kristie a stern glare "—don't you think it's time to stop idealizing Ray? *He* called *me* to cover up a killing. To falsify evidence. He lied to the president of the United States. And he lied to you. Not such a hero after all, is he?"

Kristie remembered his tortured face on the plane ride. And his glowing account of his new affair with a redheaded beauty named Miranda. "No. Not such a hero after all."

"Don't you want to know what he gave me in return?"

Kristie shrugged. "He's going to be the director of the FBI. I imagine having him in your pocket was a pretty enticing proposition."

Jane laughed harshly. "Ray Ortega won't last six months in that job. The guy's on a self-destruct course. You know that as well as I do." Her tone grew wistful. "He was the best once. Now he's just a shell. The day he turned his back on his instincts—the day he decided a maze of rules would protect him from the truth—he was finished."

Abandoning her mournful tone, the CIA recruiter added brightly, "Fortunately for Ray, he had something else to offer me in exchange for my cleanup services. Something I really had my heart set on."

Humiliated, Kristie stared down at her hands before murmuring, "Me?"

"That's right. Not that you were his to give—at least, not exactly. But he promised to be neutral. To let you make your own decision. If you were leaning toward taking my offer, he promised not to talk you out of it."

"Hey, Goldie," McGregor murmured, nudging her with his thigh. "He only agreed to that because he was confident you'd never leave SPIN."

She raised her eyes to his, grateful for the kind words, and grateful also for the opportunity to confirm for herself that she and McGregor were on the same page. He had suggested that she devise a scenario to help Jane and Pritchert, but she was almost sure he was hoping for something much sweeter—to buy them time, so that she could come up with a way to overpower the CIA agents without risking Ellie's life.

And so she smiled at him through her tears, and was relieved at what shone back in his eyes. Commitment, confidence—and integrity.

They were definitely going to take these bad guys down. Together.

"Don't kid yourselves about your boss," Jane advised Kristie, her eyes dark with contempt. "We can do anything to you and McGregor we want. And do you know what Ray will do about it? Not a thing. He's our coconspirator. Which means, our crimes are his crimes. He may have been thousands of miles away when we kidnapped Ellie and took those pictures, but he'll go to prison for it the same as us. If we have to kill you to cover it up, he'll go along with that to save his own hide. In fact—" she paused to glance at her watch "—one of my operatives already briefed him on the situation a few minutes ago."

"What?"

"They're on their way here as we speak. My plan was to have Ray pull the trigger—just to be doubly sure he understood his role in all this. Now of course that won't be necessary. He'll be relieved to know you're going to design another solution."

"You actually believe Ray Ortega could shoot me? In cold blood?"

"I think he's capable of it," Jane retorted. "In fact, I know he is. But I wouldn't ask it of him. My plan was for him to shoot McGregor. Pritch would do you. But now," she acknowledged lightly, "you're going to wow us with your brilliance, and we'll all walk away without any blood on our hands. Right?"

"Yes." Kristie gave her a confident glare. "Like McGregor said, it's what I do. I hate the idea of saving your hide, but it's not going to be too difficult. Nothing compared to Palm Springs. So…" She arched an eyebrow in Pritchert's direction. "Pull in the driveway, then uncuff McGregor and walk up to the house with him. The dog won't think anything of it. Jane can drive the van into the garage, and the other guy—Evan, is it?—can pull the pickup in behind us."

She turned back to Jane. "The last thing I need is for Nugget to start barking and attracting the neighbors' attention. We need a low profile for my plan to work."

"Are you saying you've already come up with something?" Jane eyed her with skepticism. "That's impossible. I've been over it and over it—"

"You're not me. You're not even *half* as good as I am." Kristie laughed with sincere contempt. "For one thing, you're sloppy. If you'd just made Pritchert wear a mask when he abducted Ellie and faked those pictures—or if you'd used an agent I'd never met to do it—we wouldn't be in this mess right now."

"She was drugged—"

"Drugged enough to make her compliant. But she wasn't out cold. And she's got an eye for detail. *I* would have anticipated that." The spinner waved her hand, dismissing the subject. "I still have a few loose ends to tie up, but I think I've got the gist of it. So pay attention, and do exactly what I say, and everything's going to be just fine."

Chapter 16

They settled down at McGregor's dining table as though they were about to have tea—three CIA operatives, an FBI agent and a spinner. The handcuffs had been removed, but both Evan and Pritchert were pointing pistols at Kristie and McGregor, who were seated side by side across from their captors.

Pritchert spoke first. "Let's hear your brilliant plan."

"But first…" Jane smiled grimly. "Let me guess. You're going to suggest that we can threaten your aunt and uncle's safety to ensure your silence, the same way we could use Ellie against McGregor. Correct?"

Kristie rolled her eyes. "Give me some credit. I have a reputation to protect, you know."

Jane shrugged. "Go on, then. Dazzle us."

"It's so simple, I'm surprised you didn't think of it. But then again—" Kristie sighed "—we've already established you aren't in my league, haven't we?"

"Just tell them the plan," McGregor suggested.

Kristie admired the hint of concern in the FBI agent's tone. He was so good at this. She could rely on him, as she'd done so many times in the past six months. All she had to do was give him something—*anything*—and he'd make it work.

And in this case, her "something" was pretty darned good.

"You need something on us," she told Jane. "Something solid. The whole idea that you could use Ellie's safety to control McGregor is ludicrous. All we'd have to do is get her into some sort of witness protection program, then we'd be free to come after you. And the same goes for my aunt and uncle. Right?"

Jane nodded.

"You need something on us that can't be hidden away. Something with teeth. Something so solid, so gripping, you'll own us forever. And I know just what that is."

"Tell us," Pritchert demanded, clearly enthralled.

Kristie ignored him, turning instead to McGregor. "We've got to murder someone."

She wasn't sure if he was just acting, or was truly stunned, but his response was perfect when he demanded, *"What?"*

"It's okay." She patted his cheek. "We'll kill someone bad. Someone who deserves it. But we'll do it in cold blood. And we'll videotape it. Just so there's no misunderstanding over who pulled the trigger."

"You'd actually murder someone?" Jane's blue eyes twinkled. "Any candidates?"

"There's only one." Kristie paused for effect, then elaborated. "Ray Ortega."

She was pleased when even Jane flinched.

Then the spinner leaned forward. "Don't you see? It's

perfect. This is all Ray's fault. He almost got me and Mc-Gregor killed because he didn't take responsibility for what he did to Payton. Ellie went through that whole ordeal because of him. He lied to the president of the United States! And like you said in the van, we'll really never know if he killed Payton by accident or on purpose."

All visible signs of blood had drained from Jane Smith's face. "You could do that? Kill Ray?"

"Couldn't you?"

"What happened to the bright line?"

Kristie shrugged. "*He* crossed it. If someone has to pay for that mistake—if I have to choose between Ray and Mc-Gregor—then it has to be Ray. Not us." Turning to Mc-Gregor, she sandwiched his clenched jaw between her palms. "I can do it. Can you?"

"Yeah. I can do it," he assured her, his voice hoarse but devoid of hesitation.

Then Kristie fixed Jane with a stare. "What about you? He's your friend."

"He meant a lot to me once, but that Ray Ortega doesn't exist anymore. And the simple truth is, I don't need a friend. I need a spinner. That's the deal, correct? Once the investigation is over, you'll come to work for me?"

Kristie sucked in a breath, then nodded.

"Fine." Jane leaned back, folding her arms across her chest. "Let's hear the details."

"Well obviously, we need to stage it as self-defense. The idea being, I had begun to suspect Ray of killing Payton. I was miserable about it—believe me, I know how that feels. So I came here to run my theory by McGregor, hoping he'd talk me out of it. We made some calls to double-check Ray's alibi. Ray found out about those inquiries and came here to confront us. He had a gun. We shot him in self-defense. End of story." She fixed Jane with a cool stare. "Can your redheaded operative—Miranda, right?—handle this on her end?"

"Yes."

"Have her tell the authorities she had several dates with Ray, but not on Saturday night. She'll say he told her he was working undercover, and asked her to lie for him. But no one checked the alibi until tonight, when I left her a message on her answering machine. She immediately called Ray and asked what to do. That's all she knows."

"That should work," Jane admitted, nodding.

"It's all pretty simple, but we can't afford any loose ends, so I need a little information. First, how will Ray be armed? I know he carries a Glock in a shoulder holster. Will he have any other weapons?"

Jane frowned. "It's been years since I worked with him. And in those days, he was an operative, not a bureaucrat. He always had a small backup revolver strapped to his leg. But these days? I just don't know."

Kristie turned to McGregor. "What do you think? Would he have a loaded backup revolver as well as his usual sidearm?"

She had tried for a casual tone, but desperately hoped McGregor would understand what she was really asking him. She didn't care about Ray's guns. She wanted to know if McGregor had a loaded weapon somewhere in the house. If he caught on—and he usually did—he'd find some way to let her know. A tilt of the head. An oblique reference. Something.

He pursed his lips. "Ray's been out of action for a while, but old habits die hard. It's like—" he paused to grin "—even if I were a ninety-nine-year-old widower, I'd probably keep a fresh stash of rubbers in my nightstand.

Any possibility of action—however remote—and I'd want to be ready."

As Pritchert roared with laughter, Kristie rolled her eyes, pretending to be disgusted while silently cheering. McGregor had a loaded gun in his nightstand. It was perfect.

"You said Ray and your operative are on their way here? What's their ETA?" she asked Jane.

The agent looked at her watch. "Ten minutes. Fifteen, tops."

"Let's move then. We need to set things up. And if possible, I'd like to do a run-through once, to get the bugs out. McGregor, do you have a video camera and tripod?" When he nodded, she told Evan, "Help McGregor set it up in the bedroom."

Jane's eyes narrowed. "The bedroom?"

"It's the logical spot. Wasn't that *your* plan? To stage this so that it appeared McGregor and I had a deadly lovers' quarrel because I wouldn't cover up his crime?"

Jane nodded. "That was the plan."

"I'm guessing you would have forced us at gunpoint to pretend to make love in his bed before you staged the actual killings, right? The investigators—McGregor's fellow agents, and my friends, like David Wong and Justin Russo—would have been so unnerved by the intimacy of the crime scene, they would be more likely to miss things." She met Jane's gaze directly. "You used that tactic on us, didn't you? Those pictures of Ellie—they were so…well, so distressing, we didn't examine them as professionally as we should have. It was too painful. So we were less likely to pick up on tiny imperfections."

Jane nodded, smiling. "It almost always works."

"And it'll help explain the video camera. Lovers filming their first sexual escapade. When Ray gets here, you'll be waiting for him here in the dining room. You'll tell him McGregor and I are having simulated sex in the next room, at gunpoint, courtesy of Pritch and Evan." She arched an eyebrow. "Trust me, Ray will want to see that."

Jane nodded again. "He's got a thing for you, that's for sure."

"So, he'll walk into the room. McGregor and I will be going at it pretty intensely. Pritch will say hi to Ray. That'll be our cue. McGregor will grab his gun off the nightstand and shoot Ray right between the eyes." She glanced down at the duffel bag filled with their belongings. "His gun is in there, right?"

"You think we're going to let you have a gun? You must be nuts," Pritchert said with a growl.

"No, it's fine," Jane murmured, digging in the bag until she had found McGregor's holstered weapon. "Leave them one bullet, Pritch. Empty the rest."

She gave Kristie a knowing smile. "It's a good plan. I especially like the idea that I'll have a videotape as insurance. But I want *you* to pull the trigger. Not McGregor."

Kristie had expected the objection, but still pretended to disagree. "I've never shot anyone."

"It's like you said—Ray will be distracted by the sight of you naked with McGregor. Even if he has his gun drawn, he's not going to be alert. Just aim carefully, right between the eyes. You can do it."

The spinner hesitated, then shrugged. "I'll do my best. But I'll only have one bullet. If I miss—"

"If you miss, I'll have to shoot Ray myself," Jane agreed. "Once he realizes we gave you access to a weapon, he'll know I set him up. But after I shoot *him,* McGregor gets my next bullet. And then you."

"That's fair." Kristie squared her shoulders. "I'll hit him. I can't guarantee I'll kill him, but I'll hit him. I'd be crazy not to try my best, since he'll probably shoot back at us."

"True." Jane arched an eyebrow. "Just make sure to aim at his head. I doubt if he'll be wearing a vest, but he might."

They moved into the bedroom, where McGregor had just finished setting up the camera, placing it on the left side of the bed.

Kristie knew that was another message—his way of telling her his backup revolver was in a drawer on the bed's right-hand side.

"Put McGregor's gun on the nightstand closest to the camera so we get a good shot," Jane told Pritchert briskly. "Kristie, I agree we should do a quick run-through."

"Yeah, get undressed, spinster," Pritchert said with a wink.

Kristie glared at him. "This is just the practice round, pervert." Kicking off her tennis shoes, she began to rumple the sheets and blanket, then patted them in invitation to McGregor. When he had slipped under the sheets, she told Pritchert, "Give us a minute or two to get worked up. Then say, 'Hi, Ray.' That'll be my cue. I'll grab the gun and point it toward the doorway. But I won't fire this time. Unless *you* happen to be standing there, of course."

"No more bickering," Jane said, her intonation terse. "Let's see how this is going to work. And, Kristie?"

"Yes?"

"Don't get any ideas about that gun. One bullet's not going to do you any good against three armed professionals."

"Don't worry," Kristie told her. Then she turned her attention to McGregor, who was propped up on one elbow as if waiting for instructions. But she suspected he knew exactly what he needed to do. They had worked enough cases together for him to know how her scenarios flowed. And in turn, she knew his capabilities.

From here on out, this was all up to him. Her spinner brain had done its part. Now it was up to McGregor's toned, agile body and his superior marksmanship. Once he had the fully loaded backup pistol in his hand, he'd be responsible for taking out Jane and Evan. All Kristie had to worry about was using her one bullet to hit Pritchert, then she'd stay out of the line of fire until McGregor had finished with the others.

But first, she needed to put Pritchert off his guard. And perhaps she could distract Evan as well. The younger man had taken every opportunity to manhandle Kristie's body while moving her from Ellie's house into the van. That was a good sign.

So she pushed McGregor back into his pillow, then straddled him and began to playfully unbutton his shirt. After using her fingertips to explore his muscled chest, she knelt up straight, then pulled her silk tee over her head with a flourish, revealing a lacy bra. McGregor slid his hands up, fondling her breasts gently.

With any luck, Pritchert and Evan were imagining themselves in McGregor's place, feeling the same sensations he was pretending to feel. But Kristie knew McGregor's mind was otherwise engaged. He was going over the plan one last time in his head, as was she. They had to get it right. Their lives depended on it, and so did Ellie's.

Taking McGregor's hands, she pressed them more solidly to her breasts, then leaned her head back and murmured his name. Hoping that the other men were suitably impressed, she then instructed breathlessly, "Do you have a condom nearby, McGregor?"

"I thought this was a *dry* run," Pritchert complained, his voice hoarse, his eyes fixed on Kristie's chest.

She ignored him, but explained in McGregor's direction, "These tiny details will make or break this plan. We need to set things up now, before we forget."

"I agree," Jane murmured.

Kristie heard McGregor inhale sharply, and she braced herself as well. This was it. He would reach into the nightstand drawer for a condom, but he'd come out with a loaded pistol. He'd shoot Jane—the only alert villain in the room—and then he'd take out Evan, who was positioned on McGregor's side of the bed. Meanwhile, Kristie would grab the other pistol and shoot Pritchert in the head. Then she'd hit the floor and scramble to safety.

As McGregor leaned away and opened the drawer, Kristie plumped her breasts in the cups of her bra, knowing Evan and Pritchert would be watching her. She could only hope Jane would be watching her as well—not out of sexual curiosity, but because Kristie was so close to the loaded gun on the nightstand. In any case, the spinner didn't dare watch McGregor, but she was acutely aware of his movements.

Those movements were leisurely as he reached into the drawer, and then in an instant he sprang into action. But to her horror, there was no gun in his hand.

In that instant she knew that the CIA must have swept the house earlier that evening, removing all weapons, leaving McGregor defenseless for the massacre to come.

Still, McGregor didn't hesitate. Instead, he lunged for Evan with clear plans to confiscate *his* pistol. And Kristie sprang into action herself, scooping McGregor's Beretta off the nightstand just as Jane opened fire on McGregor.

More than anything, the spinner wanted to turn her single bullet on Jane, but she forced herself to stick with the plan. McGregor—if he was still alive—would be expecting her to neutralize Pritchert.

Two shots sounded from the far side of the bed, and since neither bullet hit Kristie, she allowed herself to believe they were fired by McGregor and not by Evan. Somehow he had managed to overpower the CIA agent and get his gun.

Firing her one precious bullet straight into a stunned Pritchert's head, Kristie jumped from the bed and grabbed his body before it could slump to the ground, just in time to use him as *her* human shield against a volley of shots from Jane's gun. The bullets pummeled Pritchert's vest, sending him and the spinner flying backward against the wall. Two shots connected with flesh—*his flesh*—opening his upper arms on both sides of his dying body. His pistol had long since dropped out of sight.

Another shot rang out from McGregor's location, and Kristie saw Jane's weapon sail out of her hand, thudding onto the carpeted floor and under a chest of drawers. Now both women were unarmed, and as their steady gazes locked, the world seemed to freeze to a halt. There were no sounds and no movement from the far side of the bed. And while the room contained half a dozen weapons, Kristie wasn't sure where most of them were, or which ones still had ammo. And it seemed as though Jane wasn't quite sure either.

"McGregor?" Kristie called out warily.

"He's dead," Jane assured her, shifting her position slightly, beginning to circle her prey. "So is Evan."

A chill shuddered through Kristie's body. "McGregor? Are you okay?"

"I told you. He's dead." Jane winced as she examined

her bloody hand. "He got off one good shot though. Just not good enough."

"Bitch," Kristie whispered.

"What exactly was your plan?" Jane said, taunting her. "You really thought McGregor could wrestle Evan's gun away and neutralize me?"

"I thought he had a backup pistol in the nightstand. But you swept the place, didn't you?"

"Who's sloppy now, spinner?" Jane flashed an evil grin. "Gabe stopped here on his way to Ray's. He never mentioned finding a pistol, though. I'll have to remember to give that boy a raise."

Kristie bit her lip. Jane had been very thorough. And she was still being thorough, trying to buy time until Ray and Gabe could rush to her assistance.

And while Kristie still wasn't convinced Ray would side with Jane against her in a gun battle, she wasn't about to find out. Not with McGregor unconscious on the other side of the bed, possibly dying.

Possibly dead already...

She couldn't afford to think that way, though. She had to believe there was still a chance, if she could just subdue Jane before the others arrived.

The ruthless recruiter was still circling, and now Kristie joined the game. Slowly, but with confidence. She only wished she could call a time-out, just long enough to put her shoes back on. Then she was sure she could win.

But she had trained in bare feet, hadn't she? And even if she ended up pulverizing all ten toes, there would be a certain satisfaction in knowing she'd broken them on Jane Smith's jaw.

Jane must have seen something in the spinner's eyes because she murmured, "You're really going to take me on?" Then she reached down inside her black leather boot and pulled out a tiny jeweled knife.

Kristie grimaced. More than her bones were now at stake. The blade was only three inches long, but she had no doubt about its razor-sharp edge. If she didn't aim her kick just right, that little blade was going to slice her foot wide open.

But at least her right hand is out of commission, thanks to McGregor's bullet, the spinner reassured herself. *She won't have optimum control using her left. And she won't be able to switch hands like Ray did in your apartment. So actually, this is no biggie...*

Kicking the knife was the only logical move, which meant Jane would be expecting it. That—plus the prospect of severed toes—was enough to convince Kristie to try another tactic, so she fixed her stare on the knife but aimed her kick at Jane's chin instead.

It caught the agent by surprise, knocking her onto her backside, but when Kristie's second kick tried to reconnect with Jane's jaw, the agent was ready for her, burying the blade into the spinner's instep. Kristie shrieked in agony and jerked her foot away, sending the knife flying into a corner. Then she tried to jump free, but Jane grabbed her by the ankle and felled her.

There was a vicious snarl on the CIA agent's face as she straddled the spinner and began punching her in the face with her bloody right hand as well as with her left. Livid, Kristie summoned every bit of adrenaline-laced strength she could muster and threw the agent off of her. Then she crawled a safe distance away, desperate to regroup.

And even more desperate to find a weapon—any kind

of weapon. Unfortunately, the only one within reach was McGregor's Beretta, which she knew was empty.

Jane apparently had the same idea, but had spied a better option, and now lunged toward the bed, thrusting her hand underneath to recover Pritchert's Glock.

Knowing she had less than a second to act, Kristie didn't hesitate. Instead, she returned to the only ploy that had ever really worked for her. Grabbing the empty Beretta, she took careful aim and sent the heavy implement flying, end over end, toward the back of Jane's head. In an instant, the familiar sound of a skull cracking filled the air.

A violent tremble coursed visibly through Jane's prostrate form. Then she lay still and silent.

With no time to waste, Kristie called out McGregor's name, but there was no response. Dragging her sliced, unusable foot behind her, she crawled around the bed and found the FBI agent buried under Evan's limp body, which she tossed aside without pity.

Gathering McGregor into her arms, she saw that both his shoulder and midriff were bloody. Pressing her palm against the stomach wound, she insisted frantically, "McGregor? Can you hear me?"

He started to moan, and she kissed his mouth in relief. "Just a sec. I've gotta call 911, okay?" Leaving him where he lay, she scrambled to the nightstand, retrieved a cordless phone and returned to cradle him again as she dialed.

"Kristie…"

"Shh. Just relax. I'm calling for help."

"Listen to me," he insisted hoarsely. "Neighbors heard shots. Reported already."

"I'm sure they did, but—"

"Get ready for Ortega. Here any minute. Find Evan's gun. Lock yourself in the bathroom—"

"Ray won't hurt me, Will. It's all over. I promise. Just close your eyes. Try not to worry. Just let me hold you—"

The agent's eyes widened. "Kristie!"

He was looking at something over her shoulder—something that horrified him—so she spun around, just in time to see Ray in the doorway, aiming a gun in their direction.

She howled as two bullets whizzed by her ear, then she swiveled to see Evan, who had pulled himself up to a crouched position, crumple back to the floor.

Then Ray strode past Kristie, as though he hadn't even seen her there. Standing over Evan's body, he stared down for a long moment. Then he fired a third shot right into the CIA man's head.

As Kristie watched, exhausted and mesmerized, Ray walked past her again. And again, he seemed not to see her. His sole focus was now on Pritchert's motionless body, which he nudged with his foot. Then he robotically fired two bullets into the agent's brain.

Finally he moved to Jane Smith and shoved her body with his foot, coaxing from it a soft, pitiful moan. Then he aimed his pistol at her head.

"Ray, don't," Kristie whispered, her throat tight with conflicting emotions. She wanted Jane dead more than anything in the world. But she had to stop Ray for *his* sake, so she managed a louder, more authoritative, "Ray! That's enough. It's over."

He raised his head and gazed over toward her and Mc-Gregor, then he nodded and dropped to one knee, cuffing Jane roughly. Kristie thought he was going to leave his weapon there, but he carried it over to her instead and relinquished it, the barrel pointed in his own direction.

Then he knelt beside McGregor and pressed his

fingertips to the FBI agent's neck. "Good pulse," he told Kristie.

McGregor struggled to sit up. "My sister…"

"She's safe." Ray looked directly into the agent's eyes. "There's a SPIN team with her at her house. The bastard who threatened her is dead. And the paramedics will be here any minute. Close your eyes. Try to rest."

"Thanks."

Ray winced. "Don't thank me. All I ask is that you believe me when I say, I never, *never* suspected anything like this would happen.

"We know that," Kristie said, stroking his arm.

"I take responsibility," he continued stubbornly, his voice choked with emotion. "But I swear, Will. I didn't know until tonight that that bitch involved your little sister—or you—in any of this."

Then he turned to Kristie. "I made a deal with her. I wouldn't stand in your way if you chose the CIA over SPIN."

"I know. And FYI? I decided to choose SPIN."

Ignoring the gentle joke, he stood up. "I'll be outside. Waiting for the paramedics."

"Ray, don't go." She was alarmed by his miserable expression. "Stay with us."

"I've got some thinking to do."

The idea of him alone with torturous thoughts frightened her. "You're not going to do anything crazy, are you?"

You mean, take the easy way out again? Like I did when I called Jane in to clean up my mess?" He exhaled sharply. "I just went to Payton's to talk, Kris. He came at me like a madman. I hit him without thinking, and he cracked his head on the fireplace."

"I know. I *know* it was self-defense."

His eyes glistened. "All I could think was, I could do some good—serve my country well—at the Bureau. Why let a stupid accident ruin all that? So I did what we used to do in the old days—the *bad* old days. I called Jane."

"It's okay, Ray. Everything's going to be okay."

"No, it isn't," he corrected her. "But don't worry. I'll face the music. Much as I'd like to blow my brains out, I won't. I promise."

"I didn't mean that," she protested. "Just stay and talk—"

"Take care of Agent McGregor. That's your only job right now. Keep him quiet and warm," Ray instructed. Turning his back to them quickly, he strode out of the room.

"Talk about demons," McGregor murmured. Then he reached up and brushed a stream of tears from Kristie's cheek with his thumb. "Are you gonna be okay?"

She hadn't even realized she was crying. Wiping both cheeks with her palms, she smiled sheepishly. "I'll be fine. But look at you."

"Look at *you*," he whispered in return, resurrecting the romantic wordplay that had preceded their first kiss.

Kristie stared at him in wonder. It had only been hours since that first embrace, yet it felt like weeks. Weeks of danger—to their love affair and to their very existence. Now both were going to be just fine.

Leaning down, she brushed her lips across his just as sirens began to wail in the distance.

Chapter 17

"The president will see you now. Please follow me."

Kristie stood up and smoothed the skirt of the exorbitantly expensive charcoal-gray suit she had purchased just that morning for this occasion. She had also bought a pair of four-hundred-dollar black leather shoes with low heels, but, unfortunately, was only wearing one of them. Her other foot was cradled in an embarrassing but comfortable white sheepskin slipper pending her recovery from Jane Smith's knife wielding.

She stole a glance at McGregor, mostly to be sure he was steady on his feet. After all, he had just been released from the hospital six hours earlier. Even so, he looked pretty good, despite the fact that he hadn't bought something new and special for this meeting. In fact, he had scoffed at the suggestion, pointing out that having his arm in a sling would ruin any attempt at appearing stylish.

But he was wrong. He looked perfect, sling or no sling. She especially loved the way the subtle blue pattern in his tie brought out the hunky perfection of his eyes. And that square jaw!

She laughed at herself, realizing that this trip to the Oval Office was taking a back seat to the event they'd been anticipating for six excruciating days—getting him out of the hospital and into bed. With *her.*

With a wink, he took her by the arm and they followed the president's executive assistant through a doorway and into the stately, ivory-toned office, where President Standish was waiting in front of his desk with Director Oakes of the FBI.

The commander in chief strode forward and offered his hand to Kristie. "Be careful on that foot now, darlin'."

"I'm fine, sir." She shook his hand eagerly. "It's such an honor to meet you in person."

"It's mutual, believe me." He surveyed her face for a few seconds, and she suspected he could see the last vestiges of Jane Smith's pummeling, even through two generous coats of makeup.

So much for blowing her paycheck to look good.

Then Standish shook McGregor's free hand. "I've heard great things about you, son."

"Thank you, sir. But all the credit goes to Dr. Hennessy here. She masterminded everything."

"She's a special woman," the president agreed. Then he stared directly into McGregor's eyes. "I deeply regret the turmoil you and your family were subjected to, Will. And I appreciate your discretion in regard to Colonel Payton's idiosyncrasies." Sighing, he added, "Yuley was a flawed man, but we had some good times together."

"I'm sorry for your loss, Mr. President," McGregor assured him. Then he looked past Standish and said, "It's good to see you again, Director Oakes."

"Hello, Will." Oakes stepped forward and shook his agent's hand.

Kristie remembered what Ray had told her about the FBI director's heart condition. She also remembered it was a secret, so she tried not to let sympathy show through as she smiled at him.

But Oakes apparently wasn't going to pull any punches. Instead, he demanded in a booming, jocular voice, "So I finally get to meet the infamous S-3?"

Infamous? She grimaced. "It's a pleasure, sir."

"Let's sit, shall we?" President Standish suggested, directing them toward a pair of semicircular silk sofas that formed a cozy conversation pit in the center of the room. Kristie and McGregor sat beside one another, taking care to leave a generous amount of space between them.

Across from them, the president took a seat next to Oakes. Then he leaned forward and announced, "I asked the two of you here for a couple of reasons. The first is obvious. I owe you a lot. The county owes you a lot. So thank you."

"You're welcome, sir," Kristie murmured.

"I figure you've got questions about what's going to happen next."

"We're worried about Ray," she admitted. "I've tried calling him, but all of his lines are disconnected. He helped us at the end, Mr. President."

"That's right, sir," McGregor added forcefully. "The minute Ortega figured out what was really going on, he dispatched a team to my sister's house to ensure her safety. And he took out two of Smith's men himself, at great personal risk. He could have just sat back and done nothing—"

"That's not Ray's style. Never has been, never will be."
The president's green eyes clouded. "I've granted him a
full pardon for any and all crimes related to the incident
in Los Angeles, starting with the accidental death of my
friend, and ending in the apprehension of a renegade CIA
agent."

"What a relief!" Kristie beamed. "Is he coming back to
SPIN, sir? Or…?" She glanced toward Director Oakes,
wondering if he was there for the purpose of officially announcing that Ray was going to take his place.

The president pursed his lips. "Director Oakes and I
have decided SPIN should be absorbed into the Bureau."

"No!" Kristie flushed and added quickly, "Please don't
punish everyone else for my mistakes. I was reckless. I
admit that. But the concept behind SPIN is still sound."

"I agree," Oakes told her. "I have big plans for the SPIN
Division. Starting with the selection of an assistant director to head it up. That would be you, Will. Assuming
you're really ready to give up fieldwork."

"Me?"

Oakes laughed. "Ortega has been bending my ear for
months about you. Telling me that aside from himself, you
were the only person with the right set of skills. The field
experience, the analytical ability and the understanding of
the relationship between spinner and operative. It's the reason he kept assigning S-3's cases to you. That backfired
for him a little toward the end, but I spoke with him yesterday, and he reaffirmed that you're his number-one
choice."

Kristie watched with delight as McGregor considered
the offer. And while she had assumed the job would go to
David Wong, she realized Ray was right. His field-opera-
tive experience had been invaluable in the evolution of

SPIN. Under McGregor, that could continue. She had a feeling David would agree.

But McGregor wasn't exactly jumping at the opportunity, and she suspected he had Ellie on his mind. Would his sister agree to move to Washington? Otherwise, his whole purpose in seeking a desk job—even one this prestigious—would be undermined.

Oakes didn't seem to notice the lack of response. "During the transition over to the Bureau, I've asked David Wong to act as interim director of SPIN. That should free you up, Will, to take on a special project for me."

"A project, sir?"

"SPIN's expansion to the West Coast is long overdue. You'll go out to L.A. and establish the new office."

McGregor smiled in relief. "That sounds terrific, sir."

Oakes turned to Kristie. "For the time being, you'll report directly to Wong. However, any informal on-site assistance you can provide for the West Coast project would be greatly appreciated. Once it's up and running, we'll reevaluate your assignment."

Kristie bit back a smile, convinced that Ray had come up with this plan. He knew Kristie and McGregor wanted to start dating, and so he had made sure her lover wouldn't also be her supervisor. As usual, Ray was looking out for her. And being his usual controlling self in the process. Not that she minded this time.

McGregor was nodding. "Sounds like a great opportunity, sir. I assume Ortega will be available to consult?"

"Actually, no. Effective immediately, he has asked not to be contacted regarding SPIN. Or anything else for that matter."

Kristie shook her head, instantly panicked. "What does *that* mean?"

The president gave a weary smile. "He's gone into se-
clusion. Did it once before, when he left the CIA. This
country asked a lot of him back then, Kristie. I'm sure he
never told you the half of it, but it scarred his soul. He went
off to a cabin, put himself through a couple of years of
cleansing rituals, training and contemplation. Came out of
it a new man. Stronger. More centered. With a fire in his
belly to establish a new agency called SPIN." His voice
cracked with emotion. "I pray he comes out of it again one
day. But this time, I'm not so sure."

"He's hurting!" Kristie exclaimed. "We can't just let
him be all alone with that pain."

It's his choice, not ours," Director Oakes told her.
"You're going to have to let him go. If you or anyone else
tries to see him—well, take my word for it. They won't be
welcome."

"Poor Ray. All he ever wanted to do was serve his
country."

"Speaking of serving your country..." The president
gestured toward three square envelopes that had been laid
out on the coffee table between the sofas. "I've got some
doodads for the two of you."

One envelope had Kristie's name on it in neat hand-let-
tering, so she picked it up. When the president nodded for
her to continue, she opened it to find a beautifully em-
bossed certificate of commendation signed by both Standish and Oakes.

"Wow." She bit her lip. "Thanks."

"This means a lot," McGregor murmured, staring at his
own document.

"So...?" Kristie eyed the third envelope, which had no
name on it. "I assume that's for Ray?"

"Actually, it's for one of the spinners from your office

who provided some pivotal support. I'd like you to deliver it for me if you don't mind."

"Okay." She reached for the envelope and started to open it.

"You can do that later, can't you?" Director Oakes chided her. "The president and I are already late for another meeting."

"Oh!" She flushed and jumped to her feet. "Thanks again for everything. And when you talk to Ray—"

"I won't."

"But if you do, *please* tell him to contact me."

The president stepped over to her and took her hand in his own. "He's gone, darlin'. Just let it be, for everyone's sake. And take care of yourself." Turning to McGregor, he added cheerfully, "Take good care of her, son."

"So far, it's been S-3 taking care of *me*," the agent assured him with a laugh, flapping his arm in its sling as if to emphasize which of them had fared worse in the battle. "But we'll both do our best, sir. That's a promise."

As soon as they were settled into the limousine that would carry them to Kristie's apartment, McGregor closed the privacy glass between them and the driver. Then he gently pushed the spinner's shoulders down onto the seat until she was almost fully reclined, all the while nuzzling her neck.

Kristie wanted nothing more than to submit, but reminded him dutifully, "We promised Dr. Hall we'd take it slow. She wanted to keep you for a few more days, remember?"

"I feel great. And you feel *really* great."

"Mmm…" She slipped her hands behind his neck, ready to enjoy a long, leisurely kiss.

But McGregor hesitated, then stroked her cheek with his free thumb. "Sorry about Ortega, Goldie."

"He'll get in touch with me. I'm sure of it. He just needs a little time alone. To think."

McGregor seemed about to disagree, then shrugged instead. "So? Aren't you curious to see who gets the other certificate?"

"I'm sure it's David. He did all the legwork here while we were in L.A."

McGregor reached for the envelope and peeked inside, then murmured, "Not exactly."

"Really?" She took it from him. "Let me see."

"I don't think you're gonna like this."

Intrigued, she turned her attention to the beautiful gold-embossed letters and was surprised to see that they spelled out the name MELISSA DANIELS.

"He's kidding, I'm sure," McGregor told her gently. "Everyone knows it was all you."

"Why should I be upset?" Kristie gave a dismissive shrug. "Melissa doesn't even exist anymore. But when she did, she was me. So either way, it's not a problem."

McGregor arched an eyebrow. "Melissa doesn't exist anymore?"

"Well obviously, she *never* existed," Kristie corrected herself with a laugh. "But to me, she was real, at least in a sense. I can see that now."

"Because she's gone?"

"Right. It was just like David predicted. As soon as I discovered that *her* limits were *my* limits—when she couldn't destroy that postmark any more than I could—I finally understood that we were the same person. With the same moral code. The same skills. The same person in every way that counts."

"She always *was* the same person as you. But she still existed," McGregor reminded her. "What makes you think she's gone now?"

Kristie bit her lip, wondering how to explain it to him. "It was an amazing moment, really. When Jane Smith pulled that dagger out of her boot—when I knew for sure things were going to get rough—that was exactly the kind of situation I instinctively turned over to Melissa in the past. But this time, I didn't. I wanted it to be *me* who kicked Jane's ass. Even more importantly, I knew I could. At that moment, as they say, the assimilation was complete."

McGregor seemed unconvinced. "Shouldn't you discuss this with Wong? He seemed to think it was a little more complicated than that."

"David is my supervisor now," she reminded him. "He wouldn't be comfortable counseling me. Plus, it's not necessary. Melissa's gone. Case closed."

When McGregor pursed his lips, Kristie had to laugh. "Let me guess. You're remembering that one-night-a-week with Melissa I promised you? Are you saying I'm not enough woman for you?"

McGregor rallied promptly, his blue eyes twinkling. "As long as I can have Kristie, Goldie and S-3, I'll be a satisfied man. Wouldn't want to be greedy," he added with a wink.

Kristie laughed. "Go ahead. Be greedy. I dare you." Then she pulled his head down until their lips were almost touching, assuring him in a throaty whisper, "We're all here. And we're ready whenever you are."

ATHENA FORCE

Chosen for their talents.
Trained to be the best.

Expected to change the world.

The women of Athena Academy
share an unforgettable experience
and an unbreakable bond—until
one of their own is murdered.

The adventure begins with these six books:

PROOF by Justine Davis, July 2004

ALIAS by Amy J. Fetzer, August 2004

EXPOSED by Katherine Garbera,
September 2004

DOUBLE-CROSS by Meredith Fletcher,
October 2004

PURSUED by Catherine Mann, November 2004

JUSTICE by Debra Webb, December 2004

**And look for six more Athena Force stories
January to June 2005.**

Available at your favorite retail outlet.